The Mirror House Girls

A psychological thriller

Faith Gardner

MIЯROR
HOUSE
·PRESS·

Be the first to learn about Faith Gardner's upcoming releases by joining her newsletter!

To anyone who has ever gotten lost
trying to find themselves

Author's Note

This book features a character who is a singer/songwriter and contains original music written to accompany the text.

You can hear the songs by scanning the QR code below:

Excerpt from the documentary *The Mirror House Girls: One Year Later*

LOCATION: Former Mirror House property in Bodega, California

SHOTS: Ocean cliffs under a cloudy gray sky; crows descending into cypress trees; a sea breeze bending the grasses back; waves churning violently over the jagged rocks below

VOICEOVER, recording of a 911 call.

DISPATCHER: 911, what is your emergency?

CALLER: (Voice shaking) I think they're all dead.

DISPATCHER: What's your name, sir?

CALLER: I—I just want to phone in an anonymous tip.

DISPATCHER: Can you please tell me what's happening?

CALLER: There's a … a group, living out at the property, 221 Hitchcock Road. I think there's been a mass suicide.

DISPATCHER: Police and paramedics are on their way. Is anyone still breathing?

CALLER: No. They're gone.

DISPATCHER: Sir, can you—

CALLER: They jumped. (Choked sob) They jumped, together. Every single one.

SHOTS: News footage of thirteen pairs of shoes on the cliffside; shoes are arranged in a circle with thirteen severed braids of hair laid behind them. Camera fades to the image of a plaque that now rests here, overlooking the ocean.

The plaque reads:

Here the mysterious group informally known as "Mirror House" ended in a mass suicide.

1
Two Years Ago

I'm LOST, both literally and figuratively, wandering the mildew-stinky hallway of a church basement when a girl pops out of the shadows and asks, "Looking for the death thing, dude?"

Spooked, I put a hand to my chest and stop in my tracks. "You mean the Transcending Grief workshop? Yes."

"Did I scare you?"

"Also yes."

"Sorry." She offers a sheepish smile. This girl looks like a Santa Cruz stereotype: tattooed stars above her eyebrows, hippie clothes, sunny energy, a stoner twang in her voice. She's about my age, early-to-mid twentysomething. "Me too. It's the last door at the end of the hall. I'm debating bailing though. That's why I'm lagging here."

"Oh no. Why?"

"Guess I'm nervous." She bites a fingernail. "I'm here because my grandma passed but I don't know if that's ridiculous. You know? Of all the tragedies, a grown woman mourning her grandmother."

Instantly, we are connected. The sad sparkle in her eyes, the uncertain loneliness, the quiet burden of grief—it's like looking in a mirror.

"I'm here because my grandma died too," I say with a little surprise.

She's visibly relieved. "Seriously?"

I nod. "We were really close. I lived with her for a year before she died."

Her eyes widen. "Same. I lived with my grandma up until a couple years ago. She basically raised me."

"Well, you have every right to be here."

The girl peers down the dim hall at the door, seeming to reconsider.

"I'm Winona," I say.

"Dakota," she says, with a dimpled grin.

"Don't worry, it's just a one-day workshop and then it'll all be over," I tell her, hoping she'll come too now that we've got our grief in common.

"It's not just that," Dakota says, smile faltering. "I've got a fear of public speaking."

"Oh." I scrounge for words of comfort. "I think there are only going to be a few of us in there?"

"I know. It's supposed to be practice." She swallows. "Exposure."

"You can always get up and leave if it's too much."

She nods and blows out a long, even breath. "Okay. Yeah. Thanks."

Together, we walk into the room.

The walls are painted with rainbows and flowers, the room perfumed with jasmine tea. There are six people on the floor sitting on meditation pillows. All of them have graying hair and at least a generation on Dakota and me. A woman with a burst of curls and cat-eyed glasses welcomes us, pointing to the unoccupied pillows.

"Namaste," she says. "I'm Elaine, group leader. You must be ..." The woman squints at a yellow pad of paper on her lap. "Is one of you Winona and one of you Dakota?"

We nod and introduce ourselves.

"Welcome," everyone murmurs.

I settle into my pillow next to Dakota, whose face has whitened. I give her arm a pat and whisper, "You okay?"

She nods, but the deer-in-headlights expression says otherwise.

The solemn quiet of the room gives me tingles. Elaine leads a short meditation exercise, focusing on our breath and inhabiting our bodies. I was nervous about coming today—not as nervous as this girl Dakota, clearly, but I wasn't sure what to expect. Immediately, though, I exhale and relax into the group.

One by one, everyone introduces themselves and explains what brought them here. One man lost his wife, one woman lost her sister, and two people recently lost their moms.

"My name is Winona," I say when it's my turn. "I'm here because I lost my Grandma Jane this year." I swallow a lump. "I took care of her for a year while she was dying of cancer. She and my mom don't get along super well, so it kind of all landed on me. It's been hard, because I uprooted myself and dropped out of college in Iowa to move back to southern California and care for her—and now I don't know what to do with myself and what comes next." I wipe my eyes. "Grandma Jane loved it here in Santa Cruz. It was one of the last places we visited together. I moved here just last month, kind of on a whim. I don't know anyone here and am kind of trying to figure it all out ..."

A flood seems to pour out of me as I tell everyone about myself. Last year was hard. It was hard to finally go away to college in Iowa only to come back to Escondido, my California hometown glittering between foothills and a short drive to the beach. As soon as I returned, I was miserable there for a multitude of reasons beyond Grandma Jane's cancer. Stupid Dean, a married man who strung me along with empty promises. And my mother, a human migraine I learned to tolerate during all the stress, an endless barrage of emotional breakdowns via text message even as I was busy changing bedsheets, fixing twisted tubing, and calling insurance companies on Grandma Jane's behalf.

Suddenly I realize how long I've been talking and cut myself off. "Sorry, I'm rambling."

"That's why we're here. Ramble on," Elaine says, fist in the air that reveals an infinity symbol tattooed on her wrist.

Dakota goes next, keeping it short and simple. "My name is Dakota. I lost my grandma too."

I shoot her an encouraging smile and she returns it, looking relieved.

Elaine hands out journals with rainbows on them where we can jot our feelings down throughout the day. Our first assignment is reflecting on happy memories of the people we lost. As I sit listening to the song of scribbling and occasional sighs, I remember Grandma Jane with an ache. I chase the words down with my pencil, letting it all out.

Grandma was crooked hot-pink lipstick, Kentucky bourbon, and hell on an electric-powered scooter. She was girl-group music and a loud voice yelling at her soap operas the way some people might yell at a sports game: *Dammit, Calliope, ya dumbass! That's his evil twin brother!* We had always been close. While my mom is fretful, my grandma sprinkled lightheartedness everywhere she went. My mom raised me on health food, but my grandma gave me my first taste of ice cream. She's taken me on trips since I was a kid—and she's who showed me Santa Cruz for the first time.

And now I'm here without her.

Dakota and I walk to a bagel shop to eat lunch during our

break. Waiting in line, we both start singing with the Grateful Dead on the stereo. Somehow, she feels like an old friend just because we spent a couple of hours in grief group together. Nothing like bonding over losing our grandmas to cement a friendship. Well, that and the fact we're both Deadheads, I guess.

"Thanks for helping me chill this morning," Dakota says as we sit down together with our food. She unwraps her veggie bagel. "Today's been hard, but I'm glad I didn't bail."

"Same."

"I didn't know you were new here. You said you don't know anyone in town?"

My mouth's full. I shake my head.

"We should hang out together sometime," Dakota says excitedly. "You can meet my housemates. We're going foraging this weekend. Want to come with?"

After swallowing my bite, I ask, "Foraging?"

"Yeah. For, like, mushrooms and other edibles that grow up in the hills."

I'm amused by the idea. It sounds like the hippie-est hobby imaginable. I can totally imagine Dakota wandering the mountains, scouring nature for treasures.

"Sounds fun," I say. "I've never foraged before."

"We don't usually invite people along, but I'll talk to Simon." She brightens up, showing off her dimples. "I have a feeling they're all going to love you."

2

Life is a beautiful wilderness.

Stop right here, right now. Savor it.

In the shady redwood forest, ferns explode like green fireworks. I smell deep, sweet earth and hear a waterfall trickling somewhere. Nature halts me in my hiking boots. It vacuums my worries, steals my breath, and prickles my eyes. It's quiet enough here to remind me of the electric beat of my heart. Mighty enough to remind me how tiny I am.

It's been a rough year. These reminders offer profound comfort right now. A beautiful line from Henry David Thoreau echoes in my brain: *I took a walk in the woods and came out taller than the trees.*

"All right back there, dude?" Dakota calls.

Dakota lingers behind for me as her four housemates walk farther up the path. I take a deep breath and catch up.

"Yep. Just taking it all in," I tell her.

"First time in these mountains?"

I nod.

"Hella cool, right?"

"It is."

Such a change of scenery—this forest, these people. I still get lost in my own neighborhood. I haven't made new friends since I left Des Moines over a year ago, unless you count Dean, but don't. Dean was never a friend. And he's nothing now.

"Up here," Dakota's housemate Simon calls from the front, beckoning the rest of us.

We hurry toward where he squats in the trail. He's pointing to the ground at what look like miniature green flowers, round heads with buttons in their middle.

"Sounds like he found something," Dakota whispers. "Simon's a foraging genius. When the zombie apocalypse happens, I know I'll be spared, living in a house with that dude."

I've long accepted that when the zombie apocalypse happens, I'll be first to die. I don't think there's going to be much need for bookstore cashiers and college dropouts who studied twentieth century poetry.

Simon brushes his fingertips over the plants. "Miner's lettuce," he says. "*Claytonia perfoliata.* Native to California. Perennial succulent." He picks a sprig and eats it. "Try it! It's got a fresh taste and a crunch to it. You can use it as a salad green."

Everyone leans down, picking a piece and chewing it. It reminds me of spinach. I study Simon, impressed. He's been leading this trek today with the knowledge and confidence of a forest ranger. I've never understood how some people can store things in their brains like the scientific words for plants and animals. I consider myself a word person, but I can't tell you the plot of a book ten minutes after I finish it.

As if Simon hears my thoughts, his eyes meet mine for a moment. They're bright and green-brown and wide with wonder. I feel startlingly seen as he looks at me. And I'm

7

confused about whether I find him good-looking or not. That mop of brown, curly hair. That sun-bronzed skin. Those round glasses and Birkenstocks and a T-shirt that says SAVE THE PLANET. His gaze hangs for an extra-long second and I almost squirm until he breaks eye contact and lists a passionate litany of facts about the lifespan of the redwood tree (*sequoia sempervirens*).

"That means *sequoia ever-living* in Latin." He touches a tree trunk gently. "They're communicating beneath our feet right now, interconnected through roots and fungal networks."

It's humbling to think that this species of tree can live to be over two thousand years old. To think that these giants have been standing here in this earth longer than me, my mother, my grandmother. These trees were here before this state and this country existed. Before the invention of the computer, the typewriter, and maybe even the printing press. Before Shake-speare wrote his plays.

And they'll be here long, long after I'm gone.

3

I PLUCK a stem of Miner's lettuce and chew it. The sharp green taste is one I've never had before. I have so much to learn. So many plants I never knew were edible, subjects I've never studied, people I've never met.

"Can I say something, Boss?" Maude asks.

I'm confused by the word *boss* when she says it, unsure of who she's addressing. Then I realize she's asking Simon.

"Of course," Simon says.

"This stuff is delicious with a little bit of Dijon dressing," Maude says to me, grinning.

Maude is the oldest person in this group, probably my mom's age. But she's nothing like my mother. Despite her soft, heavyset figure, she has muscular legs and arms. She doesn't dye her graying hair. She has a nose piercing and a faded tattoo of a hen on her arm. Dakota told me that Maude used to be in a women's motorcycle gang. I'll bet Maude has some stories.

"You cook?" Maude asks me as she takes a mesh bag out of her backpack. She gently pulls handfuls of Miner's lettuce from the earth and stuffs the bag full.

"Little bit," I say.

The group, still gathered at this spot, all turn heads toward me as if they're waiting for me to elaborate. Their full attention is so strange and intense. Simon and his unflinching gaze. Dakota and her encouraging, dimpled smile. Maude, pausing her foraging. The others stop whispering to one another to listen.

"I wouldn't say I'm a *good* one, though, so hold onto that Michelin star for now," I say to them all. "I almost burned my grandma's apartment down making a quesadilla last year, so ..." I perform an exaggerated wince.

They laugh, which relaxes me.

Simon beckons everyone forward on the trail, saying, "I *might* know where to find some black trumpets."

"Hell yeah." Maude zips up her mesh bag and follows him. "Pasta for dinner."

Dakota and Simon put their arms around each other's shoulders and lead the way. I'm not used to the affection this group shares. My Delta Theta Kappa sisters at Drake University were all sugar and toothpaste-ad smiles. But behind closed doors, they let homophobic shit fly out of their mouths about not wanting lesbians in our chapter. I was terrified that if I hugged too hard, sat too close on the couch, they'd think I was one. No, Dakota and her housemates remind me of my friend group in high school, who I miss. That's the problem with befriending overachievers—they dispersed all over the country to Ivy Leagues as soon as those graduation caps were tossed in the air.

"Dakota said you were funny," Kristin says, walking next to me.

Despite her California-girl appearance, Kristin has a gravelly voice. It gives her an extra dimension, along with her skateboarding company T-shirt and skull baseball cap.

"Dakota's bar for funny must be pretty low, then," I say.

Kristin laughs. Scarlett, who joins us on my other side, laughs too. I suddenly feel like the funniest person in the world. "What do you guys do?" I ask them.

"I'm just a barista," Scarlett says.

Scarlett's adorable and plucky. She sparkles. She's got a Southern twang in her voice, her red hair is wild and everywhere, and she wears a little bandanna around her neck.

"Come on, don't undersell yourself, Scar," Kristin says. "You're a *killer* singer and guitar player."

"Really?" I ask, impressed.

"Are you kidding?" Scarlett scoffs. "I know like four chords." Then to me again, "But yeah. I write silly little songs sometimes. What about you, what do you do?"

"I work at Chapters, that bookstore downtown."

"Oh yeah, I know that place."

"As for me," Kristin says. "Funemployed. Just got out of rehab last September. My twenties are honestly kind of a blur."

I glance at Scarlett, who studies the ground as we walk.

"Oh." I swallow, taken aback by how real things just got. "You okay now?"

"Yep, alive and still kicking," Kristin says cheerfully. "Alcohol-free for two hundred days and counting."

"Congratulations," I offer.

An awkward silence spreads between the three of us as we near where everyone's gathered off the path. Simon's pointing and Maude is plucking something from the ground. She holds a clump up in the air.

Kristin shouts, "Jam out with your clam out!" and hurries away to join them.

Scarlett cringes and calls after her, "Kristin, yuck. Stop *sayin'* that."

I smile at their dynamic.

11

Scarlett gently touches my arm. "Dakota's told me a little about you."

"Really?"

I'm not that interesting. My favorite ice cream flavor is chocolate. My favorite holiday is Christmas. The most fun I've ever had, my face was stuck in a book. And besides crying together in one grief workshop, I don't even know Dakota that well.

Scarlett nods. "She said you lived in Iowa?"

"Just for a year."

"You like it out there?"

"I tried. I failed."

She laughs. I like the way her hand feels on my arm and I'm suddenly aware I haven't been touched by anyone since Dean tucked five hundred dollars in my purse and kissed me goodbye like some kind of polite John.

My stomach turns. Fuck him.

"What about you?" I ask. "Where are you from?"

"North Carolina. Moved here last year looking for a fresh start."

"I love your accent."

"What? I don't have an accent, y'all have an accent," she says teasingly.

"Touché."

"You'll come over to eat the foraging feast tonight, right? That's the best part. Maude makes the most incredible food. She used to own a vegan catering company, know that?"

"I didn't."

Damn, a motorcycle gang member with a vegan catering company? Maude contains multitudes.

"I'll come for dinner," I say. "Thanks for inviting me."

There's a pinch on my upper arm and I slap it automatically.

When I look at my hand, horror: a smashed mosquito, a deep red smear.

My worst fear. My phobia. That thing that makes me want to turn inside out. It's why lab tests at the doctor are misery, why I couldn't be in the room when Grandma Jane had an IV, why a paper cut might as well be a mortal wound.

Blood. Mine or someone else's. *Blood.*

Blood. I can feel it. *Blood.* My insides wanting to spill outside. *Blood.* Ugly red and glistening. *Blood.* Panic.

Blood, blood, blood, blood, blood.

4

MY VISION SPARKLES and my neck prickles. I might pass out.

"You all right?" Scarlett asks.

"Do you have a napkin?" I whisper, trying to not look at my hand, trying to focus on a tree trunk near me. The sky. The air in my nostrils. Anything but blood.

With a worried look, Scarlett opens her backpack and pulls out a tissue. "You need a first aid kit?"

I shake my head. Ironically, the sight of blood feels like it has drained all the blood from my face. I take the tissue and wipe my hands and, without looking at it, stuff it into a side pocket on my backpack. I'll deal with that later. I look down at my palm. It's shaking. But it's clean.

"A mosquito bit me," I explain to Scarlett. "There was blood on my hand. The sight of blood gets me. I'll swoon like a Victorian woman."

"Oh wow. Sorry. I had no idea."

"Yeah. Thanks. I hate it."

She smiles. "Next time I'll bring my smelling salts."

Next time. That's sweet.

"How in the hell do you deal with having a period every month?" Scarlett asks curiously.

"Weirdly, that doesn't bother me. It's not the same as people bleeding and being cut."

Scarlett studies me as if I'm an alien.

"I know. It makes no sense," I say.

She pats my back. "Well, we've all got our quirks."

Maude and the others are gathered around a dead alder tree at the edge of an embankment. A babbling brook and birdsong fill the air. Simon spots us and hurries over excitedly. He has something in his hand.

"Hey, open up," Simon says.

Scarlett opens her mouth like a baby bird and he tucks something inside. She *mmm*s and nods, then runs to where the others are to investigate where it came from. Dakota, Maude, and Kristin are pulling mushrooms off the alder tree and popping them in their mouths.

Simon turns expectantly to me now.

"Open up!" he urges.

I can't tell what he has in his hand. I squint. "What is it?"

"I'm asking you to trust me," he says.

He says it so pleadingly. As if it really matters to him. As if I'm going to let him down if I say no. In a flash, a memory of going to church with my friend when I was twelve and taking communion even though it felt wrong, because I didn't know how to say no. A memory of Grandma Jane making me my "favorite dish" of meat loaf and me not having the heart to tell her I didn't like it anymore. I ate it anyway and told her how good it was when I was done.

I open my mouth and Simon puts something inside. It's tender, chewy, and my first instinct is to gag and spit it out— but I keep chewing and give him the thumbs up.

"What is it?" I ask after I swallow.

"*Psilocybe cubensis*, or psilocybin," he says with a bright smile.

It's like someone pushed me down a flight of stairs.

What the hell? This man just fed us psychedelic mushrooms without permission? Just popped it into our mouths, no question?

A cold sweat breaks over my forehead. And it hits me—shit. I'm out in the middle of nowhere with a bunch of people I hardly know. With no cell reception and no vehicle of my own. I'm stuck here with them and now I'm about to have a drug trip I didn't ask for.

"Hey, hey, hey," Simon says, rubbing my back, as if he can sense my panic. "It's okay. I'm kidding. I'm pulling your leg." He holds the rest of the mushroom up, which itself looks psychedelic, wavy and wild, like something you'd see on a neon blacklight poster. "*Pleurotus ostreatus*. Oyster mushroom. A hundred percent edible. Not at all like psilocybin."

I exhale a sigh that tells him exactly how much his prank scared the shit out of me.

"Oh no, Winona, I'm so sorry," he says, offering a quick hug. He smells like sandalwood and sweat. "I really freaked you out, didn't I?" He pulls back to observe me like someone studying an accident victim for signs of injury. Up close, he's got crow's feet and I'm guessing at least ten years on me. "Are you okay? I feel terrible."

"No, I'm fine," I laugh weakly.

"Not a fan of magic mushrooms, huh?" he asks with a grimace.

"I've never taken them, actually."

He takes a deep breath as he adjusts his glasses and studies me. "You're inconceivably dazzling. When I first saw you today, my pulse skipped a beat."

I prickle with joy. Who says that? *Inconceivably dazzling.* The elegant phrase just rolls from his lips as if he's the leading man in a romance novel. And it works, reader. A cherub might as well have shot an arrow to my heart. There's zero creepiness in his lingering stare and in his words. Coming from another man, they might feel that way. Not with Simon, though. This isn't lust. This is pure, unadulterated sincerity.

I've always been a sucker for a man who can casually utter four-syllable words. But I've never learned the art of gracefully accepting a compliment.

"You might want to see a cardiologist," I say. "I hear arrhythmias can be dangerous."

He raises his dark eyebrows. "She's clever, too."

"Who is?" I ask, jokingly looking behind my shoulder.

He has a wry smile on his lips, like he wants to say more. Is this flirting? Are we flirting? I can't tell.

"You're coming for dinner, right?" he asks.

"If you'll have me."

"Well, you'd better pitch in then," he says, pulling my sleeve toward the tree. "Help us pick oysters."

Everyone waves at me when I join them, as if I'm one of them. As if I've been miles away and they missed me. Maude hands me my own mesh bag and Kristin and Scarlett are jokingly hip bumping each other like teenage sisters and Dakota's smiling at me with a sparkle in her eye like, *See? See why I wanted you to meet my amazing housemates?* When she raved about how they were like a family, I didn't believe her.

But I believe her now.

Excerpt from the documentary *The Mirror House Girls: One Year Later*

LOCATION: Interviewee's home, Raven's Landing, California

SHOTS: Exterior of pink cottage crawling with vines; interior of the sunny living room; a floral sofa near a window

Settling into her seat, SCARLETT BEALE adjusts the tiny mic clipped to her collar. She has curly strawberry-blond hair to her chin, glossy heart-shaped lips, and wears a daisy-patterned shirt with an orange ascot. She looks at the camera and speaks.

SCARLETT: Okay, so, I—I just look into the camera then? And … talk?

INTERVIEWER (off camera): Start by introducing yourself, if you don't mind. And then you'll tell your story.

SCARLETT: Lord. Where do I begin? I don't know where to begin. (Nervous laugh, bright smile) I might need a moment. (Puts her hands together in a prayer position and closes her eyes. Her smile slowly melts. When she opens her eyes again, they're full and glassy) My name is Scarlett Beale and I'm the only survivor of the original group that lived at Mirror House.

5

As we ride down the mountain in Dakota's Volvo with the bumper duct-taped on, she cranks the Grateful Dead with one hand on the wheel and we sing along. It's spellbindingly bright every which way, a redwood eternity, sky so blue you could cry about it. Reminds me of summer camp. And it's not just the trees everywhere—it's the butterflies in my belly, the time spent with strangers who feel like easy friends. I'm reminded that life's still young and anything can happen.

I roll the window down and put my arm out, fingertips surfing the warm summer wind, and catch a glimpse of myself in the side mirror. The sunshine pinked my cheeks and I'm smiling. This is not the shattered me I've carried like a heavy load this past year. Not the swollen-eyed, frown-lined me exhausted from a year of watching my grandma waste away. Not the foundation-thick face with false eyelashes from my sorority days in Iowa and my nights out with Dean in San Diego. This is someone new and I'm thrilled to meet her.

After a gorgeous twenty-minute drive back to town and a quick stop at a dispensary, Dakota brings me to her house.

And it's ... not what I was expecting.

To be fair, would anyone expect to pull up to a house covered in mirrors?

"Here?" I ask as Dakota pulls her Volvo to the curb. "You live *here?*"

"Yep," she says. "You've seen this place before?"

Even I, new to Santa Cruz, know about the weird mirror house. I heard someone saying once they thought a religious group lived there. You'd think Dakota might have mentioned it on the drive down from the hills. *Hey, by the way, we live in that gigantic bizarro house with mirrors all over it.* Then again, Dakota has a three-foot bong belted into her car's back seat like a precious baby. She has star tattoos on her eyebrows. Maybe living in a mirror house is no big deal to her.

"I wondered what weirdos live here."

"It's us, dude. We're the weirdos." Dakota pulls her keys and unbuckles her seatbelt. "Welcome to Mirror House."

This place is a funky landmark: a wind-bleached, lavender Victorian two blocks from the lighthouse and a five-minute walk to the boardwalk. The hundreds of mirrors covering the house are hung so tightly together you can barely see the color of the shingles. A framed mirror mounted to the front door, disco balls hanging from the porch, hand mirrors stabbed into the overgrown lawn like strange flowers. Tiny compact mirrors dangle from the bushy laurel tree in the yard.

This isn't a house; this is performance art.

"It was Simon's idea," she says. "Brilliant, yeah? Took us a few weeks. It was an *adventure.* Hella scavenging thrift shops for mirrors."

"I'll bet."

I'm surprised there are mirrors left on this planet at this point. There are even mirrors on the *windows.* What a sight.

"How do you see through the windows?" I ask as we get out of the car.

"Oh, that's one-way mirror film. Kinda like shiny contact paper? You can see out, but you can't see in."

Clever. As I sling my backpack over my shoulder, I gaze in wonder. It's like an inside-out funhouse. It blazes and blinds in the setting sun. If you squint, the house almost disappears, nothing but jagged reflections. A week or two ago, on a dark night as I rode home on my bike with the wind in my teeth, I heard guitars and bongos and laughter wafting from the open windows and wondered what oddball people lived there and what it was like inside.

Well, guess I'm finding out.

I follow Dakota to the front door, exchanging a dubious look with my own dim reflection. Behind me, twilight and palm trees. A lazy yellow grin of a moon. Then the door swings open to a gale of laughter and warmth and the smell of curry and peppers.

Maude's there to greet us, waving a wooden spoon ecstatically. "Come on in! What took you so long?"

"Made a dispensary stop," Dakota says. "What's cookin', Ma?"

I close the door behind me. The foyer has a familiar, comforting smell beneath the deliciousness—woody, dusty, like a library or a church. The floorboards creak, the wallpaper is black with pastel pink flowers. Lanterns and fairy lights give the air a magical glow. A rainbow of coats, purses, backpacks hang along the wall, shoes lined up on racks below.

"Can you lose your kickers?" Maude asks. "We're a barefoot house."

"No problem." I slip my hiking boots off, leaving them at the end of a long line.

Dakota and I follow the sound of laughter and music through the hallway and into the living room. There, Scarlett sits on the couch with a guitar, her bare feet tapping on the Persian rug as Simon and Kristin watch on. Scarlett chugs her beer and puts it down, lit up as if we're her audience.

"Okay, I'm going to play you the first thing I wrote when I came to Cali," she says.

Scarlett strums her chords softly, a familiar song almost like something I've heard before but also somehow totally new. Everyone goes still. We sit on the floor, cross-legged. A magic swallows the air in the room. Scarlett closes her eyes and sings in a hauntingly sweet voice.

> My home's my home. It lives with me
> It does not carry, it's carried
> My home can cry and laugh and bleed
> My home's my home. My home is me
>
> It is a shell that fits me well
> I keep it clean, I give it hell
> Then it forgives. What else to do?
> My home's my own and it'll do
>
> Nevermind the neighborhood
> You are lovely and good
>
> My home's my home. That's what it is
> It isn't theirs. It isn't his
> I inherited its shape and space
> But chose its paint and gave it taste
> My home's my home
> It's no mistake

As her last chord rings out and Scarlett's eyes open, a sheepish grin lights up her face, as if she just realized we were all here. Kristin and Dakota and I applaud and I covertly wipe the tear from my eye.

"Did you write that?" I ask in astonishment.

"She writes everything she sings. See? She's amazing!" Kristin says.

My jaw drops. I've spent my life pining after the profound words of strangers, poems and books and songs—but I've never actually known someone who could spin something like *that*. It wasn't fancy. It was just effortless and heartfelt. The way every incredible poem in the English language is written from twenty-six letters in the alphabet, every song is made of just a handful of chords and yet people like Scarlett can somehow make them seem new.

"Damn, Scarlett, you should be on the radio!" I say.

"Aww, shucks, I can't even write a bridge," Scarlett says. Her eyes float to Simon, who sits in the corner, contemplating her as if he's still chewing on the song. "What did you think of that one, Simon?"

"Fine, as always." He gets up and stretches. "Going to go see how dinner's coming along."

He walks out of the room and Scarlett's face falls, as if she had hoped for a better response. I hurt for her even though I don't understand the dynamic. She puts her guitar down as though she lost interest in it.

Dakota unpackages a vape pen and puts it between her lips. "Want me to show you around?"

"Yeah, definitely," I say, so intrigued by everything around me. The tiny oil paintings on the walls, wildflowers and mermaids. The mismatched furniture. The beanbag chairs on the floor.

Dakota nods toward the back door. "Let's go outside for a minute. Simon doesn't like vaping in the house. Then I'll give you the grand tour."

We sit on the back porch in hanging chairs and watch the pink lemonade sunset over their yard. They have fairy lights and a giant trampoline, the kind I always wished I had as a kid. My mom was too worried about broken bones to ever let me do anything like that. Too worried about razors—and sugar—in Halloween candy to let me trick-or-treat. Too worried about me being molested to ever allow me to sleep over anywhere. Too worried about her own mental health to take care of Grandma when she was dying of cancer. My mother's worry was a cage and even though I'm twenty-two, I still feel sometimes like I haven't escaped it. Like I've never quite learned how to be free even though I've pined for it all my life.

In the backyard of Mirror House, there are raised garden beds in bloom, fresh soil and rows of seedlings. Dakota explains that they forage in the forest on weekends and grow a lot of their produce themselves and they want to get chickens and bees soon. There are random sculptures throughout the yard that she tells me Simon makes out of garbage and recyclables. Along with their mini-farm, an assortment of curiosities: a bald, naked mannequin, an inflatable alligator, and a rainbow-painted pedicab.

"Maude drives it on Sundays," Dakota says when I ask about it. "It's her career."

Career. I take a hit of the vape pen, even though I don't usually smoke weed, and we sit out here a while in the quiet. A comfortable, shared quiet, which is a gorgeous and rare thing. I think about how content I am at this moment. How striking the sight of the rising moon. And I can hear my grandmother's voice: *Be happy, Noni. Be happy.* Her last words.

Faith Gardner

"This place changed my life," Dakota says to me, breaking the silence.

I turn and study her profile, the billowing smoke as she stares at the sky with her own thoughts. Maybe she hears her grandmother's voice too.

"Yeah?" I say. "What do you mean?"

"Mirror House, it's just ... there's no place like this." She turns her hanging chair with a bare foot and lets it go for a single spin. "I've never had friends like this. Or lived anywhere like this. I feel so lucky to be here, every day."

Envy winks in me. "It seems really special, what you all have."

"I mean, you know about my family situation, dude. It's bad. My mom's ..." She circles her finger around her ear. "My dad's useless."

"I can relate."

My dad's beyond useless. He doesn't even know I exist. I can't bear the thought of him.

"We have a room opening up," she says. "Did I tell you that?"

I shake my head in surprise.

"Yeah. It's fuckin' dope, too. Want to see it?"

"Sure," I say with a shrug.

I try to bat the hope away. My thoughts speed ahead of me. Could I live here? Is this fated? I don't know where I'm going to live long-term yet. I'm in a shitty sublet situation trying to figure out my next steps. Have I stumbled upon something special today, some gift from the universe?

Be happy, Noni.

I stand and stretch, pausing for a moment on the porch as Dakota slips back inside. Sharing a secret smile with the moon. Then my focus falls to a strange structure in the corner of the yard I hadn't noticed before. It looks like a doghouse, a waist-high wooden box with a boarded-up door that has a lock on it and a heavy chain. I don't know why, but my stomach turns at the sight of it.

"What's that?" I ask Dakota.

But she's already headed back inside.

6

DAKOTA GIVES me the grand tour. The lemon-yellow kitchen, swept and counters clean, Maude listening to Guns N' Roses out of her phone in a silver bowl as she cooks. My mouth waters at the smell of sautéed onions and garlic filling the air.

The kitchen might be cluttered, but it's well-organized. Pots and pans hang from the ceiling, shelves stacked with labeled containers, counters wiped down and floors swept. I notice this kind of thing because I'm currently renting a room in a disgusting house full of college boys who never do dishes and don't own a broom and ignore the ant problem in the kitchen. This, in comparison, is glorious.

"Showing Winona the house," Dakota says loudly over a wailing guitar solo. "She might be interested in the room."

"Rad," Maude says, raising a hand and giving me a hi-five.

"So nice in here," I say, my eyes following a hanging plant that slithers up the kitchen wall. "And whatever you're cooking smells amazing."

"You a fan of curry?" she asks, stirring the pot.

"Love it," I say. "Can I help with anything?"

"Look at this one, already wanting to pitch in." Maude comes and gives me a side hug that smells of patchouli. "Nah, go, go, finish the tour. See the rest of the house."

Dakota keeps walking and I follow. She points out the closed doors at the end of the hall where Kristin and Scarlett live. She tells me about when the house was built (1904) and how long they've lived here (less than two years) and the "co-op style" living they do, sharing chores and meals and having house meetings. I'm getting sorority house déjà vu, but this place, of course, is nothing like that. The Delta Theta Kappa house had a temporary air about it. We all knew it was just another place we'd graduate from. My mother lives in a condo so clean I'm scared to set foot in it. Dean's apartment was just a fuck-closet he rented because he had a wife and family. I was startled to find one morning that it didn't have real dishes in it, that the cupboards were as bare as a movie set. But this is a bona fide home—a colorful, full home, one loved and lived in. I haven't seen one of these in a long time.

"The other bedrooms are upstairs," Dakota says, beckoning me.

We climb up a dark staircase, my pulse picking up speed. A whisper inside me asks, *could* I live here? Among friendly people who eat dinner together and hang out like friends? My current lifestyle includes eating frozen dinners while sitting alone on my bed reading books; popping my head out occasionally to ask the howling monkeys I live with to keep their voices down; leaving notes on the fridge about stolen oat milk. Long nights spent stalking Dean on social media and then plummeting into self-pity. That kind of shit.

"Simon, me, and Maude live in these rooms," Dakota says.

She pops open the nearest door, showing me her room. It's just what I would expect Dakota's room to look like: giant poster of Bob Marley on the wall, a comforter on her bed printed with a shirtless Jim Morrison. A bong on the night table. She moves to the next bedroom and points to the door, which is ajar.

"Damn, Maude left her door open," she says. "She keeps doing that."

We peek inside. It's tidy and tiny as a monk's room. Nothing on the walls. Not even a bed frame, just a mattress on a box frame and a giant snake slithering across the floor. And I mean *giant*. I startle at the sight of it. There are a couple of snake turds on the otherwise clean floor and the room has a smell I can only describe as reptilian. I've never had anything against snakes, but I shiver.

"That's Harvey," Dakota says. "Five-foot ball python."

I crane my neck and scan the room again. "Does Harvey have a terrarium or something?"

"Nah," Dakota says, shutting the door. "He just lives in there." Leaning in, Dakota adds, "It's part of Maude's exposure."

I'm not sure I heard her right. "Exposure?"

Dakota nods and says, in almost a whisper, "It's *mind*-blowing what Simon can do. He's a therapist. Or used to be. Maude is a chick who used to be so afraid of snakes she wouldn't go on *hikes* when she first moved in. She couldn't look at a picture of one without gagging. Now she lives with Harvey. It's incredible."

Dakota watches me, as if waiting for a response. Maybe it's the vape pen's fault, but my mouth is suddenly so dry.

"That's wild," I say.

"I'm about to up my own exposures and I cannot fucking *wait*."

Dakota turns the other way and pops open a door at the far end. We start up another set of narrow stairs that creak and moan under our footsteps. A third story! Mirror House is a waking dream.

"Up here, this is where the open room is," she says.

It's all still spinning around in my head: the room for rent; the loose enormous snake; "exposures." I'm about to ask a follow-up about Harvey when we get to the top and Dakota pushes open the door. And then my train of thought gets derailed.

This isn't a room. This is an entire *floor*.

She flips the lights on and dust sparkles in the air. I spy stars out of the window on the opposite end. The walls to the right and left of me are slanted and the ceiling overhead is tall, beams exposed.

"We just cleaned this out. Refinished attic room. Hella big," Dakota says.

"It's enormous."

"You've got a half bath there at the end, the door," she says, pointing. "No closet, but there's a wardrobe. This is the only room on the third floor. Views are killer. Minus is, it'll probably get stuffy in the summer." She turns and points to a small second window behind us. "But Simon just installed the window box AC."

"How much?" I blurt.

"Twelve hundred a month."

I can't believe a room half the size of the house I'm living in is going for the same amount I'm paying to live in my current mousehole.

"Is it haunted?" I ask jokingly.

My whole life I've eaten up haunted house novels like candy and this rings eerily close to the beginning of one of those twisted tales—where a family scores a Gothic mansion for pennies, then finds themselves shocked to be sharing the house with ghosts.

Dakota's eyes widen. "No, but we could, like, sage it if you're worried."

"I was kidding."

"Oh." She wheezes a laugh and slings an arm around my shoulder. "What do you think? Could you see yourself here?"

I'm getting the tingles. I've been touched more times today than I've probably been touched in months. This stroke of good luck seems serendipitous. And to think, it all happened because my grandmother died and I joined a grief group. Ugly accidents can produce unexpected gifts.

"I see myself here," I say, a smile spreading over my face.

Excerpt from the documentary *The Mirror House Girls: One Year Later*

LOCATION: Interviewee's home, Raven's Landing, California

SCARLETT stares off-camera for a moment, as if collecting her thoughts. (Cut to B-roll footage of the view from her perspective: an oak tree dancing outside her windowpane)

SCARLETT: (Looking at the camera again) I cannot describe how weird it is to hear the world call the people you love most a "murderous death cult." We weren't. I never thought of us as a cult. We were just friends, that's all. I mean, that's how it was for … for most of the time we knew each other, I'd say.

You think "cult." You think, "That could never be me, I'm smarter than that." But what a lot of people don't understand is how slow the process is. We weren't trying to start a movement at first. We were just a house, you know? And my housemates were some of the most gorgeous, talented, hilarious, brilliant folks I'd ever met. I mean, I had some of the most fun I've ever had in that house. And there was healing going on, actual healing. It wasn't fake. The love was real as all get out. That's what makes me so sick. (Scarlett's eyes water up and she turns the other way) Excuse me, I need a moment.

(Camera cuts out, then back on. Scarlett's eyes are pink and puffy and she holds a tissue in her hand)

SCARLETT: The worst part of it is the guilt. I should have done something more. I played a role in it. We all did. And we thought we were doing everything for the right reasons. And that's the worst kind of evil—the self-righteous kind.

7

MY MOTHER ADVISES me not to take the room at Mirror House when I tell her about it because she scrutinized the house on Google Street View and it looked "weird." We're on a video call. She's power walking on her treadmill in Escondido, I'm packing my room into boxes here in Santa Cruz. A gorgeous spread of four-hundred-fifty miles divides us.

"It's *weird*, Noni," she tells me, a little out of breath, her high salt-and-pepper ponytail bobbing up and down. "Who glues garbage all over their house? Looks like someplace a sociopath would live."

Years ago, I discovered that the best way to navigate my mother is to do the opposite of whatever her advice is. This reaction of hers, in a backwards way, is reassuring. *What Wouldn't Janine Do?* is the game I've been playing my whole adult life.

"Well, I met the people who live there," I say as I align paperbacks in a milk crate. "Sorry to tell you, no sociopaths. And I get an entire floor to myself, two blocks from the beach."

"Something about this stinks. If something seems too good

35

to be true, it is." My mother, ever the optimist. "How did you even *find* that place? They advertising for it at a carnival? Looks like a funhouse."

"This woman I know, Dakota, she lives there."

"How do you know her? She another *bookstore clerk*?"

She says *bookstore clerk* with such disgust. My mother's never needed words to convey her emotions; her tone does the work for her. I cannot get off the phone fast enough. But we have this agreement where we talk on Saturdays at 9 a.m. and by keeping to this agreement, she mostly stays off my back.

"No, she's not from the bookstore. I know her from a grief workshop."

My mother squints at me. "Why do *you* need a grief workshop? She was *my* mother."

I bite my lip, not saying what I want to say, which is that *I* was the one who took care of Grandma for a year. *I* was the one who moved home to live with her and drive her to chemo treatments and then move her to hospice. *I* was the one who was there with her when she died. But I don't have the energy for argument.

"It's not a competition. We're both allowed to grieve, Mom," I say quietly.

"Sometimes I can't believe how much you continue to worship her. You know, she wasn't that great a mom. I did my best to give you everything she never gave me."

"I know your relationship was complicated. But she was still my grandma."

"And how do you think I feel?" my mother asks, with a quiver in her voice. "First my mom left, then you left—I'm an orphan."

"Aww, you're okay," I say, but without real conviction. "Hey, I'm sorry, but I need to get packing. My new housemates are coming to help me move in thirty minutes."

"You should keep pepper spray with you until you know more about these people." Earlier in the call, my mom tried to pump me for everyone's full names so she could snoop on them online, but I admitted I didn't know their last names. A tirade commenced.

"Go ahead. Go move into your new weird house. Good luck with *that*." Her tone softens. "Stay safe, baby. Call me if you need anything, anything at all."

"I will. Love you."

"Love you more."

We hang up and I let out a held breath.

"Pepper spray," I mutter to myself. "What the fucking fuck."

8

MY FIRST NIGHT in Mirror House, they throw me a party.

No one has thrown me a party in longer than I can remember, since the days of pigtails and cupcakes. It truly melts me. Maude cooks chana masala ("I remember how much you love curry!") and Dakota gifts me a chenille blanket ("For couch chillin'! You gotta have a blanket for couch chillin'!") and Kristin bakes "special" brownies ("Start off with a half of one, because these babies are TKOs") and Simon offers to give me a "free session" soon ("He's a healer!" they tell me, and I can't tell if they're kidding) and Scarlett sings me a version of "Hallelujah" with her ukulele in a voice so startlingly soulful I have to fight tears in my eyes.

"Damn, I feel like it's my birthday. Why are you all so nice?" I joke. "Are you secretly recruiting me for your church or something?"

They laugh and start throwing out names. "Church of Mirror House!"

"Church of the Holy Mirror!"

"Saint Simon!"

"The Virgin Scarlett!"

"Maude Magdalene!"

They're doubled over, hiss-giggling. I'm getting flashbacks of junior high sleepovers, nights when I laughed so hard at everything and anything my sides hurt. What is it about this house, these people? It's a place of pure joy and camaraderie. I've barely seen any salty interactions since I met them all, not a note of bitterness, not a bad mood or a cutting remark. No messes anywhere. I haven't even seen anyone slink off to their room for solitude—they truly seem to enjoy one another's company all the time. I've never met people like this. Even in high school, my volleyball team had cliques within it. The girls at the sorority were all sweetness in the living room, but there was sniping and shit-talking behind bedroom doors.

My mom's nagging voice whispers, *If something seems too good to be true, it is.*

I push the thought away.

"More vino?" Kristin refills my chipped ceramic mug with a comically large bottle of wine. Costco wine. She doesn't wait for my answer, filling it to the brim.

"That'll do," I say, and she moves on to top off Maude's glass.

Kristin doses out refills with the cheerfulness of a restaurant server. Isn't she a recovering alcoholic? Wouldn't that be some kind of temptation? I watch her make her way around the room in fascination.

Brownies might be kicking in. I'm quickly turning into a pile of goo on the couch.

Dakota, who's sharing my "chillin' blanket" with me, gives my back a pat. "You all right there, soldier?"

"I might be stoned. Or drunk."

"Droned?" Dakota tries.

"Stunk," I reply.

We cackle like a couple of merry witches.

"So stoked you're moving in." She cheerses me. Her face is shiny, cheeks pink, all smiles. Nothing like the weeping girl I met in grief group. "You just like—you belong here in Mirror House."

"Fuck yeah, you fit in." Maude pumps a fist in the air while wiping down the dining room table. "It's the destined divine."

Everyone agrees, nodding and saying yes.

"Hey, I want to show you something," Simon says.

The room goes completely silent. Scarlett stops her ukulele plucking to turn and listen. Simon's standing above me, extending his hand.

I float my palm up to meet his. "Yeah?"

He pulls me to my feet. "Come on. Bring your blanket."

In any other situation, I'd be hesitant if a man whose last name I still didn't know told me to come with him and bring a blanket, housemate or not. But all the women in the house are looking at me and nodding and grinning, like they're in on it too and whatever he's promising is going to be amazing. Like Simon holds the world.

"Do what Simon says," Maude says, almost impatiently, hands on hips.

I go with him, wrapping my blanket around me, the room slightly spinning.

As he leads me to the back door, I note that he's the only man here, living with five women. *Do what Simon says.* Am I imagining it, or every time he speaks, does everybody stop to listen?

9

I'M LYING on my back on the trampoline next to Simon under a blue-black sky screaming with stars. The pounding surf, the cricket's song, the salty bite of the night air. Simon's leg rests against mine under the blanket. We listen together. We don't talk. My head's spinning, drunk girl carousel.

I have a history of desiring men I shouldn't: my best friend's boyfriend in high school; my graduate student instructor at Drake University; Dean, a married man twice my age who was such an obvious slimeball one had to squint hard to see a decent man. And now I can feel that turn in me, that desire. That heat in my lips and tingling between my legs. It's the worst idea in the world, but I'm attracted to Simon.

"*Sic itur ad astra,*" he murmurs. "You know that phrase?"

I shake my head.

"Latin for 'thus one goes to the stars,'" he says. "But really, it's about how you achieve immortality."

Simon's a strange one. Thoughtful, solemn, deep. There's a quiet command about him. When he chooses to speak, he does so slowly, deliberately. I can't tell what he thinks about me, but every time I'm around him, I'm compelled to impress him. Or crack him open somehow, make him laugh. I've yet to make him laugh.

"I know about your grandma," he says, turning on his elbow to look at me. "I'm sorry to hear about what a rough time you've had."

My mouth suddenly feels very dry. The smile evaporates from my lips. "Oh. Yeah."

"Dakota said you spent an entire year caring for her. Dropped out of school, too? That's incredibly generous."

I squish the sadness down. "Well, what are you going to do."

"Are you going back to school, or ...?"

"Not sure," I admit, aiming my gaze up at the stars again. Deriving comfort from my smallness, my not mattering. "Maybe. I was going to become a teacher. Then I thought about switching to nursing after taking care of my grandma but ... I can't stand blood, so, not sure that's gonna fly."

"Can't stand blood," he repeats, as if turning the phrase around in his mind.

"Makes me all queasy. I'll pass out if I see it."

He nods in understanding. "Ah. Hemophobia. It's not uncommon."

Of course he knows the scientific names for phobias. He reads textbooks for fun. An amateur mycologist. The man apparently speaks Latin. Under the blanket, his warm hand discovers mine. He slips his fingers between my fingers and a delicious shiver walks my spine. Because he's brilliant. Because he's important. I start playing sex chess in my mind: If he makes a move, shall I rise to the occasion? Will I do the noble, smarter thing and turn him down? Dare I devour him, here and now, simply because I want to? Maybe a kiss, but that's it. He's my housemate and this is my first night here, for crying out loud. Calm your loins, Winona.

But he doesn't do anything except hold my hand.

I fill the air with questions. I ask how old he is and he tells me he's thirty-three. He must think I'm a child. I'm ashamed to say this makes me want him even more. I ask about his job and he reminds me that he's a "former therapist." But now he's "on pause."

"So you're a healer," I say curiously. It sounded silly when someone said it earlier but now I don't know. Simon seems wise and full of surprises. "What does that mean, exactly?"

"Please, not my term. *Healer*. That's a vast exaggeration of my abilities," he says with a humble half-smile. "I just—I help people transcend their fears."

I wait for more. Instead, he lets go of my hand and sits up.

"I'm grateful you found us, Winona," he says, running his hands through his hair to tame it. He peels the blanket away and slides to the edge of the trampoline. "You're a delight in every way. I meant what I said about that session. Let's do it soon, all right?"

Then, in one quick hop off the trampoline, he's gone. I sit up and watch Simon as he walks barefoot up the porch stairs, where a figure waits in the darkness, arms crossed and elbows cupped in her hands like she's cold. When she speaks, I recognize the voice. Scarlett. Soft and pleading. In the soft glow of the fairy lights, Simon puts his arms around her. I get an odd flutter of envy as they go back inside together. Then I'm left staring at the house, nothing but mirrors.

If I look hard enough, I can see myself there in the shining dark.

10

I'm fascinated by Simon.

There's an air of mystery about him. He's the unspoken leader of the house. He deals with rent and utilities and the landlord. His room is the master bedroom and I've only seen it in glimpses: an altar next to a king-sized bed, a photograph of a smiling, brown-skinned man wearing a blanket. Buddha statues on the windowsill next to burning incense.

"What do you do, Simon?" I ask him one morning as I eat yogurt at the kitchen table, ready for work at the bookshop in my beige Chapters vest.

He looks up from the book he's reading, *A Brief History of Time* by Stephen Hawking. Those brilliant eyes of his, behind his glasses, are framed with thick lashes. They're the brown-green color of the forest and his pensive, wrinkled brow lends his gaze a brooding charm.

"What do I do." He smiles. "Well, right now, I'm speaking to you."

I can never tell if he's kidding. I offer a soft laugh, just in case. "For *work*. Since your psychologist career is on pause."

"Oh." He shuts his book, as if this is going to take a minute. "Currently, I'm consulting as needed—software engineering stuff. Not very enthralling, but my new edict is to work as little as possible. Eventually I'd love to not work at all."

"That's the dream, isn't it?" I say, stirring my yogurt.

"I find it utterly tragic that most Americans slave away in soulless careers their whole life hoping they survive long enough to enjoy their retirement. Is that truly living? I'd rather be hungry and authentic than full-bellied and spiritless."

I could kiss him.

"Psychologist." I put my spoon down. "Is that spiritless work though?"

He exhales, as if this is a heavy question. "You'd be surprised how inhumane it can be."

"Yet you still do this—healing work. Isn't that psychological?"

"Entirely different. That's educational and voluntary. I would never charge anyone for it. Once a gift becomes monetarily exploited, it's not a gift anymore."

My lips tingle as I imagine them on his. Intelligent *and* humble. Devour me now on this kitchen table, Simon.

"It's not healing work, anyway," he says, laughing a little. "Don't call it that. It's just—you want a little taste of the kind of thing I do?"

"Yes," I say automatically.

He pushes his mug of tea to the side and takes his phone out of his pocket. He scoots closer to me on the bench, murmuring, "Hope you don't mind."

"Don't mind at all."

His wallpaper is a white background with the words TURN OFF YOUR PHONE AND LIVE YOUR LIFE. He scrolls through his photos and I find myself studying his long fingers, his square fingernails, remembering how it felt when we held hands the other night. Wondering if it meant anything.

"Here we go," he says, showing me a picture.

It's a portrait of a smiling man, close up. Clean-cut, middle-aged, striking blue eyes.

"This is my dad," he says.

"Aww," I say, looking a little more closely.

"Would you guess he was my dad, looking at him?"

I scour the man's features for resemblance. It's there now that I search for it—the dark eyebrows, the full shape of their bottom lips.

"The mouth, the shape of the eyes maybe?"

"I'm pulling your leg. That's not my dad."

"Oh." I bite my tongue, feeling foolish.

"But when I said he *was*, you started seeing it, right?"

"I guess so."

"And how did you feel about the man when I changed the context?"

"I mean ... I don't know."

"You don't know? You said, 'aww.' Why'd you say that?"

"Because ..." The temperature rises in my cheeks. It's like I'm back in school again and I'm being called on by a teacher unexpectedly to answer a question in front of the class. "Well, I guess I thought it was sweet. That he looked sweet, because he's your dad."

"Right. I saw it in your body language—your posture slackened, you looked at him closer, you smiled a little. You were at ease. Well, as I said, it's not my dad. This is actually a picture of a man who kidnapped and murdered three children last year."

I gasp.

"Okay. Study the picture again and tell me what you see," he says.

I hesitate, disgusted, not wanting to look at the picture again now that I know this information.

"You're taken aback," he says. "Your lip is curling, your posture is rigid."

"Because that's *horrible*."

"Of course it is. Can you see it, though? See it in him, now that it's contextualized?"

He zooms out on the picture, makes it go from close-up to medium. It's a mugshot.

"Really study his face. What changes for you in terms of emotionally processing this image?"

"I don't like looking at it."

"No, dig deeper. What don't you like about the *image*? Be specific."

The man's red face, now too red. His smug smile, his sharp-blue stare.

"I—I don't like his eyes," I say, wanting to look away. To think of what those eyes have seen makes me want to scream.

"Because you know he's a murderer. Because the story changed."

He turns off his screen and pockets his phone.

"That was actually an AI image, don't worry," he says, laughing, petting my arm to assure me. "You don't need to be this disturbed."

Finally, I made him laugh. And all I needed was to be flabbergasted.

"My head is spinning," I say.

"Exactly. Because the story keeps changing. And that's all life is—stories. Narratives. If you change the story you tell yourself, you can change anything. I'm sorry." He tousles my bangs. "I didn't mean to make your head spin."

"No, it's an interesting exercise. Definitely something to think about."

"An addendum, if you don't mind?"

An addendum. I love him.

"Go ahead," I say.

"The strings pulling the puppet here are simple. There's just two of them. There's fear and there's love. And everything else stems from there. It was love that made you say *aww*. It was fear that made you recoil. All the other emotions—hate, guilt, shame, jealousy—they stem out of those two emotions. My sessions, my teachings, are just meant to explore that. How you can move from one to the other, from fear to love. How you can be the writer of your own story."

"So interesting," I say.

He adjusts his glasses and goes back to reading his book. The conversation's over. But all day long, I'm replaying it. I'm watching the world a bit differently and trying to pinpoint the stories I might be telling myself. I'm turning over this idea in my mind about fear and love being the roots of all emotions.

Maybe there's something to that.

Excerpt from the documentary *The Mirror House Girls: One Year Later*

LOCATION: Interviewee's home, Raven's Landing, California

SCARLETT crosses her arms as if a cool breeze just blew in. Her eyes dance and her brow creases as she watches the air.

SCARLETT: Tell you what, we were all a little in love with Simon. He had this lure, this way of seeing just what it was you needed and giving that thing to you. He changed my life—*all* our lives—for the better at first. And it was *real* what he did. He could … dig deep, find what it was you were most scared of, and he could teach you to conquer it. He worked psychological miracles. I saw it happen with my own eyes. He did it for me. In our sessions, I confronted the worst, I confronted it head on. (Her voice drops to near a whisper) I was victorious. For a bit. Losing battle, I suppose.

(She wipes her eyes, visibly shaken, and looks at the camera) Fear always wins in the end though, doesn't it?

11

MY FIRST COUPLE of weeks in Mirror House, I wake up to skylight sunbeams and the distant noise of the curling surf. Drink pour-over coffee, listen to Scarlett playing guitar in the other room. Swing on the chair out on the porch with a paperback splayed on my thigh. Thrift shop with my bubbly housemates. Paint furniture. Dry wildflowers between the pages of heavy books. Weed the garden, fingernails charcoaled with dirt. Sink my teeth into whole tomatoes that explode like delicious grenades. Guzzle cheap wine from chipped mugs. Devour vegan feasts. Dance around a beach bonfire. Burn candles in old wine bottles, learn three chords on Scarlett's guitar, read my favorite page of the *Rubaiyat* to everyone.

> I sometimes think that never blows so red
> The Rose as where some buried Caesar
>   bled;
> That every Hyacinth the Garden wears
> Dropt in its Lap from some once
>   lovely head

Maude nods, Kristin murmurs "Noice," and Dakota wipes a tear from her eye. Scarlett jots it down in her journal. Simon silently mouths the words as if memorizing them. They know what it means. Until now, poetry has been a mostly solitary indulgence. If not solitary, it's been a withered academic spewing it to a sea of bored faces in a classroom setting. What a gift to indulge in poetry as a peer group, swept up in the words at once, hearts rhyming.

The poem speaks and we get it: life is never so beautiful as when you have known its opposite.

I adore every person here. Kristin with her brash, say-anything ways, her self-deprecating humor, and manic energy. She spends a Saturday morning teaching me to ride a skate-board and we glide through town, over a footbridge, along the beach, Ferris wheel in the background, wind in our ponytails. She treats me to lunch at a restaurant on the wharf, a bistro that is all windows, white tablecloths, and waiters who call us "ma'am" as if we're not wearing cutoff shorts and bathing suit tops.

"Can I order you a drink?" Kristin asks.

"I'm okay."

"It's part of my exposure. Can I order you what I'd order? Vodka tonic?"

I part my lips, unsure what to say.

"Come on, bitch! It's good for me. Simon wants me to."

"Okay," I finally answer.

After ordering, my phone *hum-hum-hum*s in my pocket and I sneak a peek. My mother. Again. I forgot about our weekly call. Her first text was at 9:08 this morning: *Are you alive??* When I replied that I was out with ones of my housemates, she asked if my housemates are more important than she is now. Grandma Jane used to dare me to block my mother's calls and I can't deny that the temptation's there sometimes.

"Grandma!" I'd say, horrified. "She's your daughter."

"*I* would never block her. But *you* should. Just for a little spell, make her loosen the damn leash already."

And then she'd cackle. No one made my grandma laugh like my grandma.

"... and so it's about fear, at the core," Kristin's saying. I can feel her leg jiggling under the table. "Isn't everything? Jealousy, guilt, shame, all the more complex emotions? That's what you discover when you start breaking everything down."

What she's saying sounds familiar, but I spaced out and missed her last few sentences. If only conversations were like reading and I could silently just back up a paragraph to catch up.

"Simon reframed it for me in session, that addiction's fear in victim's clothing, and it's been kind of a revelation to me." Kristin folds her hands on the table. Manicured hands, despite her baseball hat and cargo shorts. What was she like ten years ago? I can imagine her on the volleyball team with me. "Sorry. Am I making you uncomfortable? I'm an oversharer." She laughs loudly—a *hee-haw* laugh that reminds me, endearingly, of a donkey. "Sometimes I don't know when I've crossed a line."

"Nah, not at all."

I love oversharers. They're easy conversationalists.

"My parents have spent more money on rehab for me than they did to send my brother through medical school," she says almost proudly, but her smile falters. "I could have died a year ago. Rehab helped me detox, but it's Simon who keeps me clean. He really is a healer."

The gleam in her olive-green eyes borders on worship. I'm guessing there's more to this story—she's attracted to him, they've hooked up, something. I have yet to fully untangle the backstory of Mirror House. Then again, every time I suspect that Simon might be flirting with me, I see him doing the same to someone else and realize it's just the way he is.

The server, a man in a button-up shirt with GOOD and EVIL tattooed on his knuckles, delivers my drink. Kristin asks me if she can take a selfie with my vodka tonic, such an odd request that I answer her like I'm asking a question. "Sure?"

"Just need to send him a copy." Kristin snaps a selfie and sends it off on her phone. Her hand is shaking. When she's done, she raises a glass of water with such energy, a drip splashes on the table. "Please! Cheers!"

I clink my glass to hers, a little uneasy and a lot confused.

The meal is mediocre, the drink is weak, but the view is sublime. She pays for the check with a silver credit card, the name KEVIN PARK embossed on the front. Same credit card that bought our groceries earlier this week and all that soil from the nursery. Her family's pockets apparently run deep.

We walk the length of the wharf and spend a long while leaning on the wooden railing, taking in the glassy, choppy ocean. Kristin's ponytail whips back and forth and when she thinks I'm not looking, her face relaxes into a forlorn expression.

I gaze at the water again, a quivering green. Full of sharks and murk, yet all we see from here is sparkle.

* * *

Later in the week, I wake up at three in the morning and head downstairs to refill my water bottle. I'm spooked by the sight of Maude sweeping the kitchen floor at this hour. I blink back at her in the darkness.

"Maude?"

"Hey, Winona."

"What are you doing down here?"

"Just ... can't sleep." She lets out a long sigh. Her eyes are bright but puffy from exhaustion, her hair in an unkempt braid. She's in a long nightgown with a lace collar. "Figured I'd clean up a little."

Maude's always in the kitchen, always picking up after everyone. Sometimes people call her "Mom."

"You don't have to do that," I say as I watch her.

"I want to!"

I fill up my bottle at the refrigerator, watching as she sweeps. It feels like an hour goes by. My water bottle is huge.

"Whenever I have trouble sleeping, I read something boring," I offer. "Like *Moby Dick*."

"Eh, I'm no intellectual. I'm a doer, not a thinker." She reaches down with a groan, picking up a dust bunny and tossing it in the trash. "My daddy used to always say, 'if you're gonna be miserable, at least get some shit done while you're at it.'"

Footsteps bound down the stairs. It's Simon in his plaid robe and slippers. He's squinting. "Maude?"

"I know, I know," she says defensively. "I already know what you're going to say."

"Then don't make me say it," he says.

His tone is gentle, but his words are a command. I don't know exactly how to read him. There's this long, loaded moment—one where Simon stares at her as if waiting for something and Maude stops sweeping and gives him a pleading look. Finally, she turns and puts the broom back in the corner.

"Okay," she says, heading up the stairs.

"Do not let fear rule your life," Simon says as he follows her. "You're stronger than this."

The stairs creak, their voices disappear, and I'm left alone in the kitchen. As I head back to my room, I overhear soft sounds behind her door—Maude crying the high-pitched words *thirty years!* And Simon comforting her in a low voice.

I've always been a greedy reader. I want to know the deeper meaning. I want to know the whole story.

12

I'M NOT A BIG DRINKER. I was the designated driver at my high school prom. I order cosmos when I go to bars because I can only handle girly cocktails. The first time Dean gave me whiskey, I gagged; he licked his lips, declared me cute. But since moving into Mirror House last month, I've started drinking to keep up with everyone.

The wine's ever-flowing here, bought by the case. White in the afternoons, red in the evenings, mimosas at breakfast. And a lot of weed, though Simon says it irritates his lungs and that we need to keep it outside. The wine only adds to the Dionysian vibe of the house. Scarlett belts her songs a little louder, Simon paces the house and philosophizes, Maude cranks her music and mops the floor, pretending the handle is a microphone and she's singing along with KISS. Kristin, of course, embraces her role as the cheerful enabler. We even call her that as she wanders around topping off glasses.

"Enabler! Thank you," Maude says, kissing the side of her head.

"You're most welcome," Kristin says with a smile.

"Come, smell my glass, enabler." Simon says one night, holding his COOL GRANDMAS HAVE COOL GRAND-KIDS mug in the air.

Kristin slides his way and puts her nose in his glass.

"Mmm," he murmurs as he draws it to his purpled lips. "Imagine how good it tastes."

She nods, her face still close to his.

"It's delicious," he says quietly to her.

Then he kisses her. Fully. Tongue in her mouth and everything. I gape in shock. No one else seems startled, but a faint *mmm* escapes from Kristin, like a hungry woman who just got her first taste of food. He pulls back and glances at me as he wipes the edges of his mouth with a finger.

"Exposure," he says, wiggling his eyebrows.

Won't lie, the whole exchange was kind of hot. Then again, I'm drunk, a pile in a beanbag chair. When I'm a drunk pile on a beanbag chair I'm not the best judge. The room's beginning to tilt and I get up for a glass of water, gulp it down in the kitchen, fill it up again. Dakota's got control of the stereo now, I'm guessing, because "Friend of the Devil" comes on in the living room. Kristin comes in behind me and puts the giant wine bottle on the counter.

"Are you and Simon a thing?" I ask.

Kristin seems startled by the question, as if she had been daydreaming and didn't know I was even here. In a blink, her expression warms. She snickers. "No, no. Oh, that? We're just silly sometimes."

A moon grins goofily at me through the window. Beneath it, there's that weird doghouse no one seems to know the story about.

"Isn't it hard for you?" I ask Kristin. "Serving everyone, when you're sober?"

Self-awareness prickles. I realize how drunk I sound—nosy questions and slurred delivery.

She probably thinks I'm an idiot.

But she doesn't let on, offering a tight smile. "If it isn't hard, it isn't work worth doing."

I admire her deeply at this moment. I don't know that I've ever worked too hard at anything. That's not entirely true; I did care for Grandma Jane, hardest work I've ever done. But loving someone makes hard work easy. What I mean is this: I'm not sure if I've ever worked a damn to better *myself*.

Back in the living room, Simon suggests that we play a game of Truth. Everyone *ooh*s and *ahh*s and finds seats, three squeezing in cozy on each couch. Dakota turns off the stereo. The fairy lights and flickering candles and the hush that settles throughout the room all lend the scene an air of holiness, like I've stepped into a chapel. I sip my icy water, thinking ... Truth? As in Truth or Dare? What's next, Spin the Bottle and cootie catchers? I'm a grown-ass woman. I left games like that back in the age of first crushes and training bras.

"Top me off one more time before we begin, Kristin?" Simon asks, putting his hands together in a prayer position.

"You got it," Kristin says.

His tolerance is astounding. While other people drink and get flushed and giggly and sentimental, Simon can drink wine like water and never waver. He can't be ruffled. His focus and self-possession are untouchable.

"We're really playing Truth?" I ask, my question directed at him. He's seated in the middle of the other couch with Maude, sharing a blanket.

"Fuck yeah we are. Get with the program, man," says Maude. She's got a grin cemented on her face as she knits. I can tell she's tipsy because it's only when she's tipsy that she smiles wide enough to reveal her silver teeth.

"It's a Mirror House thang," says Scarlett, who is seated next to me and braiding her wild strawberry hair. "Can I share your blanket?"

"Of course!"

As we cuddle closer, I can smell her—vanilla and campfire smoke. I'm still getting used to the unabashed affection this group shares. There's this feeling in the air that you can hug anyone at any moment, tell them you love them, say anything and be accepted fully. I've never felt that before, not anywhere. I've spent my life watching what I say carefully and molding my responses to fit other people and situations. Here, we're just ourselves, plain and simple. It's so freeing.

"All right," Simon says after Kristin's refilled his wine. She settles next to him on the couch, sipping her sticker-covered water bottle. "Good girl."

She gives a thumbs up. Her mouth might be smiling, but her eyes aren't. Despite her cheery disposition, something is underneath—a sadness, a tenseness—and I feel sorry for her, being the only sober person in the room. I know she wouldn't want my pity. She's choosing to be here and to play the role of barmaid. To do "hard work." But still.

"I know it might seem juvenile, but I promise, it's a lot of fun." Simon looks at me and smiles. A silence floods the room and I hear a few deep breaths, as if everyone's about to watch me jump into a cool body of water. They turn their heads my way. My neck prickles in anticipation. "As the latest addition, you're going to go first."

"Me?" I ask, my mouth going dry.

The room is so quiet I can hear the crackle of a candlewick.

"Tell us something you've never told anyone before," he says.

I snicker nervously. "Really? Seriously?"

"You can do it, dude," Dakota whispers next to me.

Everyone waits. I feel like I've been slapped, my thoughts spinning, the wine clouding my head. What am I supposed to tell them? They're watching me with shiny, expectant stares.

"Something I've never told anyone," I repeat. "Okay."

Think, brain. Find something funny. Shatter the agonizing seriousness that has overtaken this party.

"Once I had a dream I went skydiving with Chewbacca," I say.

But no one laughs. They're still staring at me.

"Come on, Winona." Simon shakes his head, as if I've disappointed him. "No cheating. No hiding behind humor. Dig deep."

I don't know what to tell them, how to please them. I steal a sip of wine to stall.

"Mmm." I put the mug back down. A memory surfaces with a jolt of shame. "Okay. When I was in school in Iowa, I once stole a block of cheese from a supermarket."

Nothing. Everyone's waiting for more.

"You think that's deep?" Simon chides. "Then there must not be much to you."

"Come on, bitch, we want dirt," Kristin says playfully.

"It has to be real," Dakota says from beside me, nudging me with a socked foot.

"That is real!" I say. "I really did that."

"So what? You stole some cheese, so fucking what?" Simon almost shouts.

I've never heard Simon raise his voice. Simon speaks in whispers, in calculated statements. He's collected. But right now, he seems pissed.

"Tell us something that scares you. That truly matters." His expression softens. "Give us *a box full of darkness*."

I'm a sucker for poetry and the man knows it. How dare he

use Mary Oliver's words against me. I lock eyes with him. He perks his purpled lips into a half-smile.

"We will still love you, no matter what you tell us," he says, "and whatever you say, it stays in this room. It expires at midnight like fairy godmother magic. It goes nowhere."

I'm so on the spot and wine-sloppy, my eyes sparkle with tears. I blink them away.

"We've all done it," Scarlett whispers, her hand finding mine under the blanket and squeezing. "You can too."

In the long silence, I consider my options. I could make up a salacious story to please Simon. Somehow, though, he'd know it's not real. He can see right through me. I could announce that I've become uncomfortable and don't want to play this game, but imagining the disappointment of the five lovely people in the room makes me want to implode. I could pretend to be sick and run to my room—too pathetic. There are plenty of options to get out of doing it. But somehow, I know this is a fork in the road. And I want to take the one less traveled.

My mind is stuck, so my mouth takes the lead.

"All right, all right." I clear my throat and squeeze Scarlett's hand back. Blow out a long breath. Tell my tear ducts to keep their shit together. "I'll tell you a story about my father."

13

I GREW up revering my single mom, a businesswoman in the pharmaceutical industry. She was my champion—the one who packed snacks and parked herself in the front row at every volleyball practice. Who stayed up late to triple check my homework. Who made me gluten-free, vegan, raw breakfasts, lunches, and dinners. But the older I got, the more oppressive her attention became.

Sylvia Plath has a line in a poem, "Widow. The word consumes itself," and it makes me think of my mother. She's not only a widow, but one who thrives on that identity and the sympathy it elicits. A woman who lives in a cage of her own sorrow and worry.

My mom is someone who pays for apps to tell her about every crime that happens in her neighborhood. Who sees someone in a hoodie walking near her house and jumps online to report a suspicious person sighting. Who stays up to date on obscure viruses spiking in regions all over the country. And yes, it's a lot, but I learned why at the age of six. My father, absent all my life, died in a car accident when my mom was pregnant with me. I've assumed the shock and loss shaped her into the woman she is today: the widow who consumes herself.

Widow isn't the technical term, because my parents never married. Still, my mom has called herself one all her life and hasn't dated anyone since. Even though my parents were only together for three months. Even though I never knew his last name, only his first. When I asked questions about him, she cried. I hated making my mother cry, so I stopped asking questions.

But when I was fourteen, I found a picture of him in her vanity drawer while snooping for eyeliner. It was him, I knew it was, because on the back of the picture she wrote the name "Sawyer" and a heart.

That was his name.

And those were my eyebrows, and my dark brown eyes, and there was the cowlick just off the center of my hairline. He had a jagged scar across his entire left cheek like a startling pink slash. I longed to know the story of his scar. I longed to know him. He perched on a sofa I recognized—the floral antique that had always been in our living room—and wore a sharp blue suit, his thousand-dollar smile like a man who won a prize.

The sight of it made me ache, but I couldn't stop staring.

I never asked my mother about it, but I took a picture with my phone. A picture of a picture. I can't count the number of times I gazed at that picture of a picture over the years, wondering what life would have been like if he had survived.

At seventeen, I got a job bussing tables at an Italian restaurant called Cugini's in Carlsbad. My mom disapproved; she didn't like me having to drive on the freeway at night. She didn't like the idea that I might get sexually harassed by patrons. She used her app and cited murders that had occurred in the area. But I wanted, more than anything, to be independent, and so I took the job anyway, leaving my phone tracking on so she could know exactly where I was as a compromise.

I absolutely loved that job. It was my first taste of freedom, the first activity I had where my mom wasn't there. She had been the leader of my Girl Scout troop growing up, the chaperone at every field trip and school dance, my volleyball cheerleader. And she now became a regular at the restaurant. But otherwise, this was *my* space. I was the youngest employee and I blended in with the grown-ups. I overheard the cooks' dirty jokes and listened to the servers complain about their dating lives and sometimes I had a beer when my shift was over, always making sure to eat breath mints and wash my face so my mom couldn't smell my breath and clothes.

A few months after I started that job, I leveled up from bussing tables to hostessing. I got to dress pretty and wear lipstick and earrings. I didn't have to pick up dirty napkins or scrape half-eaten plates of pasta or haul tubs of dishes anymore. One night, a family walked in for dinner and when the man asked to be seated, my mouth dropped open.

He was the man in the picture in my mother's vanity.

It was impossible—a ghost sighting—it defied logic. But it was him, I knew it was, because I had stared at that face longingly for years and years. He was older now, plumper, some wrinkles, salt-and-peppered hair.

But that scar on his cheek.

Eyebrows like my eyebrows.

The matching brown of his eyes.

"Table for five?" he repeated, as if I was stupid.

He had no idea who I was.

I felt myself falling while standing still. Finally, I found my voice again. "Right this way."

After I seated him, my chest tightened so badly I asked for a break. I went to the back of the kitchen. I stood in the walk-in freezer, stunned, and took deep breaths of arctic air. I finally collected myself and returned to the floor and passed by the man's table to steal another look at him. I was a hundred percent sure. And they were clearly a family—two grade-school-aged boys and a girl who was probably thirteen. His wife had an easy beauty about her, graying blond hair and a floral dress that reached the floor. They shared a bottle of wine and smiled and chatted. The boys pushed each other and the dad—my dad?—threatened to take away their screen time. He pushed the bread basket toward the girl and said, *mangia, mangia* in an Italian accent like a dorky dad.

He was real.

I took note, out of the corner of my eye, of everything I could about him. The shiny watch on his left wrist. The fact he ordered linguini and clams and drank chardonnay. The way he gesticulated when he spoke and the boom of his laugh. Part of my hostessing duties included ringing up checks, so when they wrapped up their meal, I took their card with a shaking hand and rang it up.

Sawyer Woodward, it said in embossed lettering.

I felt like I had swallowed a stone.

I asked the server who had been at their table about them and she said they were regulars. *Regulars.* They lived close by. I couldn't even wait until my shift was over, I faked a stomachache and fled to my car and looked him up online. I spent an hour in my parked car, scrolling my phone and hyperventilating. He was an ophthalmologist at a clinic not ten miles away from my house.

I drove home practicing how I was going to ask my mom about this. I rehearsed, controlling my tone, cool and collected, clutching the steering wheel so tightly the bones in my fingers hurt. But when I got through the door and she looked up at me—she was running the vacuum on the already

65

clean living room floor—I saw my own panic reflected back like a mirror image.

"What happened?" she gasped, switching it off. "What's wrong?"

"You lied," I croaked.

"About what?"

My mouth hung open. I racked my brain for eloquence, for complete sentences, for logical questions. But all I could get out was his name.

"Sawyer Woodward," I said.

The name was a knife that sliced through the air. We held ourselves still, neither one of us blinking.

"I saw him," I said. "At the restaurant. I've seen the picture in your drawer. He's my dad, right?"

My mom covered her mouth with her hand. Her eyes filled with tears. Mine didn't—I felt something else rising in me, a tidal wave of rage.

"What the fuck is wrong with you?" I said, louder. "You said he died. Why would you say that?"

"Please don't scream at me in my house."

I bit my tongue until the pain was too much.

"If you sit down and stop shouting and cursing at me, I will talk to you," she said, in a tone like she was talking to someone with a grenade in their hand. "If you remain calm, we can have a conversation."

We sat down on the sofa—the same one in the picture of my dad—and she hugged me and burst into tears. She cried and cried until my shoulder was wet, murmuring things like *I never wanted you to know* and *I was only trying to protect you*. She told me the story, hammering the points out like a chronological shopping list: She and Sawyer had a "passionate, whirlwind affair"; when she got pregnant, he didn't want to be a father; he gave her money for an abortion and broke it off; they went their separate ways; she never saw him again.

"I thought a dead father would have been better than one who never wanted you at all," she said. "I figured it was simpler to say he died."

I studied her crumpled and quivering face and wondered what other lies hid behind there.

"It was wrong, but everything I've done, it's been for you." She put a hand to my cheek. "To protect you. You *know* that."

She wrapped her arms around me. As she shuddered with sobs and I patted her back, I went numb, empty. And I thought, first chance I get, I'm moving the fuck out of San Diego County and I am never, ever going to return.

Never told anyone that story. Not my friends, not my sorority sisters, not even my Grandma Jane.

Until now, anyway.

14

My Mirror House audience is rapt as I wipe tears from my silly, disobedient eyes. A pause swells in the living room as the candlelight dances in shadows on the walls. Everyone watches me with such sadness. I'm a puddle. I'm too much wine and tears. Make it stop.

"Bless your heart," Scarlett says, pulling me in for a hug. "You sweet girl."

I don't want to cry. Don't want to be the center of attention, to be a soggy, sentimental mess, for this party to have somehow devolved into group therapy. I wish I could eat my words again and steal my story back. But suddenly it's not just Scarlett comforting me. Dakota wraps her arms around me, too. Then everyone comes and surrounds me, into a group hug, five people, ten arms, and my vision goes black from the tight embrace. And then the oddest thing happens. I feel an electricity, a thrum. A buzzing like I'm a bee in the heart of a hive.

They're all humming together.

mmmmmmmmmmmm

One long droned human didgeridoo note.

mmmmmmmmmmmm
Vibrating and tickling and worming inside me.
mmmmmmmmmmmm
The rich sound radiating like a train passing through my ghost.
mmmmmmmmmmmmm
The skin of my eardrums to my blood-buried bones.
mmmmmmmmmmmmmm
In my lungs, in my lips, in my heart.
mmmmmmmmmmmmmm
Time stops and my tears dry.
mmmmmmmmmmmmmmm
And now I'm humming, too.
"Mmmmmmmmmmmmm..."
This is one of the strangest experiences, one that sparks every emotion at once. I'm scared in the darkness of this collective embrace, of why they're doing this to me. I'm amazed at the droning sound, I'm in ecstasy because something about it feels physically good. I'm sad because of what I just shared. The overwhelming droning goes on and on. Minutes tick by and I'm dizzied from the lack of oxygen. When everyone pulls away from me and the humming stops, I gasp like I've just been born.

They're looking at me with expectant, shining eyes. My skin tingles and my ears still ring from the humming.

This is the weirdest fucking moment of my life.

"How do you feel?" Simon asks.

I don't have the correct words. I'm not sure what happened, but it was incredible. Like someone just poured a bucket of light and love on my head.

"Fortified?" he offers.

I nod, slowly. A bewildered laugh escapes my lungs.

"We call that a Resonance," he says.

My head is swimming.

"Transcendent, isn't it?" Dakota asks, petting my arm.

"You did great," Maude says.

"You're a rock star," Kristin says.

Dazed, I keep nodding, a real-life bobblehead, then murmur something about needing to go to bed. I make my way upstairs and collapse onto my mattress without brushing my teeth. I'm not sure if I'm more drunk or baffled but either way, my brain is a merry-go-round and I need it to stop.

It's not until I'm drifting to sleep that it occurs to me that I was the only person who played the Truth game tonight.

Excerpt from the documentary *The Mirror House Girls: One Year Later*

LOCATION: Interviewee's home, Raven's Landing, California

SCARLETT stirs a cup of steaming tea and sits back in her chair.

SCARLETT: "Parties." They weren't much fun, looking back on it. But in the moment, they were a blast. In the moment.

They'd start out normal. Dancing, drinking, loud conversations. Bump music, jump on the trampoline. It would end with someone in tears and then the Resonance. Which … y'all have seen the videos.

I still remember Winona's first party, few weeks after she moved in. We were all nice and buzzed, gathered around the living room for a game of "Truth." (Finger quotes) Led by Simon, of course. Though somehow he made it feel like it was all our idea, *our* ritual.

Winona had to tell us about something she'd never told anyone before. (A teary-eyed pause) Can I have a minute?

(Cut. SCARLETT now has a box of tissues and

she's no longer crying; her eyes, however, are puffy and pink)

Her first game, her first Resonance, Winona was blackberry-lip drunk, you know? Only Jesus's disciples liked wine more than Mirror House, so we were all tipsy. Seems unfair to booze somebody up and then get them to tell you their secrets. But that's what happened. I had this weird déjà vu the entire time watching it through the haze. Realizing that this was maybe some kind of ritual I was part of and right now I was just standing on a different side of the fence. 'Cause they'd done the same thing to me a few months back.

Winona moving in shifted my perspective for the first time. Just the first lil' inkling that something about this wasn't right, you know? The doubt, the devil on my shoulder whispering in my ear. But I dismissed it, because to question what we were doing was to question my friends, my life, my living situation, my community. My family. The only people I really had.

I had been the last one to join the house, about six months before, so I was pretty fresh myself when Winona joined Mirror House. It was eerie the way the same things seemed to happen to Winona that happened to me. It's strange how you don't notice manipulation when it's happening to you. But it's obvious when you see it happening to someone else.

I wish I'd listened to the devil on my shoulder, 'cause he was onto something.

15

THE NEXT MORNING, Simon visits me in my room with a cup of tea. Earl Grey, with a teaspoon of honey and a dash of oat milk, the way I make it every morning. I'm touched by the gesture. He's still in his pajama pants, scruffy-faced, hair fluffy and wild.

"Just came to check up on you," he says softly, studying me.

I wrap my hands around the warm mug. "Oh, I'm fine."

"I'm proud of you for being so open and honest with us last night. It takes strength to be vulnerable, to surrender," he says with that therapist energy of his.

His handsome seriousness makes me squirmy.

"Thank you, kind sir," I say, to try to break the ice.

I sit up, propped against pillows under my quilt. I'm still waking up, at a loss for words as the details of last night float back to me. The long-lost-dad sob story—I cringe. And the bizarreness of the "Resonance." The humming, the group hug that swallowed me in something resembling a holy moment. Now, in the light of day, I don't know what to think about it. I feel awkward.

"It was a weird night," I say finally, because Simon seems to be waiting for me to say something.

"What happened was important," he says. "You finally let something go that has been holding you back for years. You can release that memory and the grief and resentment. What do you think is at the root of choosing to keep that memory to yourself, of letting it fester? Where did it stem from, Winona?"

I haven't had enough caffeine yet for psychoanalysis. I'm at a loss. "Embarrassment?"

"Dig deeper," he says. "It's *fear*. If you deconstruct embarrassment, it's simply the fear of rejection."

I nod slowly, his words sinking in. I never thought of it that way.

"Every negative emotion comes down to fear." Simon's eyes light up as he continues. His passion is contagious. "Anger: the fear of losing control. Jealousy: the fear of not being loved. Anxiety is simply an overreaction to fear."

I consider what he's saying as I sip tea. In the pause, the distant sigh of the ocean drifts from my open window. Sunshine slants through my skylight, sparkling the dust in the air. I picture Grandma Jane's ghost. "What about grief?"

"Mmm," he says, as if his interest is piqued. "Grief is love bent backwards. Have you ever noticed the pitch in your stomach you get, that physical sensation of being overwhelmed by grief? Really located it in your body? It sends you into a state of arousal of fight, flight, or freeze in the same way fear does. You follow?"

I nod, fascinated. I'm getting a TED talk in my own bedroom.

"And fear is almost *always* located somewhere in the past or future. For example, your story last night—your past. That is done, that is over, that happened and it's unfortunate but the negative emotions you feel are about something that literally does not exist anymore. The past does not exist. The future does not exist."

It's freeing to imagine.

"Shame?" he continues. "That's fear of other people's reactions—reactions that haven't even happened, by the way. The *future*. Hypotheticals. But you know what is always, always located here in the now? What is ever-pure and ever-present? Love. Which is the antidote to fear."

My eyes are locked with his. This guy is so fucking smart. Not just book smart, although he's that, too. Simon is the most emotionally intelligent person I've ever met.

"You should be a guru," I tell him.

He pushes me playfully. "Stop."

Our eyes lock again. If I didn't know him, I'd wonder if he has a thing for me. But Simon looks at all of us this way. Everyone in this house looks at each other that way.

"We have something so unique here in Mirror House," he says.

I blink. He might even be able to read minds.

His expression goes solemn. "We're collectively enlightened. And as individuals, we've worked toward a life without fear. Everyone is doing the work to overcome the burden of it. You can feel it here—pure acceptance, pure love. I see the look on your face. The doubt. But there's an energy in this house that you can't deny. And last night, the Resonance? That was you becoming a part of it."

"It was definitely an experience."

"What does that mean, exactly?" He reaches for my toe and squeezes it through the quilt. "An 'experience.' Be more specific."

My brain reaches for the right word. "A spiritual experience, I guess?"

"You 'guess?' Are you not sure?"

"No, I am." I flash him a smile. "Sorry. I haven't had caffeine yet."

"It was beautiful to see. And I have a feeling it's only the beginning." He smiles at me. "I offered you a free session. When are we going to schedule a time for it?"

I bite my lip. After last night, I'm dying to know what these sessions are like. Are they anything like how the Resonance felt? Or is it going to be cathartic, like therapy? I have to find out.

"I have Wednesday afternoon off," I say.

"Does two work?"

"Sure. What do I need to bring?"

"An open mind. That's all."

"My place or yours?"

"You never run out of quips, do you, Winona?"

He stands up and stretches, revealing a little patch of hair under his belly button. With a spark, I suddenly wonder where it leads.

"We love you," he says when he leaves my room.

We.

16

CHAPTERS IS a soulless chain bookstore mostly stocked with airport paperbacks and decorated in various shades of beige, but it's air-conditioned in the summertime and slow enough that I'm able to sneak a few pages here and there. My boss stomps around with a vein ticking on her forehead and an eternal train of coffee-breath sighs escaping her mouth as if she's about to blow her top over the fact that someone messed up her cookbook display. But I get along with the rest of my co-workers, a handful of literary nerds and prose snobs and wannabe poets like me.

Sunday, I get a ride home from Daphne. She wears black lipstick and sings in a band called Rotted Corpse, and she's read every Stephen King book ever written. I invite her inside to see Mirror House. She can't believe I live here.

"You fucking freak!" she says, with admiration.

I'm excited to show it off, my strange and artistic and wonderful house, and as we step inside, I recognize the wonder painting her face. I felt the same wonder when I first stepped inside. And even though I've only paid two months' rent at this point, I'm proud of my home like I built it with my own two hands.

Scarlett pops around a corner with a towel on her head, in her bathrobe, and startles. She looks spooked. I'm about to introduce Daphne but Scarlett turns and disappears—*poof*—as quickly as she arrived.

"Fucking freaks," Daphne murmurs again.

I choose to take it as a compliment.

"Anyway, thanks for letting me inside." Daphne heads toward the front door. "I've always wondered about this place."

"Have a good one," I say with a wave.

After Daphne takes off, Scarlett emerges from her room. She's dressed in shorts and a T-shirt, her hair still wet. "I'm about to head down for beach cleanup, wanna come with?"

"Sure," I say. "Can I change out of my stupid work shirt?"

"Aww, come on. You look like a cute little golfer."

I scoff and bound up the stairs for a quick wardrobe change.

When we head out of the house together, our flip-flops slapping the pavement, Scarlett asks me about the girl I brought over.

"Oh, she's just someone I work with. She wanted to see what the house looked like inside."

"Ahhh."

A couple laughing surfers in wetsuits pass by us on the sidewalk.

"You check with Simon about that?" Scarlett asks, stopping to smell a geranium in someone's front yard.

"About what?"

"Your friend coming over?"

I'm so confused. I block the sun with my hand, trying to better read Scarlett's expression. But it's hard with her heart-shaped sunglasses.

"Should I have?" I ask.

"Never mind. What's done is done." She nods up the block toward the eucalyptus trees that overlook the ocean. "Race you to the beach?"

She starts counting off before I can even respond and when she hits three, we break into a run and speed toward the ocean as fast as our legs will take us. Our sprint only takes thirty seconds and then we're there at the top of the steps overlooking the beach, laughing and catching our breath.

"Hey, slackers!" Kristin yells below, waving with a grabber tool.

Scarlett and I head down the rickety wooden staircase. The whole group is picking up trash along the beach. Maude drags a bag so massive she reminds me of Santa Claus.

"Leave any trash for us, Maude?" Scarlett jokes. "Don't get greedy, now."

"Hey, don't piss off a lady with a bag full of broken bottles," Maude jokes back.

We get a couple grabber tools and scour the sand for cans and bottles and cigarette butts. As the ocean waves break against the rocks, that odd interaction with Scarlett floats back to mind. Was she serious? Was I supposed to ask Simon about Daphne coming inside? I must have misunderstood. But soon I forget about it. Because everyone's laughing and tiptoeing in the waves and chasing each other with grabber tools. Somehow, these people can make a blast out of something as mundane as cleaning up a beach.

17

I'M SITTING at the breakfast table with Dakota and Maude, eating oatmeal. Dakota's in her mechanic shirt because she's headed to work soon to be her badass lady self who fixes cars. Maude's playing solitaire. She's cheating, moving piles willy-nilly, and I bite my tongue to refrain from telling a silly joke about her only cheating herself.

"I hear you've got your first session with Simon today," Maude says with an encouraging nod.

"You got this, dude," Dakota says, reaching out for a hi-five.

"I have no idea what to expect," I tell them.

"That's the best way to go in," Maude says. "With an open mind."

"It's rad." Dakota says through a mouthful of oatmeal. "I've only done a few sessions and the progress I've made is, like, monumental."

"What are you working on?" I ask.

"Glossophobia, I guess it's called? Fear of public speaking. Remember? I told you about it when I met you. We started out with just talking in front of a mirror, then moved to recording me and listening back, and then—"

"Hey, sis, session confidentiality," Maude says.

Her tone is friendly, but it's also got a note of alarm in it.

Dakota stirs her bowl and nods. "Oh yeah. Anyway, without spilling exact details of the sessions, just saying—five-star review. Dakota stamp of approval. Shit works."

"Sure does," Maude says, smiling with tired eyes.

Kristin joins us soon after that, trudging into the kitchen. Muttering to herself and banging cupboards open and shut. We can't see her through the door that connects the dining room to the kitchen, but the mood is palpable.

"Good morning, sunshine," Maude sings.

"Blah," Kristin says back in her gravelly voice.

"Starting her new job today," Maude whispers to us.

I raise an eyebrow. Kristin comes in and joins us, not meeting our eyes. She has cereal in front of her and greets us by saying, "These Grape Nuts are like eating guinea pig litter."

Oddly specific. So many questions.

"Later, skater," Dakota says, getting up and clearing her place at the table.

"*Wish* I was skating," Kristin mutters. "Instead of slaving away at a smelly-ass pub."

Maude rolls her eyes. "Welcome to capitalism, princess."

"I don't see you working. Who are you to talk?" Kristin shoots back.

Maude's smile melts. "Excuse me, I have a pedicab career."

"Oh, right." Kristin rolls her eyes. "That."

"Who does your dishes, trust fund baby?" Maude's tone rises and I see a flash of Biker Gang Maude. "Who sweeps your floors and does your laundry?"

"Sorry, Mom."

I'm at a total loss as to how sarcastic or genuine they're being. I guess when you're close you can be both.

Maude reaches out and squeezes Kristin's shoulder. "You're gonna do great, Krissy."

"What's your new job?" I ask her.

Kristin adjusts her ball cap over her eyes. "Barback. You know, like a bartender's assistant? I have to go in to fill out a bunch of boring paperwork. I don't want to talk about it."

Barback. Interesting choice. Must be more of her exposures.

"Maybe I'll get lucky and be hit by a bus on my way there," Kristin says.

Kristin is moody—sometimes a fireball who wants to go run to the ocean for a midnight swim, sometimes a girl who doesn't get out of bed all day. I've noticed her extremes more and more lately and have learned to tiptoe around her when she's like this.

Nobody's perfect, of course. One day Dakota kept telling Maude how much better her veggie burger would have been with mustard and Maude snapped, *Well, get the fuckin' mustard then, bitch.* Kristin and Scarlett are like sisters, sniping with each other about space in the bathroom, occasionally exploding at each other with a fierceness that ups my blood pressure, then they're perfect chums five minutes later. Dakota gets unreasonably grumpy when hangry. And once I saw Simon not speak to Maude for two days until she begged him his forgiveness in tears.

But overall, it's just like any other family.

18

Simon's room gives me happy chills.

I've passed by it, of course, and spoken to him from the doorway. But he's never invited me in until today.

How special this is, to be sitting across from him: me in a cushy chair covered in a knitted blanket that Maude gave him, Simon seated at his desk where there's nothing but a laptop and a stick of incense burning. Above him, that picture of a guru who Simon says is a Hindu saint who taught a simple message— "Sub ek," or "all is one." On the far wall, there's a floor-to-ceiling bookshelf that puts my personal library to shame. Books on psychology, cosmology, Buddhism, evolution, every subject you could imagine. The spines are well-worn and splintered. I'll bet he's read them all cover to cover. Multiple times.

Simon sits up straight, puts his hands on his knees. He's wearing a boho V-neck shirt, linen pants, and a beaded crystal necklace I've never seen him wear before. "What we're about to embark on is something like shadow work. Are you familiar?"

I shake my head.

"In Jungian psychology, the 'shadow self' represents the unconscious, repressed parts of you. Your emotional blind spots and deepest fears. What you told us, about your father? The shame attached to that memory? All part of your shadow self."

A heat flares in my cheeks.

"Now we can't see a mirror in the dark," Simon says. "We can't study our dreams if we remain unconscious. We can't reflect on our shadow self unless we bring it in the light. So that's what I do: I bring you the light. I help you confront your fears. You follow?"

My stomach turns. "I think so."

"You look uncomfortable."

"No, this is great," I say, giving him a thumbs up. "Can't wait to dive into the fear."

It comes out sarcastically. I didn't mean it to. The look on his face tells me he is not amused.

"If we're going to do this work today, you need to discard the façade," he says. "Hang the wisecracking armor up at the door or this is pointless. I have many other things I could be expending my energy and time on today."

I correct my posture and swallow. "I want to be here."

"Okay, then." He opens his laptop. "Let's get started."

Simon explains that this is confidential. His services are something that a therapist would charge hundreds of dollars for, but he feels called to do this work for free, in service of humanity.

"I get nothing in return for the work I do," he says with a smile. "Which is how it should be. Non-transactional. An act of love."

The man beams. I've never known anyone like him—someone with their head in the clouds, whose idealism is infectious, who's driven to some greater purpose that I've never even contemplated. He's the reason we all go out every week or two to pick up trash or deliver sandwiches to the homeless. He's why Mirror House is a work of art and why we live with a philosophy of self-improvement and community.

I would do anything to impress him. Even if it means baring the ugliest parts of me, the guts of my soul.

"This isn't going to be easy," he says. "But if it isn't hard, it isn't work worth doing."

I've heard that somewhere before and it rings true.

Nervously, I answer his questions. They're not easy. They're ... strange. One moment he asks me if I have any siblings and the next he's asking if I've ever been molested.

"Have you ever traveled outside the United States?"

"Um, I went to Cabo with my grandma in high school."

"Have you ever injured yourself on purpose?"

My mouth hangs open. I'm dizzied by the sharp turns his questions keep taking. "On purpose? No, of course not."

"I'm curious about your hemophobia. Have you ever received treatment for it?"

I shake my head.

"What initially triggered it? Was there an event, an injury you remember that might be the root cause?"

"I don't think so. There's nothing rational about it. I've just always been squeamish about blood." I swallow. "There's something so disgusting to me about what is supposed to be kept on the inside leaking to the outside."

He sits back, eyes twinkling, fingers steepled. "Fascinating."

Immediately, his questions take another steep change in subject. What are my talents? Do I vote in every election? How many people have I slept with?

That one makes me balk.

It's a very easy answer. One. I've slept with one person. I'm more embarrassed to say this to him than if I'd slept with a hundred.

He widens his eyes at me. "*One?*"

"Well ... my mom was very strict so I didn't really have a chance to have relationships in high school. And by the time I went to college, I was focused on schoolwork and my sorority. I mean, I made out with people at parties a few times."

Here's what I don't tell him: the last person I made out with at a party at Drake University was a girl. A hot, smoky hallway. Her peach lip gloss all over my lips, the magnetic mash of our bodies, my hands pulling her short hair, her hand up my skirt, her fingers that knew where to touch me so well it was as if they remembered. As if this wasn't the first time. My only time. The fact that I did that—and that I enjoyed it so much, that I still relive the delicious memory in the private dark of my bed— scares the shit out of me. It was an earthquake that sent my identity into seismic despair. Made me realize I hadn't the faintest clue who I truly was.

"So who's the lucky guy?" Simon asks, with a half-smile.

"Sorry?" I ask, the image of the short-haired party girl disappearing. "Oh. His name is Dean."

I offer the abridged version: I was stupid; dated a man who I met on an app; found out he was married; we broke up, I lost my grandma, I ran away from my problems and moved here. *Fin.*

"I hadn't realized how inexperienced you are," Simon says, typing. "Do you consider yourself a sexual person? Do you masturbate?"

He asks me this without looking at me, with the detachment of someone who works at a doctor's office asking for my home address.

When I hesitate, he turns to me and says, "I can sense your

shame right now. Lean into the discomfort. Don't let fear rule your life."

I swallow and nod. He's right. I'm a fucking grown up, why be ashamed about masturbation? I blame my mom for how uncomfortable I am with sexuality. Growing up, the subject of sex was always attached to a warning—everything from unwanted pregnancies to sexual assault. My mom acted like she was tolerant of gay people but told me how relieved she was that I was straight because it would be so "heartbreaking" to see me discriminated against. She also offhandedly mentioned that she thinks bisexuality doesn't exist and people who think they're bisexual are just confused or wanting attention.

But I try to ignore my awkwardness and answer Simon's questions as they get more and more detailed. Do I watch porn? Do I climax during sex? Am I sexually attracted to women?

This one stops me, because he's hit on the very thing I've never even admitted out loud to myself.

"Um, maybe," I manage. "I'm not sure."

He nods at me and smiles, like he shares a joke with himself. The discomfort of these questions—it's like I'm about to break out in full-body hives. But thankfully, we move on from sex to other subjects. To my aversions.

"This is where we start our work," he says excitedly, turning away from his laptop to face me again. Beneath his desk, a printer hums and sighs. "A known fear is the easiest starting place. You master one first, and then, in time, we can ease into deeper shadow work. With you? We're beginning with blood."

The way he says those words, with the bright grin of a man about to eat a slice of chocolate cake, does not match their meaning.

"Excuse me?" I ask.

"Blood. You have a fear of blood." He enunciates each word

carefully, as if I might not understand. Then he bends down and snatches a page from the printer.

Oh shit.

I glimpse a picture slickened with the color red.

My vision sparkles. My chest caves. My pulse leaps.

He places the page in my quivering hands, smiling. "So blood is where we begin."

19

THIS IS what the picture is of: a crime scene photo, blood spattered all over a suburban living room. Blood soaking a white sofa. Blood purpling the blue carpet. Blood smudged and smeared and streaked and dripped. My god. How many people died here and what is the horrid story, I don't even want to ask. All he told me is that it's real. It's not some slasher movie still. Not corn syrup and red food coloring.

Blood blood blood blood *blood*.

Later that week, when I first study this picture as homework, I'm pretty sure I might vomit. The second time, I fight nausea. The third, I grind my teeth and ignore the spiders in my belly.

Now that I've started my own exposure, I've become a bit more aware of the other members of the house and the exposures they're doing, even if it isn't being discussed openly. Passing by Maude's room and spotting her cross-legged on her bed as she eyes Harvey slithering on the wooden floor. Noticing the new setup in the corner of Dakota's room (green screen, ring light, and phone tripod) which she's told me is for her

TikTok channel about overcoming glossophobia. Kristin coming home grumpy from her barbacking job and slamming sparkling waters like they're beers. Scarlett ... Scarlett I haven't figured out yet.

Five minutes at a time I spend with the ugly picture. Then ten. Fifteen.

Next, Simon gives me a packet to study daily, nightmarish crime scene photos, these ones closer shots. One of them shows a woman lying on a floor with a caved-in skull and the milky, unseeing gaze of the dead, a barbell next to her head that has some kind of chunky brain matter on it. Another has a man with a bullet through his temple, his eyeball gone. A pair of wrists with razor cuts, openly bleeding. It makes me ill and I hate looking at these, but I'm amazed that I don't get dizzy.

"I don't like this," my mother tells me on a Saturday morning call.

I barely told her anything about what I'm doing, just that I'm working on self-improvement with Simon, but her disapproval is sharp. She's drinking a green smoothie at her living room table and doing a crossword puzzle. She does crossword puzzles every day not because she enjoys them, but because it prevents dementia.

"What kind of motivation does this stranger have to give you free therapy? Why would you *trust* this man?"

"He's my housemate. And he's a trained psychologist."

"That sounds completely unethical."

"He's not treating me as a psychologist, Mom."

"You just said he was!"

"I said he's *trained* as one. He's also a very spiritual person."

She scoffs. "Since when are you spiritual?"

As if I would ever trust my mother with something so delicate as my spiritual longing—like offering spun glass to a

Tasmanian devil. I glance at my watch. Six minutes. I have been on the phone six minutes. Please shoot me.

Maude knocks on my door. I know because when Maude knocks, it comes with SWAT team force that rattles my window. "Hey hon, you didn't forget the tomatoes, right?" she calls through the door. I can hear AC/DC's "Thunderstruck," frantic electric guitar and raspy falsetto wailing vocals. Maude goes nowhere without hard rock blasting from a pocket. "'Cause I'm about ready to get saucy down here."

"Um, I was just about to go pick them," I call back. "Can you give me a minute?"

"I can give ya fifteen to twenty."

"Perfect."

The music gets quieter and quieter as she thumps back down the stairs. When I turn back to my phone, Mom's scrutinizing me like she wishes she could climb through the screen.

"What now?" she asks.

"Forgot, I'm on harvesting duty today." I slip on some sneakers and pull my hair up in a topknot. "I'm supposed to pick tomatoes for a huge batch of pasta sauce."

"Pasta before noon?"

I look at my watch again: eight minutes. On Saturday mornings and Saturday mornings only, time stands still.

"We're making food to deliver to homeless folks later."

"There aren't shelters for those people where you live?"

Time. Stands. Still. I take her with me as I head downstairs, then downstairs again.

"Going down to the yard," I tell her as I exit the back door.

I take a breath of fresh, beach-blown air, slipping on my sunglasses. Dakota's out here in a hanging chair, sucking a vape pen.

"Talking to my mom," I tell her, pointing to the phone.

Dakota nods and blows vape smoke out of her nostrils like a joyful dragon.

"Who is it?" my mom asks nosily.

"My housemate Dakota." I hold up the phone. "Dakota, my mom. Mom, Dakota."

"Why hello, Dakota!" my mom says, her voice melting with honey and climbing an octave. "So nice to meet you!"

"You too!" Dakota says, then starts coughing and stands up to head inside. "Water."

After Dakota's gone back inside, my mom says, "Did that woman have *face* tattoos?"

"Yep."

I hop off the porch and head down to the garden, grabbing a basket that hangs on a plum tree. I make my way to the garden beds near the shed. That fresh smell of tomato plants hits me—zingy, grassy, spicy. I love harvesting. I get to pretend I did all the hard work to grow and nourish this food when really all I did was pick it off the vine.

"Please tell me you're not going to get a face tattoo."

"I am not going to get a face tattoo."

"Was she vaporizing cannabis?"

"Yes. It's legal," I remind her.

"It's also nine-oh-nine in the morning."

Nine minutes have passed now. Time is cruel.

"This house ... I don't know, Noni," my mom says.

One by one, I squeeze heirlooms, plucking the ripest ones. "Well, good news: you don't have to live here."

"Are you ever going to let me visit?"

I'm surprised. "I had no idea you wanted to."

"Of course I want to. You're all I have in this world."

It hurts to hear that. She means it as something resembling a compliment, but it just makes me sad for her. And it's a burden to carry—to be someone's one and only.

"Sure, Mom. Anytime. There's a gorgeous hotel right on the beach two blocks away from me."

"I see." She slurps the last of her smoothie. "So you don't want me to stay with you."

"I mean, you'd be sleeping on a couch. It's not exactly the Ritz-Carlton."

She's quiet, not responding. I try to read her, my blood pressure rising, but the silence stretches.

"I'd want you to be comfortable," I say.

Still nothing from my mother. I hate when she does this. It unleashes this weird frantic urge in me to fix everything.

"Mom?" I say in a dumb little girl voice that springs from some primal place without warning, same voice that used to call out *Mommy?*

She sits with her elbow on the table and her face in her hand, gazing the other way. This, here, is the mother-daughter stonewall dance I've done many times before, as intense as a staring contest or a game of chicken.

"You can stay with me if you want, of course," I say. "Anytime. It was just a suggestion."

Like magic, she turns to me with a sweet sigh of relief, smiling. "Well ... let me check my calendar and get back to you about it soon."

Great. Fantastic. Love it. Despair.

We chat for a few more minutes, my mom talking about the merge happening at her company and the new carpeting she's getting for her condo. The phone call ends and I let out a deep breath. Then comes the wave of complicated and oh-so-familiar feelings: relief that I don't have any obligation to call her for a week; guilt that I feel relief; gratitude for the life and love she's given me; joy that she's so far away. Guilt for that.

I fill my basket with a rainbow of heirlooms—bruise violet and sunrise peach and kiss-me red. My literary brain considers all the poems I know about produce, like William Carlos Williams' icebox plums and Christina Rosetti's goblin market. I'm in my own happy, dazed world when a sound startles me.

It's Scarlett coming out of the shed a few feet away from me.

"Oh," I say in surprise. "Where did you come from?"

Scarlett swallows. She's in a sundress, bare feet and red toenails, her hair in two braids. The expression on her face is so strange. I don't know what to make of it. Like she's somewhere far, far away from here even though she's standing right in front of me.

"Shed," she says, as if that wasn't obvious.

I laugh nervously, blocking the sun with my hand. "What were you doing in there?"

Scarlett clears her throat and steps closer to me. "Hey, sorry, but I ... I overheard your conversation."

"That's okay," I say. "I was just talking with my mom."

"Uh-huh." She puts her freckled hand on my arm. "You know, we recently stopped inviting people over. It was decided, as a house. I know it sounds weird. It's for good reason, though. You brought someone over one day real quick—from work? I should have told you then."

"Wait, what?" I snicker. "You're joking, right?"

She shakes her head.

I can't believe what she's saying. I'm getting flashbacks to Delta Theta Kappa house. No overnight guests were allowed. In fact, no visitors except on weekends. Boys were never permitted upstairs for any reason.

"But why?" I ask.

"Guess you don't know about the article in *City on a Hill*?"

I stare blankly back.

"UCSC's newspaper," Scarlett says. "One of their students came over for a party last fall—so-called friend of a so-called friend of Kristin's. They wrote an article about the house, fixing to paint everyone as lunatics. Simon got pretty upset about the whole thing and everyone decided it'd be simpler to not invite folks over anymore."

"Not even my mom?"

She does a grimacing shrug. "I mean, you could ask Simon, but I'd guess he'd tell you to just meet up with her elsewhere. If rules get bent once, they'll get bent again."

"Okay. Sure."

Still don't quite get it, but I suppose every house has rules. Though now I'm dying to know about this article painting my housemates as lunatics. I'm ready to ask about it when Scarlett beams an adorable gap-toothed smile and peeks into my basket.

"Look at all those 'maters," she says in her North Carolina drawl. "Making me hungry just looking at them. See you inside."

She makes her way back to the house and I'm left out here in the sunshine, my brain wheels turning. Why was she in the shed that whole time? She didn't come out with any gardening tools. I peer inside, to see if I'm missing something. The shed is tiny, crowded, no light—is this some kind of exposure? Or was she in there specifically to spy on me, eavesdrop on my conversation? That makes no sense. And the no guests rule ... I don't know what to make of it.

I turn my attention back to the tomato vine. Squeeze an heirloom so hard it ruptures.

Crimson gooey gory oozy juice.

Seeds, guts, splatter, gush.

I drop the fruit, lick the drip from my wrist, and push crime scene photos from my head.

Excerpt from the documentary *The Mirror House Girls: One Year Later*

LOCATION: Interviewee's home, Raven's Landing, California

SCARLETT continues talking, occasionally sipping the tea still steaming in her hands.

SCARLETT: Understand, the goalposts move so slow you don't recognize it happening until it's way too late. The control tightens in these tiny increments that make complete sense at the time. You justify everything. And if something feels off, well, you look around at all these people you love and they're smiling and accepting it and you think, well, must be me. I'll smile and accept it, too.

SHOTS: Childhood photos of Scarlett; family photos with Scarlett and her parents, parents' faces blurred; teenage photos of Scarlett with youth group, everyone else's faces blurred out

SCARLETT: Look, I grew up in a fundamentalist church so strict that if you weren't baptized, you couldn't attend. We followed the gospel "sola scriptura," the one and only authority. 'Course, once I came out, church didn't want anything to do with me and I moved to California, started over.

But maybe I just traded the devil for the witch.

Didn't realize it at the time, but Mirror House—was it all that different from the world I'd grown up in? Was there that much of a difference between the emotional revival meetings I attended as a youngun and the weepy, drunk Truth games where we spilled our guts in the living room of Mirror House?

Now, I'm not trying to compare my little country church to a death cult, of course. Lots of my favorite people in the world went to that church and nobody there bludgeoned anybody to death or made a suicide pact. I'm not talking about what happened later. Just saying, indoctrination comes in so many colors that sometimes you end up blind to it.

20

Once Scarlett clues me in on the origins of the Mirror House no-visitors rule, I Google-sleuth and find the article. Covertly. In my room, door closed, lying on my bed with my phone in my hand. I see my own face in the screen, reflected over the *City on a Hill* article. A picture that is both unfamiliar and familiar at once: Mirror House, without mirrors, lavender and undecorated.

Home.

Westside House Employs Unconventional 'Self-Improvement' Methods Led by Charismatic Former Psychologist
By Emmy Weaver

On Santa Cruz's Westside, a weathered Victorian has become the epicenter of an unusual self-improvement movement under the direction of Simon Spellmeyer, an eccentric former psychologist. Spellmeyer has attracted attention for leading his housemates through a series of unconventional practices that blur the line between therapy and social gatherings.

Attendees of recent house parties, where music, dancing, alcohol, and cannabis are common, describe the events as both liberating and unsettling. What begins as a lively social gathering often transitions into intense, emotionally charged group sessions. One attendee, who requested anonymity, shared that Spellmeyer also conducts one-on-one sessions using exposure therapy techniques, challenging individuals to confront their deepest fears and insecurities.

While Spellmeyer's approach to self-improvement might seem progressive to some, others are more cautious.

"I thought I was going to a party, bro," said Alex Chang, a 19-year-old UCSC student. "And then it ended with chicks crying about their childhoods."

During a recent party, Spellmeyer, a 32-year-old man with wild hair in a daishiki and sunglasses, spoke openly about his philosophy as he danced to "Girls Just Want to Have Fun" and drank from a bottle of wine.

"Society's approach is too soft," he remarked, his voice carrying over the music. "Everything is driven by fear avoidance. But in this house, we embrace our discomfort."

According to another attendee who requested anonymity, past parties have had disturbing elements that weren't on display that night.

"Last time I was here, there was a table set up with a bunch of roadkill on it and people were supposed to stare at it and meditate on their fear of death," they said. "So nasty. Cops broke up the party and apparently investigated that Simon guy for illegally collecting roadkill. What a bummer. I never went to a party there again."

The Mirror House Girls

Spellmeyer's parents, Amy and Kyle Spellmeyer, both respected child psychologists and professors, did not respond to requests for comment regarding their son's activities. Meanwhile, Simon's professional history is as eclectic as his methods, with past roles in private practice, art coaching, life coaching, and even insurance sales. His current position on LinkedIn is listed as "software development consulting." His Instagram, where he showcases "found sculpture and elemental art," further adds to his mystique.

The current housemates are not just focused on internal growth; they're also engaged in community service such as feeding the homeless and organizing beach cleanups. Spellmeyer has described these activities as vital to the group's holistic approach to betterment. "It's about waking up and connecting with the world in a palpable way."

Whether Spellmeyer's methods are a groundbreaking approach to self-improvement remains to be seen. For now, the Victorian on the Westside continues to be a place where boundaries are tested, fears are confronted, and evolution—at least according to Spellmeyer—is inevitable.

I'm not sure how to digest the article after reading and re-reading. On one hand, hot shame bubbles up at the mention of "chicks crying about their childhoods" because that's exactly what happened to me during the Truth game. Then there's the roadkill thing, which is gross, but makes sense considering Simon's work. Scarlett warned me the article painted them as lunatics; I wouldn't go that far, but it didn't exactly paint them favorably—Simon in particular.

All week, I mull the *City on a Hill* article along with what I'm supposed to do about my mom wanting to stay here. She's going to lay the guilt trip on *thick* when I tell her there's a no-visitors policy. Just one more reason for her to be suspicious of the house and of my general life decisions. If only she were allowed to visit and see how amazing this place is—eat a home-cooked gourmet meal courtesy of Maude, hear Scarlett singing and playing guitar, engage in a fascinating conversation with Simon, accompany us on a beach cleanup—her skepticism would probably wane. If she saw how happy I was here, the happiest I've probably ever been in my life, she might change her mind.

That's been a revelation for me since I started my expo-sures. Realizing how happy I am here. That I'm capable of more than I ever thought I was. In a little under three weeks since starting sessions with Simon, I have moved from not being able to glimpse a few drops of blood without being sick to *watching surgery videos*.

That's right. I watched a hysterectomy a few days ago.

Simon held my hand the whole time and when I told him I was dizzy, that I felt like I was going to vomit, he just kept repeating, *if it's not hard work, it's not worth doing.*

Thirty minutes. A scalpel below the navel, a slit that opened a horrid, glossy world of blood and internal organs. Wave after wave of sickness washed over me at first. But after five minutes, I started zoning out a little bit. The sight wasn't spiking my adrenaline anymore. My breath steadied; my palms dried. After ten minutes, I was unbothered. By fifteen, I was numb to it. It was like looking at red paint. There was no emotion attached to it.

Simon held me for a long time when it was done and whis-pered, "I'm so proud of you. Look how strong you are. Look what you can do."

When he pulled back, he put a hand to my cheek and studied my face. He smelled delicious. Fresh peaches and cinnamon and musk. A cold sweat of lust broke over me. God, I wanted him. The way he eyed me, like I was a wonder. The way his finger traced my jawline and he watched my lips with hungry eyes. My mouth watered. Then he took his hand away and cleared his throat.

"Carnal pleasure is a distraction," he said, as if to himself.

I suppose he's right. Because all day long, my cheek pulsed where he'd touched me.

21

JULY BLEEDS INTO AUGUST, temperatures creep, tourists dot the beaches, and I eat a bloody, uncooked steak as Simon cheers me on. He wipes my lips when I'm done.

And I'm not the only one making progress in Mirror House.

Maude drapes Harvey around her neck like a scarf in timed thirty-minute intervals. She walks stiff as the Tin Man while doing it, spraying counters, vacuuming rugs, cleaning toilets as if she's trying to think about anything other than the five-foot ball python wrapped around her neck.

"I see you," I tell her, pointing from my eyes to her. "Way to go, Maude."

"If it's not hard work, it's not worth doing," she says, wiping sweat from her brow.

Kristin's been getting used to her job and her mood lightens up, day by day. You can detect her shift in the air like weather—she's a force to be reckoned with, cackling and full of energy when she's happy. Watching skating and surfing videos on her phone and yelling, "Bro!" One lazy afternoon out on the porch, she comes up behind Simon while he's reading a book and massages his shoulders.

"Thank you," I hear her lean down and say in his ear. "I love you."

I swallow, trying to keep my eyes on the page of my own book, to pretend I didn't hear it. But a jealous little flower blooms. Why does she get to touch him like that? Can I touch him too? Is their relationship more than friends and housemates?

Dakota's metamorphosis may be the most jaw-dropping. When I pass her bedroom door, I hear her voice. She's broadcasting and building a TikTok channel as her ongoing exposure. At first, her voice is soft. Then day by day it becomes a little louder, the tone a bit more confident. I find her on TikTok and she has *a thousand* followers. Her videos have each been viewed thousands of times! She films minute-long clips about her personal experience with glossophobia. For someone who has a fear of public speaking, that is serious progress.

Today, I hurry home from work and go straight to Simon's room for our session. What a sight I must be: shiny with sweat, unbrushed hair, coffee stain on my Chapters vest. On top of that, my mom has become impossible to placate. She's settled on a date at the end of this month to visit me, and I don't have the guts to tell her she can't stay here. I settle into the chair next to Simon's desk, where he has a miniature fan blowing onto him, his hair majestic as a model in a music video, his V-neck linen shirt revealing the dark hair on his chest.

"Simon, can we talk about something before we start exposures?" I ask.

"Of course." His eyebrows furrow and he pulls his rolling chair closer. "Everything okay?"

"It's about my mom. She's coming to visit." I offer a cringing smile. "She wants to stay at Mirror House. I've been putting her off for weeks, but she's *really* set on it. I don't know what to tell her."

He gives a knowing nod. "Ah," he says, leaning back. "Have you ever tried telling her no?"

It's posed as a simple, curious question. But the truth is ... I don't say that word to her often.

"Scarlett explained why we don't allow visitors," I say. "I read the article."

Simon's nostrils flare and he does a controlled inhalation and exhalation. "A shame. I trusted people. I do what I do because I want to *help* people, because I don't believe in spiritual or psychic help ever being a transactional and then ... I was completely misrepresented."

I nod, even though I'm still not sure what was so terrible about the article.

"On top of that, Emmy Weaver's journalistic integrity should have been called into question." His voice sharpens and fire flashes in his brown-green eyes. "It's an ethical violation to quote people like that. I had no idea I was talking to a reporter. She was a so-called friend of Kristin's."

I open my mouth to say something, but apparently his ranty floodgates have opened.

"And the misinformation! The fabrications! My mother's name is Annie, not Amy. I've never been in insurance sales, I have no idea where that came from. And I have never, not once, worn sunglasses inside. I am not *that* pretentious."

Damn, even though the article was published last year, his resentment is still fresh. I feel for him. He's a gifted person who helps people for free and doesn't deserve this. Simon himself has taught me to peel back the layers; under his anger, I can see fear. Fear of being misunderstood. Fear of not being loved.

"I ask because my mom hasn't exactly approved of me living

here," I say. "I think if she actually saw what it's like here, though, she would change her mind."

He sighs, looking past me. Studying the guru on his wall.

"Why do you care about your mom's approval so much?" he asks, shifting his gaze to me again. "Are you a woman or are you a little girl?"

I unhinge my jaw, unable to respond.

"My apologies if that sounds harsh—I'm trying to get beneath the surface here," he says.

"I'm a woman," I say, quieter than I mean to.

He nods. "She's still got you tethered though. You're not truly a woman until you've told your mother to go fuck herself."

Those words spike my blood pressure.

"I'm speaking from experience. My parents have spent their lives disapproving of everything I did, Winona. Every little thing. I tried to please them—Ivy Leagues! Follow in their footsteps, pursue psychology! Nothing was ever enough. My deep-seated need for their approval had physical implications. Ulcers. IBS. And finally, I just had to cut the rope and live my life. And let me tell you what." He leans in close enough that I can smell his clove gum on his breath. "I've never been happier."

I try to imagine my mom's reaction if I told her to fuck off. Pretty sure the woman would explode into a thousand pieces, human confetti.

"Interesting," I say, not sure what the hell to do with Simon's advice.

I study him and chew my cheek. When I first saw Simon, I wasn't sure if I found him attractive. He's so gangly. His sideburns are enormous, his hair a blizzard of curls. But more and more, I think he might be the most attractive man I've ever met in my life. It's the soul blazing in his eyes. It's the beaming smile like he shares a secret with the universe. I've never known anyone who just exuded confidence and contentment the way he does. It's hard to imagine him ever being so stressed out he had an ulcer because he wanted his parents' approval. It's hard to imagine who he was before his life at Mirror House.

"Tell me what you're thinking," Simon says.

"I don't know," I say shyly, caught off guard.

"'I don't know,'" he says, in a mocking, high voice. "Come on. Don't hide behind coquettishness, it's unbecoming. You know what you're thinking."

Simon's usually so compassionate that when he delivers this remark, even though his tone is warm, it comes with an icy sting.

"I was thinking I can't imagine you worrying about what anyone thinks about you," I say. "You seem—enlightened or something."

Heat in my cheeks. Blech, I sound so fawning. But it's true.

Simon's face relaxes into a smile. He shakes his head. "I'm far from enlightened. But thank you for the compliment. Just like everyone else in this house, I'm on my own self-improvement journey."

"What are you working on, if you don't mind me asking?"

"I don't mind you asking, Winona. I'm in exposure therapy of my own. Like Kristin, I have addiction issues. Not with alcohol—with sex. I was addicted to sex for a long time."

The word *sex*, coming from his mouth, sends sparks through me. I become aware of the weight of my breasts, of a twinkle between my legs.

"Addiction—when you break it down—is fear, of course," he continues. "Fear of not having that thing. An alcoholic drinks and drinks because, deep down, they're terrified they may never drink again. A sex addict like myself lives in terror of never having sex again. So I've been committed to a state of celibacy. There you have it."

The way he delivers this information is so clinical, detached as a scientist. And really? Celibacy? Disappointing. I had secretly hoped at some point, on a wine-drunk night under a starry sky, perhaps, Simon and I might hook up. Maybe even be something more than that. Stupid, I know. Crushing on a housemate—bad idea. But my mind floats back to our first session, all those sexual questions. Did they turn him on? Was there a personal reason he asked so many?

"Enough about me," Simon says. "This session's supposed to be about you. Your first assignment this week? Tell your mom to fuck off. In your own sweet Winona way, of course." He smiles. "But we don't allow visitors, period. Even mothers. Bend the rules once, they'll get bent again."

My throat tightens but I say, "Okay."

And now we're back to why I'm here in the first place: my fear of blood.

Gulp. Every time I wonder what's coming. Every time, the dread turns my head into a lead balloon.

Simon pulls a safety pin from his desk today. He unfastens it, sharp tip catching the light, and tells me I can't look away. My pulse skyrockets at the sight of it because I know whatever's coming, I'm going to hate it.

"I'm not ready for this," I blurt. "I don't want to."

"You don't even know what's coming. Look at me. Look at me."

He uses his finger to tip my chin up and we lock eyes. For one moment, there's nothing in this world but Simon and me.

"If it's not hard work, it's not worth doing," he whispers.

I nod.

"Say it."

"If it's not hard work, it's not worth doing," I echo.

And, eyes still locked on mine, he pricks his finger. He holds his finger up and moves it slowly toward me.

"Stay," he says. "Stay here. Sit with the discomfort."

I gulp a breath as a glistening rose-red bead forms on his fingertip not six inches from my face. The bejeweled horror-shine of it. Blood. Actual blood. Serious, true blood. I shudder and dry heave. When the dizziness fogs my vision, I'm grateful. I hope I pass out.

"If it's not hard work, it's not worth doing," Simon murmurs.

Inhale. Exhale. No, they are one thing—one panicked thing—one word, not two. Inhaleexhale. Exhaleinhale.

The blood droplet becomes a trickle.

Logically, this shouldn't be hard. My brain is reminding me that I've watched surgeries. I've studied crime scenes. I've stared at pictures of corpses so long they had no meaning anymore. But this—*this*—someone's real blood, right in front of my face—makes me want to jump out of my skin.

"Lean into the discomfort," he says. "Don't you dare look away."

He snatches my arm and holds it tight with his other hand, his not-bloody hand. I tense up and try to pull away, but he says, with the assertion of a doctor, "Relax, relax, relax. Deep breath."

My heart plunges through the floor. I fight the primal urge to scream. Is he going to prick me with the safety pin, too? I work very hard to remain still, to stop shaking, to continue to direct my full attention to the blood now dripping down his hand. That red streak turning into a stream. My ears ring and my vision shadows.

"I might pass out," I whisper.

He doesn't respond or even acknowledge what I've said. Instead, gently, so gently, he puts his bloody fingertip to the swan-white flesh inside my forearm. I make a desperate pleading noise like a prey animal. But he doesn't hurt me. He doesn't poke me.

As if he is the bright-eyed painter and I am the blank easel, he draws a heart above my wrist with his blood. He fills it in, red inside red. His blood wet on my skin. Crude as a toddler finger painting.

"I'm so proud of you," he says.

I can't help it, there's a tsunamic swell of so much inside me that I shake, earthquake girl, and a sob escapes. It never occurred to me before now how salty and similar it is—the act of bleeding, the act of weeping.

All the rivers we want so badly to contain.

22

Everyone in Mirror House has aligned our schedules so we can take Saturdays off for community service. I love this about us—our shared philosophy of making the world a better place. At Delta Theta Kappa, we volunteered monthly at an animal shelter. My volleyball team in high school raised thousands of dollars for a local soup kitchen every holiday season. These were some of my fondest memories of both groups I was involved in, because there's nothing better than making an impact.

"Be the butterfly effect," Simon likes to say.

It's a concept I've mulled and repeated silently to myself since he mentioned it. It gives your life constant meaning to know small actions have big consequences. Smile at a stranger, you can lift them up for hours. Pick up a piece of litter on the ground, you could save an animal's life. Simon says it's never a question of *if* we can change the world, it's a question of *how*. We call these phrases of his "Simonisms" and Maude sometimes writes them on the kitchen chalkboard.

"Are you in love with this Simon guy?" my mom asks during

one of our weekly calls. "Is that what all this is about? I don't understand your relationship to this person."

"I'm not in *love* with him. He's my friend. My housemate."

"What is a thirty-three-year-old man doing living with five young women? Sounds more like a harem."

For the love of ...

"Maude is the oldest one in the house," I remind her. "She's in her forties."

"What's Simon's last name?" she asks yet again.

"Meyer, I think?" It's a half-lie, only the latter half of his last name, to protect Simon from my mother's nosy Googling. I don't even want to think about what my mom would say if she found that *City on a Hill* article. "You know, I have to go help make sandwiches for the homeless. Talk next week?"

"I'm still planning to come visit you," she says. "You're not going to brush me off. I'll stay in that wretched hotel if I have to."

"Talk next week," I say, punting the conversation seven glorious calendar days away.

Since moving in, I've helped remove dozens of bags of trash from the beach and fed hundreds of people. It's unexpectedly enjoyable, too. The feel-good energy on Saturdays is infectious. I'm radiating with joy and thinking, *Winona, stop and appreciate this. This is the best summer of your life.* We're happy and caffeinated and we pile into Simon's van and crank the stereo and sing along in an off-key chorus, laughing at ourselves, wind in our teeth. We come home tired and dirty but full-hearted. And then it's time to feast and drink and laugh and dance until Sunday morning. The article made it sound like the house plays Truth games or has weird group therapy parties all the time, but that's just not true. Like Simon said, fabrications. That's happened only once since I've moved in, my sad dad story, and it was never dwelled upon, and it never happened again.

What we have is special. The spirit we share is unlike anything I've ever experienced. I love these people with my whole heart, and knowing them has changed me.

One afternoon, Maude slices her hand while cutting onions in the kitchen. I'm so close to her when it happens I feel her jerk at the pain. In one second, what's inside Maude is out. Blood gushes down her hand. Usually I would turn into a pile of pudding, but this time, I reach for the paper towels and help her clean up.

This is the first time in my life I can remember responding this way. Blood always sent me running, made the room spin. Not anymore.

"Look at you, girl, you're growing up," Maude says as I wrap her hand and my heart drums.

Simon witnesses the whole thing. He's munching an apple, leaning on the doorway, a sly twinkle in his eyes. He says not a word but he positively beams and I beam back because his pride is a ray of sunshine. When I pass him in the hallway to wash my hands, he stops me, wraps his arms around me tightly, and his lips meet mine in a dizzying kiss.

"You're a marvel," he whispers.

I can still taste his apple. Then, in a snap, he lets me go and walks away.

The whole thing happens so fast, a tornado here and gone in a blink, that I'm left with my hands shaking.

I can't tell if it was Simon's kiss or Maude's blood, but it takes me a while to regain my composure.

23

THE FIRST WEEK OF SEPTEMBER, Dakota has a TikTok video blow up. It's a simple video. I don't get it. Thirty-three seconds that Dakota edited together of her picking veggies, making a pasta salad, and feeding the homeless. *How me and my housemates spend Saturdays,* it says, and then, *if it's not hard work, it's not worth doing.* She posts it one Saturday and by the next, it's had over one million views. That's more views than there are people in San Francisco. More views than there are words in the Harry Potter series. My brain can't even wrap my mind around a million random people seeing a video.

"We need to think about how to leverage this," Simon says to Dakota as we drink mugs of wine on the porch and sunset-gaze.

The sky is a flamboyant flamingo pink that will be gone soon. Every sunset I get the privilege of watching, I think of Grandma Jane. Especially right now when the sky is wearing her favorite color.

"This means something. This *means* something," Simon continues.

"I got, like, three thousand followers overnight," Dakota tells him, swinging back and forth.

Simon contemplates this, hand on chin. Despite his computer job, he seems bored by technology in general. Our living room is a laptop-free zone and we don't use our phones when eating as a group. He doesn't watch TV or movies. He only has one social media account and it's for documenting found art and strange sculptures he makes out of trash. But suddenly he's very interested in TikTok and what it can do.

"Three thousand people," he says. "Can you imagine if three thousand people came here right now? Can you imagine standing in a room in front of three thousand people?"

"Dude," Dakota says.

Dude, to Dakota, is a word that can be used for so many things. It can refer to a person; it can be an exclamation of wonder, or something akin to an expletive.

"Come here," Simon says to her, opening his arms.

I watch out of the side of my eye as Dakota gets up and moves to his swinging chair, sitting on his lap.

"You are transcendent," I hear him say into her ear. "You've not only overcome your fear, you've stumbled upon something even more valuable in the process."

It's as if the three of us were hanging out and, quite suddenly, they forgot I existed. He kisses her cheek. I try not to stare, but also, I can't stop trying to read what's going on. Is it a *kiss* kiss like our hallway kiss? Or a friendly Mirror House kiss more akin to a European greeting?

The back door swings open and Scarlett bursts onto the porch, furious. Her face is nearly as red as her hair.

"That fuckin' snake was in the fuckin' bathtub again and scared me so bad, I just about pissed myself," she says.

"Of all places to piss yourself, the bathroom isn't bad," I offer.

Scarlett gives me a deadpan look that tells me just how funny she found my joke.

"Maybe if it made you afraid, it's good for you," Simon says.

"I don't have a fear of fuckin' snakes, damn it—"

"Hey," Simon says loudly. "Cool it, Scarlett. Talk to Maude about it."

"I already have and she doesn't listen, Simon. She's doing it on purpose." Scarlett puts her hands on her hips. "This is between you and her. That snake doesn't look right, either. Something's wrong with it."

"Tell her to call a vet," Dakota says. "Simon's busy."

"Oh, I'm sorry. Am I interrupting something?" Scarlett asks, a venomous sugar in her voice. She blows out a sigh and spins on her heel, heading back inside.

In the silence, all I hear is ocean and crickets and the creaking of our swinging chairs. Simon and Dakota go inside and I hear arguing I have no interest in being part of. I can understand Scarlett's anger. Harvey pops up like an unwelcome surprise sometimes in the house. He's supposed to stay in Maude's room, but she leaves her door open.

Voices carry through the window, Maude yelling in a shrill wail that reminds me of Axl Rose, "Shut up, skinny country bitch, I'll beat your ass," and Simon calming Maude down. There's a scuffling sound, then crying, then the music stops and the party's over. Everyone scatters to their rooms and shuts their doors. Saturdays aren't usually like this, but it was a long day. A hot day. The kind that ends in arguments and sunburns. Everyone's drunker than we probably should be at eight-something p.m.

I go upstairs and lie on my bed and pass out for a little while.

Suddenly, it's the middle of the night and I'm wide awake, all the alcohol out of my body. I'm thirsty and don't know where my water bottle is. Then I remember the last place I had it—the swinging chair outside. Details float back: Scarlett yelling about Harvey and everybody fighting; Dakota sitting on Simon's lap; the million-view video. It's like I'm watching the night in reverse.

Outside on the porch, my water bottle's right where I left it. I pull a long drink from it while enjoying a private moment with the moon. I love that no matter when—day, night—I can hear the relentless push and pull of the ocean, like the world's beating heart is only two blocks away.

But there's a sound underneath it.

A piercing, heart-wrenching sound.

Like a dog whimpering. Or a child weeping. Or a woman.

That sound gives me a sick feeling. It sounds ... close. An animal under the porch? A neighbor with an open window? I can't tell. I cock my ear to the cool night air, close my eyes, trying to locate its source.

I follow my ear down the porch, descend the creaky wooden stairs. It's not coming from under the house. It's coming from our yard somewhere. Turning on my phone, I light my way with the flashlight, scanning the scene. I'm dreading what I might find. An injured possum? Rabid raccoon? No, no. As I step farther into the yard, I become quite sure it's human.

My teeth begin to chatter.

"Hello?" I say, my voice cracking.

And suddenly, the moon that I was flirting with not a moment ago becomes haunting, a glow that turns people into werewolves. I'm scared. But Simon would say, being scared isn't a reason to quit anything. In fact, being scared is a sign you should persevere. And then, my bare feet in the crab grass, tomato vines and squash blossoms tickling my legs as I pass the garden beds, I stop short.

Oh my god. No. Yes.

It can't—but it is.

I know where the sound is coming from.

I drop to my knees next to the doghouse-looking thing, the padlocked box. Someone is inside it. It's barely big enough to sit in while hugging your knees. It's *tiny*. I never knew what it was for. Everyone shrugged and acted like it was a mystery since I moved here. But someone is inside it. Crying.

"Hello?" I ask, shining my light, scrambling for an idea of what the hell I'm supposed to do.

A silence stretches so long I wonder if I imagined the whole thing. Or if I'm still sleeping and this is just a dream.

"Hello?" a muffled female voice says.

"Why are you ... in there?" I ask.

There's another long silence. "It's exposure."

Suddenly, I recognize the voice. "Scarlett?" I ask in disbelief.

"You can't talk to me right now, I'm sorry," she says.

I stand up, astounded. I have no words. "Scarlett" is all I can get out.

"I've got to go through this, okay? Don't ruin it or I'll have to do it all over again. Please. *Please.*"

She's sobbing. Begging. My stomach does a flip, to know she's stuck in there.

"How are you going to get out?" I ask, hand flying to my throat.

"Simon has a key. Please get out of here, I mean it, please."

"Can you breathe?"

"Yes, breathing just fine. Promise, I want this, okay? Now go."

I wring my hands and rack my brain. "Okay. All right."

"Don't worry. It'll be over soon."

"Right."

She sniffs. "I'll see you in the morning."

"See you."

I head inside, completely disturbed. In the dark living room, I look out at the yard through the window. That tiny, tiny thing she's locked up in. Voluntarily. I don't understand. I'm trying to understand this—I just can't. How long has she been in there? When will she get out? Has this happened before?

This is not normal, a worried voice in me whispers. *Something about this is very wrong.*

I don't sleep after that. I keep peeking out my window. At the crack of dawn, I hear Simon's door open and he slips down the stairs. Out of my window, I spot him cross the yard and crouch by the doghouse-box and open it up. Scarlett comes out. She's shivering and shell-shocked. They hug. They kiss. After a long embrace, she wipes her eyes. The sight of her smile, of Simon's arm around her as they make their way inside, relaxes me.

She wanted to be in there, I reassure myself. It was part of her exposure. It's weird, yes. Unconventional. It would be hard to explain to someone else, but when you've seen results like we've seen, you understand that sometimes extreme fears take extreme measures.

Simon said so.

Excerpt from the documentary *The Mirror House Girls: One Year Later*

LOCATION: Interviewee's home, Raven's Landing, California

SCARLETT: Simon's sessions were like getting to sit and talk with the smartest friend you ever had. Like if you had the world's best psychologist and that person also loved you with their whole heart, enough to give you advice and therapy for *free*. Tell me how often you find that in life. No, I'll wait.

My first Truth game I broke down and told everybody about getting kicked out of my church.

I grew up in a tiny town where everybody knew everybody's business. I'm bisexual and didn't hide it, either. Even though my parents were fine looking the other way, my church wasn't. My pastor told me I was going to burn in hell and the worst part is, he did it in front of the rest of my Bible study group to make an example of me. I don't know what hurt more—him tearing me down, or nobody speaking up for me.

I was still raw from this when I was scooped up into Mirror House. I told this story to my housemates out loud, in full Technicolor detail, for the first time. The love they showered on me—the instant acceptance—it was healing.

My parents still go to that church, by the way. No matter how much they love me and tell me they miss me when I call, they still sit and listen to that man's sermons every week. (Eyes filling) But Mirror House? They were my new family now. My chosen family. And when you're chosen, that means a hell of a lot more, doesn't it? Simon's words to me that night when he wiped the tears from my face, he said, "This is the first page of your new story."

I had spent my life until then trying to run away from the things that scared me. In junior high, a couple boys locked me in a janitor's closet. That was why I never went into tight spaces. Simon's sessions forced me to reckon with that part of myself. Avoidance only strengthens fear, you know? He was right about that and right about most things, honestly. So slowly, slowly, we did these exposures and we went from opening a closet and staring at the inside of it to being locked up in a box for hours on end.

(Leaning in, listening to interviewer's unintelligible question)

Oh, you're asking if I'm still claustrophobic? Yes. Hundred percent. In fact, I'm worse off. 'Cause now I'm also terrified of the exposure therapy that supposedly cures it. (Pause) Give somebody the keys to your mind, you'd better make sure you trust them.

24

IN LATE SEPTEMBER, Santa Cruz's energy shifts. The days shrink. Tourist flocks fly home and the Boardwalk roller coaster sleeps on weekdays. The fog creeps in earlier and clings to the city's streets. Still, the palm trees sway and the ocean churns and the surfers surf. There's something timeless and seasonless about a beach town, an eternal summer that just gets colder sometimes.

On the first of October, a letter from our landlord arrives and Simon tapes it to the kitchen chalkboard with the words *HOUSE SATURDAY AGENDA: Brainstorm Mirror House response.*

The letter reads:

Dear Simon Spellmeyer,

I hope this letter finds you well. It has come to my attention that the exterior of the property located on Laguna Street has been covered with mirrors.

This alteration is not in compliance with your lease, which prohibits modifications to the property without prior approval. Additionally, the mirrors are creating a nuisance for neighbors due to the reflective surfaces.

You are hereby requested to remove all mirrors and restore the exterior of the property to its original condition within 30 days. Failure to do so will result in further action, including the initiation of eviction proceedings.

I urge you to address this matter promptly. If you have any questions or need clarification, please feel free to contact me directly.

Thank you for your attention to this important matter.

Sincerely,

Paul Hamm, Property Owner

Saturday, we skip beach cleanup and instead gather around the dining room table. Simon scoots up a chair at the head.

"Am I the *pater familias?*" he asks, smiling. "Sorry, I've been reading too much ancient Roman history. Apparently I should have been researching California tenant rights instead."

We laugh together, though it feels forced. The silence that follows is heavy. The letter sits in the middle of the table, glaring back at us.

"Listen, I was going to ask permission to get my dad involved, Simon," Kristin says. "He knows lawyers who could fight this."

Simon contemplates this, his hands together in front of his mouth. "Kristin—if you don't mind—a lesson?"

"No, of course!" she says.

"And I'm going to be blunt," Simon says. "Because you wanted me to be blunt with you, remember?"

She adjusts her ball cap, turning it backwards. "Go right ahead."

"Calling *Daddy*," he says mockingly, his eyes turning to slits, his voice turning to ice, "is the oldest Kristin trick in the book. It's rich-girl bullshit. Learn a new trick."

A stunned silence expands between us. I try to read the table—how are the others feeling about this? But their gazes are averted.

Simon's expression warms and he reaches out, squeezing Kristin's hand. "Baby, you told me to be blunt."

"No, I get it. You're not wrong." She smiles, though I can tell she's stung. "Thank you."

Simon turns to us. "Anyone else?"

I'm not feeling confident enough to offer a suggestion after hearing that.

"Honestly, Simon?" Maude pipes up, her teeth grit. "I'd like to hurl a brick through that Hamm-fucker's window."

"Ahh, anger. Maude's crutch. Maude's go-to," he says, almost bored.

Maude opens her mouth like she wants to respond, but clamps it shut.

"What if we just ... removed the mirrors?" Scarlett asks.

"Just give in," Simon says. "Just cave, huh? Evade, evade! You're all so predictable."

I don't look straight at his eyes, scared he might target me for an answer when I don't have one. He bangs his hands on the table, as if trying to wake us up.

"This is an existential threat!" he nearly shouts. "This is our house. This is who we are. They want us gone. You understand that?"

I exchange a quick look with Scarlett—so fleeting, if you blinked, you'd miss it. But there's a confusion in her eyes that we share. This reminds me of the article. Something that is a mild inconvenience that Simon seems to think is a *much* bigger deal.

"Do you have any brains? Any guts?" he asks us.

He says it with such kindness that, at first, it's hard to feel it hurt.

"Or are you all just as asleep as the rest of them?" he says, softer, almost to himself.

Simon is the most intelligent person I've ever met in my life. When I don't understand where he's coming from, I feel like I've been left in the dark. Right now that's where I am: in darkness, not understanding him, not connecting what he wants me to connect. I can tell he wants something from us, like a frustrated professor trying to extract the correct answer from his class. And apparently I didn't study enough for this one.

"I have an idea, Simon," Dakota says, her eyes lighting up, two twin bulbs.

"I'm all ears," Simon says.

"Why don't we ask my TikTok audience?" she asks. "Like— what if we could get people to throw us some public support?"

Simon bites the inside of his cheek, eyeing some secret in the air that only he can see.

"We could livestream and talk about it, make videos," Dakota says excitedly. "I have almost ten thousand followers now. These people love us, dude. They think we're saints because of our volunteer work. And they hella love the mirrors. I mean, my account's called Mirror House Girl. They'll throw us support."

"Dakota, you are *brilliant*," Simon says, a smile spreading. "We campaign. That's what we do." He turns to the table, beaming. "See what happens when you face your fear? Not only do you learn to stop the suffering associated with your fear— you *master* it, like Dakota has. What was a fear before becomes a strength. Becomes love."

"Right on," Kristin says.

"From fear to love," Maude says. "Always."

The tension breaks. We hi-five and celebrate. Simon and

Dakota peel off to conspire about TikTok videos like a two-person film crew. They don't leave her room for hours. It's as if the rest of us have disappeared after Dakota made her suggestion; Simon is inspired, and when he gets inspired, he gets hyperfocused.

It might be in my head, but sometimes it's as if Simon picks favorites. On certain days, especially in the beginning, his focus was on me. But now he doesn't notice me as much. Our last two sessions, he seemed disappointed in me because I haven't been able to let him draw on me with blood without getting upset. And when he asked me to lick it, I refused.

"We can't make progress until you're ready," he said. "And sadly, you don't seem ready to part with your suffering."

I've tried so hard, though. He has no idea the things I've made myself watch. The FBI probably has me on a watch list because of my internet search history at this point. It's only at the end of the day when I pass him in the hallway and he says not a word to me that I realize he hasn't spoken to me or acknowledged me in days. Not since our last session, over a week ago now.

And I ache.

25

I LOVE MORNINGS, the air cool and salty. Silver sky through the dim windows. The sun wears a scarf of fog. The house is still, just an occasional groan of wood or footsteps pattering.

"Hi, Simon," I say brightly, coming into the living room.

Simon's often the first up. I set my alarm to catch him early today. He's relaxing on the couch in his robe and slippers, engrossed in a book. My heart flutters at the sight of him. We're not often alone, except for our sessions. One-on-one time with him is so special.

"Morning," he murmurs without looking up.

"What are you reading?" I ask.

He flips a page. "Are you unable to see the title?"

I can read the title. It's called *Using Behavioral Science in Marketing*. I was trying to make conversation, but his dry responses aren't giving me much to work with.

I hug my elbows, suddenly chilly. "Did I do something to make you mad?"

"Why do you feel the need to control other people's

emotions?" he asks, not meanly, just curiously. "What's the core fear here?"

I open my mouth, but no response comes to mind. I'm blank.

"Are you afraid of not being loved?" he asks, closing the book with a papery slap. He looks at me. His words are genuine, an analyst trying to get to the heart of the matter. "Are you afraid I don't love you?"

"No," I say.

He smiles as if to say, *we both know that's a lie.* And it is. It's a lie.

"What if I don't love you?" he asks, sitting up, as if excited for this thought experiment. "What if I never will? What if I find you annoying and weak and cloying?"

"That would be unfortunate."

He's just asking questions, I remind myself. This shouldn't hurt. Swear to god, eyeballs, if you cry right now, I will disown you.

"What if I think you don't fit in here with the rest of us?" he goes on. "What if I think you don't belong here?"

It takes a lot to not flinch and to hold my head up high. It's like Simon knows my Achilles heel and he's shooting arrows at it out of nowhere. "Are these hypotheticals or are you trying to say something?"

He sighs heavily, as if I missed the point, and goes back to reading.

"Look," I say, my pitch softening. I sit on the other end of the couch from him. I stare at his feet, which are ugly awkward hairy man feet that for some reason I still want to touch. In fact, I want to lie next to him. I want him to hold me. I want him to kiss me like he kissed me in the hall a few weeks ago. I want him to look at me the way he looks at Dakota. "Sorry my last couple of sessions didn't go well, but please, give me another chance. I've made so much progress."

The pleading tone of my voice rings within like an alarm. There's another me standing outside of me asking, why do you care so much what he thinks? Why are you begging this man for anything? But I tell myself that's just my ego. That's the false part of myself that fears being vulnerable. He's helped me make more visible progress at self-improvement in the last few months than anyone else I've ever met in my life. I thought it was an exaggeration that he's a healer, but he is. He's a mind healer.

"Prove it to me, then," Simon says.

As if he was prepared for this exact interaction, he unclips a safety pin from the belt loop of his robe. He keeps his eyes on mine as he holds it in the air and sticks it into his fingertip, not flinching, not even blinking.

A crimson bead oozes down his finger. He doesn't move, awaiting my response.

I fight the wave of disgust. I swallow it like a bad bite of food.

"Have a drink," he says, in a friendly tone, as if he's offering me a sip of tea.

The suggestion is like a sucker-punch to the gut.

My mouth goes dry.

I fight a wave of nausea.

The moment hangs so long it seems to suck the oxygen from the room. I don't know what to do. I have this fear— because it all comes down to fear, doesn't it?—that he's going to let me go if I don't do what he's asking. This is how I prove to him I'm strong enough to be here. And I realize that there's something I'm more afraid of than blood. He hit the nail on the head, what he said a minute ago.

My greatest fear is not being loved.

I scoot closer to Simon, slowly, my skin crawling and stomach rolling. And even though it's the most disgusting thing I've ever done, I put my mouth on his finger and suck the sweet iron tang of his blood. His eyes go wide, so wide. He draws in a breath of pleasure. I've never seen this look on his face—like I've blown his mind. I've knocked him off his axis. He is turned the fuck *on*. And even though I could vomit on his lap, his reaction alone has made this worth it.

I pull back to examine him and notice that he's, shall we say, *excited*. He's pitched a terry-cloth tent in his robe. Months and months of living with him and I've never seen him like this. He reaches and grabs the back of my hair, gently, playfully, and pulls my head toward his. A thrill travels through me, a tidal wave of want. And then he kisses me, long and hard, the minty taste of his tongue erasing the metallic taste of his blood. It is—besides my secret girl kiss in college—the most passionate, electric kiss of my life. I must be heterosexual after all because I've never wanted anyone more than I have wanted Simon Spellmeyer to be mine.

"You are so powerful," he says, pulling away. "You're like—you're like an electromagnetic force. I can't resist you."

"That's how I feel about you."

I want to kiss him again, but he gets up, tightens his robe. He's pink and flustered, a new look for him.

Simon runs his hands through his wild hair and takes a deep, shaky breath. "But I—I can't." He stalls, watching my mouth for an extra moment as if he's having second thoughts. He touches my bottom lip. Then there's a thumping sound, a rhythmic thumping sound.

"Let me out, Boss," I hear Maude yelling from her room.

"Oh," Simon says, as if remembering.

He turns and heads to the hall and then his footsteps clunk upstairs. I get up in a daze and follow but am intercepted by

Scarlett, who's coming out into the hall in her cat pajamas. She gives me a grimace.

"What in the devil happened to you?" she asks.

"Nothing," I say, unsure what she's talking about.

As I go upstairs, steps creaking one at a time, dust sparkling in the streaks of sunshine, I see Simon unlocking Maude's door at the top of the landing and Maude saying, "Thanks, Boss. Me and Harvey slept like beauties" despite the bags under her eyes.

I lock myself in the bathroom and immediately understand what Scarlett was talking about: Simon's blood smeared on my bottom lip.

It occurs to me it's for the best that my mom isn't visiting me here.

I don't think I could explain Mirror House to her.

26

My mother is beautiful except for the perpetual look of disappointment she wears. Frown lines that she's never been able to hide.

"She was born like that," Grandma Jane used to tell me. "She had a look on her face straight out of the womb like, 'This is it? This is all I'm getting?' Hand that woman the world on a silver platter and she'll pout and tell you she wants the moon and stars, too."

Maybe my mom was disappointed early on because, let's face it, Grandma Jane wasn't going to win any Mom of the Year awards. She left her kids for a summer to do a Babettes reunion and ended up with a coke habit that bankrupted the family. My mom liked to bring this up a lot—her early memories of repo men taking her dollhouse away.

"Christ on crackers, how many times do I have to apologize for the goddamn dollhouse?" Grandma Jane would say, rolling her eyes.

"Just once would be nice," my mom would say, so softly my hearing-impaired grandmother couldn't hear.

My grandma claimed my mother exaggerated how bad her childhood was while my mother claimed my grandma underplayed it. The truth was probably somewhere in between. I just tried my best to stay out of it.

Today, what I notice first about my mom is not her stylish jumpsuit, her art deco earrings, her four-inch pumps that she wears as easily as tennis shoes. Not the fact she took a cab straight from the airport to my job and rolled her luggage right in here even though I asked if we could meet at the hotel. What I notice first is her expression. The downturned lips, even when she smiles.

"So this is your job," she says, eyeing the beige walls of Chapters, shaking her head. "This is where you end up when you don't finish college."

"*You* didn't finish college," I point out.

She picks up a book from the Staff Picks rack. "Do I get a discount if I buy something here?"

"Sure."

"Probably still cheaper on Amazon," she says, putting the book back on the shelf.

One minute into this weekend-long visit and already I'm counting how long until it's over.

* * *

"So this is what you're wearing these days," she says when we go out to dinner at the fancy place on the wharf.

I look down at my tie-dye shirt and bell bottoms.

"I live in a beach town with a bunch of artists," I remind her.

"Have you given up on hairbrushes, too?" she asks, reaching out to smooth my hair.

So funny, because in Mirror House everyone compliments

my hair all the time. They tell me they like it wild and natural. I haven't used my flat iron since I moved in.

I duck away from my mom's hand and steer the conversation elsewhere. I pretend to be very interested in pharmaceutical sales and my mom's workplace drama. I talk up my housemates, how amazing they all are. I try to impress her by filling her in with what we've been doing on TikTok this month —how we've been livestreaming and have thousands of people watching our videos and how our landlord has been getting bombarded with emails.

"I don't understand," my mom says, cutting her salmon into microscopic pieces. "Why on earth wouldn't you just take the mirrors off the house? If I were your landlord, I would have evicted you already."

I'll bet you would, Mom. I'll bet you would.

"It's the principle." I swirl and sip my second glass of wine. "It's an existential threat against us. It's our house. It's who we are."

"What are you talking about?" my mom asks, confused. "It's not your house. You're renters."

My mouth is open. She has a point, but also ... she's missing my point. "Mom, it's our freedom of expression."

"It's a bunch of ugly mirrors."

She truly looks bewildered, like she's trying to understand. Out the window, the ocean shines under a wisp of a moon, which right now, is like a yellow grin laughing at my expense. Grandma Jane would understand what Mirror House is doing. I know she would.

"So you're drinking wine now," Mom says after I order my third glass. "Since when do you like wine?"

"Is there anything I can do—literally anything—that you won't shit on?" I ask, maybe too loudly.

My mom's jaw drops. I never speak to her this way. I'm a lifelong good girl. I listen. I don't talk back.

And I'm not finished.

I lean in, lava in my veins. "Simon said I haven't fully become a woman until I tell my mom to fuck off. He thinks our relationship is unhealthy."

"Oh, Simon says, does he?" My mom's cheeks are getting rosy. "Talk about unhealthy relationships—that man is a licensed psychologist exploiting a group of young housemates." Her nostrils flare. "I've been considering reporting him because he should *at the very least* lose his license. Thank you for making up my mind."

Panic erupts. She can't do that—Simon would hate me forever. "If you do that, I will never speak to you again."

My mother puts down her fork. "I don't think this is you, Winona."

"No, this *is* me. You just don't like me."

It comes out of nowhere, this dagger of a sentence. Suddenly the room is swollen with noise—voices murmuring and silverware tinkling and glasses clinking and mouths chewing. I burn with emotions, my sinuses on fire.

"I don't think you like me, either," my mom says, swallowing.

I suck in a little breath, spotting tears in her eyes. My mom drinks her entire glass of water and fills it up again. Her eyes are dry now. Maybe they were dry the whole time, I don't really know. I'll never quite understand what's inside of her.

"I think we can agree that if we were going to pick daughters and mothers, we wouldn't be a match," she says. "It is what it is."

It is what it is.

I hate that fucking phrase. It means nothing. It's what

people say when they don't know what to say and should just shut the hell up. What my mom said rolls around in my mind like a marble as we finish our meals in silence. It hurts. It really hurts, in this deep, undiscovered place—like if you could open my heart and there was another heart inside it. A secret heart. If I had a secret heart, it would be broken.

I'm quite drunk and hold my tongue as my mom and I walk up to her hotel, her heels clicking on the asphalt. She shakes her head at skateboarders. When a stoned, barefoot man asks if she can spare a dollar, she replies with an indignant, "I most certainly cannot." She raises her eyebrows at me and says, "So this is Santa Cruz" and gives me something resembling a smile.

I say goodbye at the hotel, but she says, "I'll walk you home."

"You can't come inside."

"I know. I'd still like to walk you home."

She regrets what she said. I hear it in the softness of her voice. But she doesn't know how to fix it. And I feel that same way. We walk two blocks, passing porches with surfboards and pumpkins. Fake graves in yards, spiderweb gauze in palm trees. And there's Mirror House: shining like a beacon, reflecting the gold streetlamps.

She regards it like it's a goddamn shame, her upper lip curled. "So this is Mirror House."

A worry whispers in my mind. "Please don't report Simon, Mom. Seriously."

She turns to me and says nothing for so long that I writhe. "Fine." The word is sharp, barbed. Her eyes shine. "This visit has been hard. I don't like seeing you like this."

"Then don't see me."

"Fine."

Another barb.

My mom's eyes linger on the compact mirrors hanging from the laurel tree. "You live your life and I'll live mine."

I swear I can hear the universe rip as my mom waves good-bye. Simon's words echo in my ears: *You're not truly a woman until you've told your mother to fuck off.*

I guess I'm a woman now.

27

Dear Simon Spellmeyer,

I am writing to address a concerning development following my previous letter, in which you were requested to remove the mirrors from the exterior of the property on Laguna Street.

Since that communication, I have been inundated with a large volume of emails from individuals—whom I do not know—expressing their support for the mirrors. While I respect differing opinions, this influx of correspondence, particularly messages that have been rude or hostile, is both inappropriate and unwelcome.

This behavior is disruptive and is only serving to escalate the situation. As the owner, I must maintain the integrity and appearance of the property. The mirrors must still be removed within the original 30-day time frame as outlined in my previous letter. Failure to comply will leave me no choice but to proceed with eviction.

Please take the necessary steps to comply with the lease terms and avoid further complications. I expect your full cooperation moving forward.

The Mirror House Girls

TWO WEEKS after our first meeting, Mirror House has another meeting. AGENDA: FUCK YOU, HAMM, in Maude's handwriting. I snicker when I read it, but no one else is laughing. They're deep in discussion about the letter at the table.

I slip into a seat next to Scarlett, who gives me a half-smile and an eyebrow raise, like *here we are again!* She reaches out and squeezes my knee under the table. She's the only person at this meeting who doesn't seem thrilled to be here. Scarlett's emotions are usually written on her face.

The energy is loud and boisterous, everyone energized by rage.

"Look, I've taken care of shit like this before, Boss." Maude pounds a fist in hand. "I know how to be discreet. I'll just ride my pedicab over to where that Hamm-fucker lives and do something small. Light a fire on his lawn, break a couple windows."

I almost snort. Who does Maude think we are? The Mafia?

"No," Simon says, his eyes widening. "Absolutely not the solution here."

"My dad knows someone who works at the *Chronicle*," Kristin offers.

Simon shoots her a look like a bullet. "Remember what happened last time we invited a reporter here?"

"Stupid idea, sorry," she mutters.

She rests her head in her hands, face invisible under her baseball cap. Simon reaches out and pulls her hat off, gently, putting it on the table.

"Let me see that sweet face," he says softly. "What's going on?"

He asks so tenderly—it's as if he sees something in Kristin right now the rest of us haven't noticed. And he must have, because when Kristin straightens her posture, she has tears streaking down her cheeks.

"I don't want to lose this, guys," Kristin says. "This house saved my life."

"Let it out," Simon says. "Let the fear out. Don't let fear rule your life."

Kristin nods and sobs openly, a wet mess of snot and tears. I'm the kind of sap who catches other people's tears like a virus, and my own eyes well up in harmony. Simon gets up and embraces Kristin, humming gently, nodding at us. He closes his eyes as if channeling all his good vibes into her. And one by one, we join in—Maude first, then Dakota, then Scarlett, then me. We hug and we hum together, a human hive that gives me tingles and chills. A lovely current runs through us. It's magic, holy, a kind of togetherness I've never experienced until I moved into Mirror House.

We stay here for what feels like a long time, but probably isn't longer than a minute. Then, one by one, we peel off the hug and exchange smiles and sit back down. Kristin's smiling too now, weakly, wiping her tears.

"Thank you all," she says.

"This is the answer, right here," Simon says, pointing at Kristin. "*This* is what we need to do. Testimonials."

No one responds.

"On TikTok." Simon points to Dakota. "We need to get each of you to go on there and talk about how much this house means to you. Create a hashtag. Make it a story."

"There's a warrant out for my arrest in the state of Florida." Maude puts her hands up. "I'll have to bow out of this idea."

This is news to me, but only me, because no one looks surprised.

Simon sighs. "Maude, no excuses. That doesn't matter."

Maude blows out a sigh. She shakes her head and leans back in her chair.

"I'll say something nice about Mirror House," Scarlett says. "Whatever y'all need."

"Me too," I say.

Simon smiles. "That's the spirit."

A tension, a sadness diffuses in the quiet that lapses between us. No—it's fear. Of course, fear, that's what's underneath. And why? Because we're afraid of losing what we love.

Fear and love, that's all there is.

Simon puts his hands on the table and says, gravely, "I promise I will not let them win. You hear me? I don't want you to get clouded by fear. Don't get sucked into their games. None of that out there—" he gestures with a hand toward the window "—none of it is real. *This* is real."

"From fear to love," says Maude, making a heart shape with her hands.

"From fear to love," Simon says. "Say it with me."

"From fear to love," we chant, the marrying of voices sending a chill through me.

"Let's get to work," he says.

28

DAKOTA AND SIMON film our testimonials one by one over the weekend with the infectious excitement of a mini filmmaking crew. They come up to my room with a ring light, scoot a chair closer to the window, and help me decide on my outfit.

"Let me just straighten this out," Simon advises, taking the sides of my floral tank top at the waist and pulling it down an inch or two.

This reveals my cleavage, which I'd been trying to cover. I fight the urge to adjust my shirt back the way it was. I've spent my life trying to artfully cover and uncover my cleavage depending on the situation. It's instinct at this point.

Simon surveys me like a painter contemplating his work in progress. "Much better. Eye-catching." He steps forward, hovers a hand over my ponytail. "You mind?"

"Not at all," I say, getting a shiver as he pulls out the elastic band and my hair hits my bare shoulders. He's so close I can smell the oatmeal he ate for breakfast, maple and peaches. If Dakota weren't setting up her phone in the tripod three feet away, I wouldn't be able to resist a taste of his lips.

"You're so alluring with your hair down," he says, running his fingers through it and smoothing it out. Brushing flyaways from my face. "There's something so irresistible about a woman untamed."

The poetic words echo in my brain.

"Okay," he says, standing back. "How about lipstick?"

"I've got lipstick."

"Blood red?" he asks with a smirk.

I answer with a smile, like we share a joke. "Sure."

This delights him. He gets an almost goofy grin on his face as I go to my makeup bag and color in my lips. I stop at the mirror, thinking that this is how I used to look when I went out on dates with Dean. I haven't had a reason to get dressed up like this until now. For just a breath, I let myself imagine I'm going on a date with Simon. That we're together. That I belong to him; that he belongs to me, only me.

"We're ready to roll," Simon says, clearly relishing this part of director he's playing. All he needs is a clapperboard.

My testimonial is all true, a hundred percent, even if it feels fake. Anything feels fake when you have to say it ten times to get it right. I just say this: Mirror House is the best home I've ever had; these are my best friends, my family; we have a philosophy of self-improvement, community service, fear to love; we're not hurting anyone by existing here; no property was permanently damaged by the mirrors; we just want to be free to be ourselves; and addressing Paul Hamm directly—please, it's in your control to do what's right. #savemirrorhouse

"Wear that to our next session," Simon whispers in my ear as he packs up the ring lights.

29

THE NEXT DAY, it hits me that I haven't had a session with Simon in weeks. Not since before our passionate secret kiss on the sofa and the thing with his finger I'd rather not think about. A sexual tension has built up between us that can't just be in my head. The way he looks at me, like I'm a piece of devil's food cake and he's ravenous. The special twinkle he gets when I walk into a room. How he says, "Why, hello, Winona," instead of a normal greeting, as if the sight of me is always a delightful surprise. That couch kiss transformed him; there's an undeniable chemistry brewing.

I want him with obnoxious constancy. My desire is a distraction. An ache when I hear him laughing with someone else. A flutter if I pass him in the hall. A jealousy when I watch him slip into Maude's room or Dakota's room or Kristin's room to comfort them, to have a private moment with them behind closed doors.

I might have accidentally fallen in love with the man.

I recognize these symptoms. I had them with Dean. I was pained and ill until I finally knew he wanted me back.

At today's session, I wear the shirt and the lipstick just like he asked me to. I'm almost sick to my stomach, full of something about to spill over. I'm both elated to be here and dreading what's next. As much as I want him, I don't want to drink his blood again. But I'm scared he'll freeze me out and I'll fall from his good graces again if I refuse.

I'm so confused.

"You wore it," he says, glancing at my shirt, smiling shyly.

The moment he shuts and locks the door with a click, I release a held breath. It hits me how nervous I am right now. I'm nearly shaking.

"Are you okay?" he asks, putting a hand on my arm. "You've got goosebumps."

"I need to talk to you about something." I take a seat on his bed, plain and blue, big enough for two. In the pause between us, I construct eloquent confessions that could probably fill a sonnet. But instead, I blurt out, "I have feelings for you, Simon."

He settles into his chair across from me. His deep-thinking face is unreadable. "Of course you do. I have feelings for you, too, Winona."

"I mean romantic feelings."

"Me too."

He says it so plainly, like it's the most obvious thing in the world. Blood is red. Water is wet. Romantic feelings. And yet he's still sitting across from me, eyeing me more like a therapist than a lover.

"But we have to separate the feelings from the work, you know?" he says gently. "Believe me, I've—I've felt it too. That kiss was something very special." He shakes his head. "Of *course* I want more than that. It's been something I've been wrestling with. You're a true test from the universe. Yet, I know what's right." He nods at his own speech, as if he's convincing himself

147

of this in real time. "We've got to maintain focus on ourselves. There's too much at stake. Us ... together in that way could thwart both of our personal progresses, considering the roles we have in these sessions. It could also distract us from our mission to save Mirror House when time and focus are of the essence."

His speech is so measured it sounds memorized. As if he really has been analyzing his feelings and arguing with himself about them and already has his answer.

I nod as I process. What he's said makes total sense, but it's also a kick to the gut.

"So for now, let's just agree we feel it, your feelings are requited, but let's keep our focus on the session. Leave personal feelings and—" he smiles, as if he can't help it "—our lust at the door. This acknowledgement should guide our session today."

"Okay," I say quietly.

This was not what I wanted, not at all. But at least I know he feels the same. At least I'm not alone in that.

"Take off your shirt, please," he says, with the casual tone of someone asking you to kick off your shoes.

I must have misheard him.

"Your shirt," he repeats, gesturing to the outfit he requested I wear. The outfit he apparently wants me to take off.

The turn in conversation has gone right off a cliff. Slapped by his request, blizzard-brained and confused, I finally respond with: "Didn't you just tell me to leave our lust at the door?"

"We're starting your session."

"But why do I need to—"

"Do you trust me, Winona?" He shuts his laptop and turns to me. "Do you believe I have your best interests at heart?"

"Of course I do, but you have to admit, it's a weird request," I laugh.

"I know. It *is* a weird request. You're not wrong. And what

I'm about to ask you to do is even weirder. Do you trust me that this is all a part of your healing?"

In the pause, in the silence, I'm so spun around I don't know what to say. Because my instinct is to say no. This feels wrong. A man asking me to remove my shirt for "therapeutic reasons?" I mean, I'd gladly do it for him for *romantic* reasons, but that's not what this is. Then again, he's not oozing creepy. It's clinical. And up until now, everything he's done has helped me. Even if at the time, it seemed like too much, too intense: the gory pictures; the gruesome videos; being drawn on with blood; drinking it from his finger. It's all been disgusting. But it has all helped me. I've made progress. Blood doesn't make me shudder and faint the way it used to.

"Of course I trust you," I finally say.

"So prove it to me," he says.

He opens a drawer and pulls something out. I gulp when I recognize it—the silver shine of a straight razor.

I'm unable to move.

I want to run.

"Freeze response," he says, because it's like my skull is made of glass with him. He can see every thought in my head. "Don't let fear control you. Look at me. Look."

I take in his warm expression, his encouraging forest-colored eyes entirely focused on me, and I thaw. He is the most compassionate person I've ever met. He's never steered me wrong. It's not normal, but not-normal is okay.

So I take off my shirt. Self-consciousness spills as I stand here objectified in a black lacy bra.

"Don't look at the razor," he says.

It's very hard to do. I try my best to keep my focus on his face, his eyes. Fear to love. Fear to love. The air on my skin sends a chill through me.

I watch his eyes drift up and down my torso. He stands up with the razor.

"Trust me," he says.

"I'm afraid."

He steps closer. "You can't let fear hold you hostage."

"Don't hurt me."

"It'll be over so fast. Lie down on the bed. Close your eyes."

I fight tears. I want to fly away. This is not how I wanted today to go.

"If it's not hard work, it's not worth doing," he says. "This—what I'm about to give you—is something that will remind you of that for the rest of your life."

I'm being tested. This is a test. I could leave, say no, but then I know that would be the end of Simon and me. Maybe even the end of me at Mirror House. And I trust him, I do. He's right. If it's not hard work, it's not worth doing.

Lying down on the bed, I close my eyes.

"Hold your hands up and keep them up," he whispers. "Don't move."

I do as he says, and all at once there's a sharp pain in between my breasts—three slashes, one-two-three—and I cry out.

"It's over," he says, kissing my forehead.

And right as I'm about to start crying because of all my mixed-up, fucked-up feelings, he kisses me. He kisses me before I can even look down to see what he did. Then we're devouring each other. We are starving people eating a feast. His tongue is along my throat and in my ear and his hands are in my hair. Our mouths kiss so long my lips go numb. I'm lost in him. I'm breathless, I want him so badly, I can feel his body hard against my softness.

"Don't look down," he tells me, cupping my chin with his hand.

"Are we—"

"I shouldn't. I shouldn't do this."

He rubs against me and breathes heavy on my neck and I moan. At the same time, I'm distinctly aware of the sticky throbbing pain on my chest. Pain, pleasure, it all becomes one overwhelming feeling. I unbutton his pants and tug them down as his hand climbs up my skirt.

"You should," I say to him.

"I shouldn't."

"Please—"

I'm about to ask about protection, but he's already inside me. I gasp, fireworks exploding as he rocks back and forth on me, in me, holding me so tightly.

"I've wanted this so much," he whispers in my ear, sending tingly rockets all through me.

"Me too," I whisper.

It's glorious.

It's so glorious I push thoughts about STIs and pregnancy from my head.

I push thoughts of the razor and what my chest looks like out of my head.

He's like Eros with his curly hair, tan arms, and chiseled bone structure. There's no world anymore. No walls around us, no space, no time. All there is, right now, is our bodies moving as one, as if this is what we were made for. As if our parts were meant to fit together. One thing. No fear. Just love.

Pure love.

I've never loved anyone as much as I love Simon in this moment and I know I will never love anyone like this again. I would do anything for him. I proved that today.

When we're done—when we've cried out in unison—we lie here for a long time, his body resting on mine. He plants kisses all over my forehead and cheeks.

"You were too tempting," he says, still catching his breath.

My heart is still beating so fast. I want to stay here forever, never pull apart. Never have to get up and leave this room. Never have to look in a mirror to see what he's done to me. Something dark passes over me—it's not regret, exactly. It must be fear. But I try to push it away. See the light. Focus on the love. I love him. I love him so much. I don't care how strange this all is, I don't care about the me outside of me, shaking her head and saying, *What the fuck?*

I stand in front of the mirror, studying myself. It's crude and swollen, but the shape he carved into my chest is not that bad, really. It's small, smaller than it hurt at the time. I'm proud that I clean my own wound and am only the slightest bit ill.

Mostly, as I eye the puffy red lightning bolt between my breasts, I'm proud.

Excerpt from the documentary *The Mirror House Girls: One Year Later*

LOCATION: Interviewee's home, Raven's Landing, California

SCARLETT continues her living room interview. Her tea is gone and she's now wearing a sweater.

SCARLETT: Simon was very seductive. He didn't *seem* it. You'd look at him, that mop of hair and his crooked glasses and, you know, not exactly the portrait of Casanova. But he had this way of slowly, slow as honey, getting you to want his attention. Getting you to somehow be the pursuer. He was "celibate." He was wrestling his own demons. Somehow that made him more attractive. He was human, too, you know?

Simon's secret sauce was this push-pull. He'd pull you in and make you feel like you were the most special person in the whole, wide world. Then, out of nowhere, he'd push you away again. And just when you were about to give up on him, he'd come back and start the whole cycle over. Pair that with the fact he played so many roles with us, you know, therapist and house leader and best friend and you were just … spun around by him all the time. Dizzied.

(Scarlett shakes her head and does finger quotes) "Celibate." That man would call an alligator a lizard. (Scarlett looks at the camera) Later, I found out it wasn't just me —he was fucking everybody in that house.

30

Dear Simon Spellmeyer,

This letter is to inform you that, as of today, 30 days have passed since my initial request for the removal of the mirrors from the exterior of the Laguna Street property. Unfortunately, the mirrors have not been removed, and I have continued to receive an increasing number of unsolicited and inappropriate emails from individuals on your behalf.

Your failure to comply with the terms of your lease agreement leaves me with no choice but to take further action. Effective immediately, I am initiating eviction proceedings. This action is necessary due to your continued noncompliance with the lease terms and the unwarranted escalation of this matter.

You will receive formal eviction documentation shortly, outlining the process and timeline for vacating the property. I regret that it has come to this, but your actions have left me with no other option.

Should you have any questions regarding the eviction process, you may contact me directly, though I must insist that any further communication be civil and respectful.

Sincerely,

Paul Hamm, Property Owner

I'VE HAD A BELLY full of bees ever since I read the letter that arrived today.

We tried our best. So many TikTok posts raving about this house, so many new followers, likes, shares, and comments. But no matter what story the analytics told and how much support we got from strangers online, this letter makes it clear it ultimately didn't save Mirror House.

There's a contemplative gloom that has hushed the house since we all read it. I've heard Kristin crying on the phone saying, *It's not fair.* Simon has been meditating about it alone in his room all day. Maude hasn't said a word, but she did punch a wall and now her hand is bandaged up. Dakota's been streaming on her TikTok channel so long her voice is going hoarse. I've been lying on my bed, too heartsick or brainsick to read, staring up at the clouds that pass by my skylight. I'm waiting for some kind of sign. What do I do next? I finally found somewhere I wanted to be, a home, and we have to leave.

I don't want to lose this place. Don't want to lose these people. With an ache, I remember Grandma Jane's words: *Wish we were just getting started.* It was her refrain, the one she said whenever we parted, whenever a holiday was coming to an end. The memory washes up like a wave: her crackly voice, the violet perfume of her hug.

Wish we were just getting started.

Sometimes I swear there must be more than this life, there

has to be, because I still feel her presence and hear her voice so vividly. It's like she's with me all the time.

I haven't called my mom since she visited me. She hasn't called me, either. What she said can't be unsaid and I suppose the same goes for me. But now, for the first time since I saw her, I wish I could reach out. That I could have someone to tell me where to go and what to do. My mom was always good at giving orders. Then again, everyone in the house agrees that my mom is toxic and I should cut her out and I can't say I disagree.

While I'm pondering clouds and my mother, a scream cuts through the air.

It's a bloodcurdling, bolt-upright-and-run-toward-it kind of scream.

Which is what I do. I scramble to my feet and run downstairs toward the earsplitting female voice knifing the air, my heart cracking open like an egg because I know whatever I'm running toward is going to be terrible.

I get to the landing on the second floor and see Maude's bedroom door is wide open. No one's screaming anymore but clearly something has happened because voices are raised and Maude's window is wide open, too. I rush inside her room, ignoring the zoo smell and the floor that has smeared feces in a corner. Rushing over to where Scarlett stands with her hands clamped over her mouth and Maude is shaking her head.

"I don't get it." Maude raises her hands in the air like I'm a Florida cop about to arrest her. "Don't know what happened. Honest."

Scarlett pries her hands from her face. "He's dead!"

"Who?" I ask, the world tilting sickly as I realize the only *he* in this house is Simon. Louder, I say, "Who?"

I push through them to peek out the open window. It's not Simon, thank god; but it's Harvey.

Poor Harvey.

The long, thick snake is lying listless on the lavender porch. He's clearly dead, inky blood spilt from his skull. It's revolting. It's testing my fear reaction. But I let out a breath of relief because for a moment I assumed something so much worse had happened.

"What's going on?" Simon asks from behind us.

"Harvey killed himself," Maude says sadly, shaking her head. "Slithered out the window, I guess."

"Stop acting like this was suicide. This was homicide and you know it," Scarlett says to Maude, nostrils flaring.

Maude glares at her. "Suicide."

"Homicide."

"Su—"

"You left the window open?" Simon asks, interrupting them. He shakes his head. "Maude, you knew this would happen."

Scarlett points at him. "Exactly."

"It wasn't homicide, you narc," Maude says.

"Criminal negligence, then," Scarlett says. "I'm sure you're familiar."

Maude looks like she could punch another wall.

"You interrupted my meditation," Simon says.

At first, I think his soft tone means he's angry. Simon either gets very quiet or very loud when he's angry. He comes to the window, putting a hand on my back. It might not look like much, but it's the most he's touched me since we had sex two weeks ago. My lightning bolt has healed to a pink scar in that time. He's basically ignored me since that session, wrapped up in his campaign to save the house. Even just the warmth of his palm on the small of my back radiates joy through me.

"This is a sign," he says, looking down at the dead snake on our porch.

"What does it mean?" asks Scarlett.

"A good sign?" Maude asks hopefully. Seeing his blank face, hers falls too. "Not a good sign?"

"Clean it up," he murmurs.

Then he leaves the room.

"It's October. Maybe if we leave it there, kids will think it's a Halloween decoration," Maude jokes, breaking the silence.

Scarlett eyes her with disdain. "Look at how happy you are. You wanted this. You hated that snake." She shakes her head and leaves the room.

"You want to help me clean up, blood girl?" Maude asks me.

"No thanks."

Something has happened to Mirror House as the end of October approaches. A spell has broken over us—the fruitless campaign, the eviction letter, and now a dead snake. A storm cloud hovers above this lovely house and threatens to rain on us and I'm so helpless. I have no idea what to do. I've wanted to ask the others if they've considered where they'll go after this, but I'm almost superstitious about it, as if speaking it out loud will make it real.

And I so don't want it to be real.

The window in my room is cracked and I can hear the crinkly-plastic noise of Maude bagging up her dead python. I can't help my curiosity. I stand near the window watching her.

"Bye bye, motherfucker," she says with a cackle, dropping it with a thump into our bin.

Then she looks up. It's almost as if she felt my gaze on her. Her grin melts into a frown.

She slips into the house and the door slams shut.

31

TONIGHT, we feast. Maude makes a corn chowder and I'm too afraid to tell her I think it needs salt. The mood is somber, candles lit, lights off, and no one is talking about the sword dangling over all of our heads: the eviction. Salt or no salt, I can barely eat anyway. I imagine soon I'll be back somewhere like I was before, renting a room in a house with a bunch of college students. Or worse, having to stay with my mother in Escondido while I figure out my next steps. I could cry.

"Eat, drink, and be merry, for tomorrow we die," Simon says, holding up a mug of wine.

We clink glasses and the screw in my stomach tightens.

"I do have an announcement." Simon reaches out and squeezes Kristin's hand. He winks at her and jealousy buzzes around my head like a gnat. They share some secret. They've been conspiring in Kristin's room for the past two hours. "Kristin and I have a solution."

Kristin squeals. "So amazing, guys." She shoves her hands in her hoodie pockets, jiggles her knee under the table. "Come on, Simon. Tell them!"

Simon's expression is blissful, relaxed, and puts me at ease. I look around—we all look around—and everyone else is visibly relaxing too. Maybe it's the wine, maybe it's his calm demeanor, but the collective mood seems to lift.

"We want to hear it, Boss," Maude says. "Lay it on us."

"It's extreme," he says. "It will only work if you're all fully committed to Mirror House as a lasting concept."

"Of course we are!" Dakota says.

Scarlett stirs her soup. "What do you mean 'lasting concept?'"

"Just keep your panties untwisted and *listen,* Scar," Kristin says.

"I had this vision when I was meditating today," he says. "I was asking the universe for a sign. And all I kept seeing, no matter how I tried to empty the mind, were trees. A lush forest, as far as the eye could see. I didn't know what it meant. Then the unfortunate incident with Harvey happened." He looks at Maude, who grimaces. "And I realized what the universe was trying to tell me."

We wait with bated breath, not a spoon moving, not a mouth chewing. All completely rapt and still.

"Escape," he says.

We look at each other, as if one of us has the answer. Instead, we're met with equally blank expressions. We turn back to Simon.

"We need to start fresh," he says. "Live somewhere away from all this. Stop pleading with greedy landlords and working silly jobs just so we can afford groceries in this soulless tourist trap." He puts his spoon down, impassioned. "Grow our own food. Connect with nature. We've dabbled in it here, but I'm talking about scaling up our operation. Truly getting off the grid. And Kristin's family has the perfect space up in Sonoma County—wine country, gorgeous hills that back into the ocean. It has a house and a ton of land."

"Literally no one in my family has used it in like a year," Kristin says. "It's just sitting there."

Scarlett squints. "Why do you have it, then?"

"One of many vacation homes for the family vacations that never happen because my dad's a workaholic and the rest of us are neurotic screw-ups," Kristin says.

I can't even imagine Kristin's upbringing. Her dad is a millionaire businessman who charters private jets. She mentions details like this as casually as I can say my mom has a pair of silver earrings.

The mental wheels turn. Land in Sonoma County. A house just sitting there, all alone. It's interesting that Simon was so disparaging when Kristin tried to offer her dad's support before, but now I guess times have changed and we're all desperate enough to take a handout. And this sounds like one hell of a handout.

"Mirror House isn't a house anymore," Simon says. "It's a state of mind."

"So we'd ... quit our jobs and move to Sonoma?" Dakota asks, with a hint of doubt in her voice.

"Why, is your spirit fulfilled by fixing catalytic converters?" he challenges.

Dakota raises her eyebrows, sinking deeply into thought.

"I'm fine with quitting my job," Maude says. "Pedicabbing's dead until spring anyway."

"We could get jobs up there," Scarlett says, as if trying out the idea.

"Yes, though what would we need money for if we grew our own food?" Simon asks.

"I don't know. Clothes, medicine," Scarlett says. "All the things we can't make ourselves."

Simon eyes her as if sizing her up. I'm not sure if he's about to get angry, but instead, he just offers, "If we grow enough food, we could sell at farmers markets. Or if you're really that materialistic, yes, get a job up there, I suppose."

Scarlett folds her hands on the table and leans in. "Look, we've got a few garden beds. But does anyone here know anything about actual farming?" she asks. "My grandma and grandpa owned a cabbage farm and let me tell you, it's not an easy living."

"Sounds like you know a thing or two about farms, then," Simon says.

Scarlett shuts her mouth, as if he stumped her.

"Listen, everyone. You all know I'm a princess," Kristin says. "I have a trust fund and I can help keep us afloat as we're figuring it out."

I can't believe my ears. Imagine having so much money you could just casually promise to support six people. Not that I should be surprised. Kristin is always paying for everything and picking up tabs.

"That is *incredibly* generous," Simon says.

Dakota puts an arm around Kristin for a side-hug. "Wow, dude."

"Hey, this place is why I'm sober. It really is." Kristin glances at her sparkly purple fingernails, twists a mood ring around. "I would do pretty much anything to keep it going."

"This could be big. Really big. We could expand—keep teaching what we teach on TikTok. Grow a *movement*." Simon shrugs. "I know this sounds wildly ambitious. If it's too pie-in-the-sky, we can go our own separate ways."

"No!" we say.

We all say it. Every one of us. A chorus of *no*s.

Simon's eyes widen. Then he seems energized, his excitement gaining momentum.

"Don't let fear be your driver," he says. "What do you all have that you're so attached to here? What is so important?"

Apparently, the mirrors are important, a little voice whispers. I can't help but wonder why we don't just take them off and stay here. Seems much easier than moving off the grid. But Simon's made it clear that isn't an acceptable solution. And it sounds like he's got a bigger and better future for us all in mind.

"What's the risk, anyway, of trying something?" he goes on. "Don't let fear of failure convince you not to try."

"I'm in," Maude says.

"Damn straight you are," Kristin says.

Dakota raises her hand. "Fuck it, dude. Why not."

Kristin hi-fives them.

"Sure." I smile. "Sounds like an adventure."

I would follow these people anywhere. In fact, the more I imagine this, the more thrilled I become. Living out on our own, off the grid? Trying to start a mini utopia? I've wanted to live a life that's worth writing about someday. This U-turn just might take me there.

"I'd like to learn a little more about the property, but ... I'm intrigued," Scarlett says.

Everyone watches her, waiting for her to elaborate. She doesn't.

"Scarlett, you have to come, bitch," says Kristin. "We could get goats. Chickens. Guinea pigs! So many guinea pigs."

"What's with you and guinea pigs?" I ask Kristin.

"Growing up, we had an entire guinea pig room in our house with these mazes and climbing structures and ramps." She looks like a happy little girl as she beams at the memory. "It was so awesome."

"Sounds like a lot of work," Scarlett says.

"If it's not hard work, it's not worth doing," Maude says.

"We can't have five out of six people go, we all have to go," Dakota says.

"It wouldn't be the same without you, Scarlett," I say.

Scarlett glances at me. There's so much in her blazing stare and I wish I knew what it meant. It's like she longs to tell me something. But her lips perk into a smile.

"Y'all are a bunch of arm-twisters," she says.

We finish dinner and Kristin makes her rounds with the wine and we party the way we used to on Saturday nights before the landlord ruined Mirror House. We look at the property together on Simon's laptop, the old house that needs work, the ten acres of land, the cypress trees and Monterey pines—a miniature forest! The creek that runs through the property. Our delight is contagious.

Scarlett sings "Across the Universe" and I read "Kubla Khan" aloud to a hushed room and then we blast eighties music and dance and jump on the trampoline and laugh and hug and Simon yells, maniacally to the sleeping neighborhood. *You're all dreamers! You're all asleep! We're the only ones awake!* And at some point, Maude goes overboard and begins shattering mirrors on the house with a baseball bat. Who cares, I guess? The mirrors are getting taken down soon anyway. We are all fall-down, slurry, sloppy drunk. Except Kristin, of course, who walks around yawning and filling glasses and drinking a thousand sparkling waters.

We're renewed tonight, knowing this isn't the end of anything. This is only the beginning. Edna St. Vincent Millay has a poem that says: *there isn't a train I wouldn't take/ no matter where it's going.*

That's me. I've always been a seeker. Eyeing the stars and wondering who made the universe. Thinking I spy my ancestors in sunsets.

I stop on sidewalks outside of churches to listen to the

choir sing. Plunk down in the sand to watch someone else's volleyball games, because I want a hit of vicarious joy. And if I hear other people laughing, I'll laugh too—even if I haven't heard the joke.

I've always longed to belong.

And now I finally do.

Excerpt from the documentary *The Mirror House Girls: One Year Later*

LOCATION: Bodega, California

Clip from LOCAL NEWS FOOTAGE

(Breaking news intro jingle)

Anchorwoman CHELSEA LEE stands on a cliff above the beach, wind blowing her hair, microphone in hand

CHELSEA: Good afternoon, this is Chelsea Lee with a breaking news update. We have just received reports that more human remains have been discovered near the site of the infamous Mirror House compound, where a mass suicide occurred earlier this year.

(Footage of the compound now: trash blowing; pedicab overgrown with weeds; deflated tents; a porta-potty on its side)

CHELSEA: Authorities are currently on scene at the now-abandoned property, located just outside Bodega, where the gruesome discovery was made earlier this morning. According to sources close to the investigation, the remains were found partially buried in a shallow grave beneath a lemon tree on the property.

(Footage: Police vehicles, officers examining the site, body bag wheeled away on gurney]

CHELSEA: Officials have yet to confirm the identity of the remains, but some speculate that they could belong to a missing woman who vanished under mysterious circumstances shortly after joining Mirror House in the months leading up to the mass tragedy.

(Cut to interview clip: police chief)

POLICE CHIEF: Our team is conducting a thorough investigation of the scene. Given the proximity to the compound and the nature of the remains, we're exploring all possible connections to the activities of the Mirror House cult. We urge the public to remain patient as we work to identify the victim and determine the cause of death.

(Cut to additional B-roll footage of the compound now: the rotten halfpipe, empty chicken coops, desiccated garden beds, and the main house with boarded windows, covered in graffiti that says things like NEVER FORGET and EVIL LIVED HERE)

CHELSEA: This chilling discovery raises new questions about the full extent of Mirror House's activities. We will continue to follow this developing story and bring you updates as more information becomes available.

(End of segment jingle)

32

"WHAT A BEAUTIFUL LIFE THIS IS," Simon says. "Stop right here, right now. Savor it."

A hush subdues the six of us as we huddle breathless on the porch and peer out at the unfamiliar scene. Our shared wonder is profound. We don't even need to say a word.

This is Kristin's family's vacation spot in Bodega: white clapboard house with a wraparound porch and a pointed witch-hat of a roof, nestled between the dramatic, blown-skirt cypresses and the rumbling ocean. We might as well be perched on the edge of the earth.

The new Mirror House.

Every one of us is carrying something—a box, a lamp, a bag of clothing. But we stop for this spell of silence. We take in the landscape, the blond grass bending back in the nippy morning wind. The fog that masks the cliffs and the ocean. A flock of seagulls descending on a Monterey pine. It's peaceful and empty as far as the eye can see, as if the world must roll on forever this way. No noise of car wheels or bicycle bells. No strangers laughing, no roller coaster whispering. Just nature, and us.

It's so peaceful I shiver.

"It's freezing, Boss," Maude says, breaking the silence.

Dakota turns to Maude. She's in a beanie, teeth chattering. "Right? Who ate the sun?"

"It's like this up here," Kristin says, zipping up her sweatshirt. "Witch-tit cold. Foggy as shit. Made me so depressed the one time I was out here I contemplated suicide." Extra chipper, she adds, "Don't worry, I'm all good now."

She opens the front door and heads in, leaving us all to exchange a look.

Inside, my heartbeat races as I set down the first box and survey the room—dusty and half-filled with furniture covered in sheets. The rest of Mirror House arrived here the day before yesterday to move another load, but I was working my last shift at Chapters and missed it.

"Don't drink the purple Kool-Aid," was the way Daphne said goodbye to me as I punched out, giving me the rock sign, devil-horn fingers.

I laughed, but since then it's bothered me every time it echoes in my ears. What the hell does that mean? She thinks I'm following Jim Jones to Guyana right now? I know I'll probably never see her again, but I still don't like anyone getting the wrong impression about me. I'm sure my mom would say the same kind of thing, if we still talked. But we haven't had a conversation since she visited me in Santa Cruz.

Maude heads straight to the kitchen, Kristin bounds upstairs, Simon and Dakota go to the backyard to film a TikTok video. I check out the living room, eyeing the tall ceilings with the wainscoted tiles, the delicate cracks in the paint like eggshells, cobwebs filmy in high corners. Smells like someone else's house, air stale and unfamiliar. For the first time, a bumblebee of doubt buzzes. It hits me that we're doing this. We are moving out into the middle of nowhere on a whim.

I turn to shut the front door and there's Scarlett still standing where we just were, out on the porch as if she stepped in glue. She's peering out at the dry dancing grass, the sky silvered with overcast clouds, and she's got this lost expression frozen on her face. I can't help but notice how quiet she's been today, barely a word since I arrived.

"Scarlett, you okay?" I ask from the doorway.

"Fine."

I shut the door and come join her. "You sure?"

The wind catches her marmalade hair and whips it around. She tucks it into the hood of her windbreaker and forces a smile. "Yep. Livin' high on the hog."

I can't keep a little laugh from escaping at that response, paired with the sight of her miserable face and hair going crazy like she's on a helicopter pad.

"You're a really bad liar," I say.

"My mama would disagree," she says with a sly smile, a real one.

"Pretty, right?" I say, nodding to the view.

"Mmm," she agrees, but her eyes are still on me.

Scarlett reminds me of a jar of fireflies, a contained bumble of frenetic light and energy. She'll be the first person to offer you a hug if you need one. She'll ride her bike singing at full volume without caring who hears. I've seen her roll around on the sidewalk to hug a dog she just met. It's hard to explain it, but I've sensed a subtle shift in her in the last month or so. There's nothing I can point to—she's still just as sweet and funny and lovely, but a touch more reserved. Or maybe I'm just projecting it onto her, after seeing her crawl out of the doghouse-box that day. Kind of hard not to project a shadow on her once I witnessed that, even if we never discussed it.

"You can talk to me, you know," I say, stepping closer to her.

"Oh yeah, doc?" She tilts her head. "How much does it cost?"

"Nothing." I drop my voice, imitating Simon. "My gift isn't transactional. It's an act of love."

Scarlett snorts. "Hey, I've heard that one before."

For one split second, panicky guilt sweeps in: I really hope that didn't sound mean toward Simon. I wouldn't want him to think I was ungrateful. He's been a little distant lately, but I'm still holding out hope that Simon and I might get close again. Maybe even sleep together.

"Want to take a walk?" Scarlett asks. "I'll give you the grand tour of the property, then show you inside the house."

"Sure."

We tread down the steps together, which need to be repainted. This place is glorious and huge, but up close, it's in need of some touch ups. I like that about it. Makes the place feel as if it's more in my league. Clean, pristine, expensive things make me nervous because no matter what I do, life is messy, imperfect, and breakable.

Scarlett and I head down the driveway, past the rental box truck, Simon's van, Dakota's Volvo, and Maude's pedicab, and walk up the dirt road we drove in on. Scarlett kicks brown dust with her sneakers and shoves her hands in her pockets.

"How are you feeling about all this?" Scarlett asks.

"It's surreal. We're so lucky, right?"

"So lucky."

We stroll along the perimeter of the property as the wind beats my eardrums. To the right of the house, there's an old chicken coop, rows of derelict garden beds, and a cattle fence dividing this property from the vacant lot alongside. To the left, a high privacy fence divides our house from next door.

"You sure you're all right?" I ask. "You're quiet today."

"Guess it's hitting me, how isolated we are. I moved three

thousand miles from the boonies to be where all the cool people are and now the cool people are all moving out to the boonies."

"Bodega's not *that* isolated."

She holds up her phone. "Yeah? I got no bars here."

This is the first I've heard this and I'm a little thrown off by it. I pull my phone out and see mine's the same, *SOS* instead of reception bars. "Oh."

"Simon and Dakota are the only ones with cars. I know Simon said we could ride our bikes into town but ... did you see that road? Tap dancing on the Empire State Building would probably be safer."

"Well," I say, kind of at a loss because I'm trying to process this myself, but we need to remain positive. "We just got here. I'm sure it'll be an adjustment. We'll figure it out together."

"Do you ever think that this is fucking crazy?" Scarlett stops me in the middle of the path back to the house.

My mouth opens, yet I'm not sure how to respond.

"I mean, moving out here like this? Not even cleaning the place out, leaving our landlord with that looking-glass hellscape and a bunch of weird-ass thrift store paintings and orphaned furniture to clean up on his own?" she asks.

"Simon didn't get his deposit—"

"I know, I know, he didn't get his deposit back, and I guess that makes it okay, right? I guess if Simon says it, then it's okay." There's a single drop of venom in her voice and I'm trying to decipher who it's directed at. Then she breaks into a grin. "You know you get this little wrinkle right in the middle of your forehead when you don't understand something. Reminds me of a puppy. You've got a puppy face."

"Thank you?" I say with a laugh.

"There you are!" shouts Simon, bounding down the porch stairs in his bare feet and waving. "I was calling for you."

"Giving her the grand tour," Scarlett says, her voice a little sweeter.

He slows as he approaches, a curious, suspicious gleam in his eyes.

"Remember? This is Winona's first time here," Scarlett says, smiling. "Just showing her some good ol' Southern hospitality."

"Right." Simon returns the smile, hands on hips, and surveys our surroundings. "Property's expansive, isn't it? There's so much we can do with it. I'm just teeming with ideas. Have you seen your bedroom yet?"

I shake my head.

"Once again, you're the unlucky girl with the ocean view ..." he says, heading up the stairs.

We follow him.

33

SIMON AND SCARLETT show me around. The kitchen where Maude is already making herself at home. The long, narrow dining room with windows that overlook the garden beds. The living room with a fireplace and a wall of windows that face the forest, so many built-in bookshelves.

"Maybe it will be your duty as resident librarian to figure out what we put here," Simon says, standing right next to me, a warmth blooming where my shoulder touches his arm.

"I can't believe this place just sat here with no one living in it. And Kristin's dad is really okay with us living here?" I ask, because no matter how many times I hear it, it never quite sinks in.

Simon nods. "We manifested this."

We bump into an awkward, dim hallway off the living room that I'd thought was a closet. Instead, it leads to a den with a low, sloping ceiling. The walls are wood-paneled, the room unlike the rest of the house and clearly an addition. It smells of mold.

"Maude's room," he says, then flicks the lights off again and we back out.

I really hope the other rooms are nicer than that one.

We head upstairs and Simon shows us the other bedrooms. Simon has the master again, off to the left, with sweeping corner views of the entire estate and a bird's eye peek into the neighbor's yard. He has his own bathroom with a claw-foot tub, which he promises anyone can use. Kristin is next door to him, and then there are two of the smallest bedrooms at the end of the hall, connected by a Jack and Jill bathroom. Both rooms are identical, with a high window that faces the ocean (somewhere, anyway; right now it's still all fog out there) and a corner closet. They're the smallest rooms in the house. My double bed will eat up half the square footage.

"You and Scarlett have these two rooms," he says. "And there we have it: the new Mirror House."

"What about Dakota?" Scarlett asks as I open my mouth to ask the same very thing.

"Oh, she's—" Simon scratches the back of his head. "She'll be with me for now. That room's too big for one person."

A cocktail of surprise and jealousy spills inside of me.

"I see," Scarlett says, her tone quieter. "Did I miss the invite to the planning committee? Who decided on all this?"

"I did." Simon turns to her. "Do you have a problem with that?"

His tone isn't mean. It's more curious than anything else. There's nothing cruel about his expression, eyes wide and blank. But there's something I'm detecting—his impatience, her poke of a question—that leads me to believe there's a history here and I'm not privy to it.

"No, sir," Scarlett says, melting into a goofy smile, as if she'd only been kidding.

He doesn't return the smile, walking away without a word. Scarlett's face falls as she watches him leave.

Is it just me or is the mood in this house tense? We're not getting our utopia off to a swimming start.

"Hey, let's go down and start moving furniture," I say.

We burn some calories hauling shit upstairs. Bed frames and mattresses and night tables and books, books, books. I unpack, slipping clothes on hangers and arrange my paperbacks in crates, alphabetical order by author name. My third time moving since the year started. I'm getting pretty good at this.

I'm grateful to have something to focus on, because then I don't have to think about Simon and Dakota sharing a room. Questions keep popping off like brain fireworks: Do they hook up like Simon hooked up with me that one time? Is he not celibate at all anymore? Are they together now? They've been spending a ton of time together, but I assumed it was all in the name of TikTok. Does Simon not care about me anymore? How long has it been since he talked to me one-on-one? Is he mad at me? Did I do something wrong?

"Hey." Scarlett pops the bathroom door to my room open. Her face is flushed, strawberry hair frazzled and in a dramatic side part. "Sorry to barge in. I should knock, right?"

"No big deal. I'm arranging my books," I tell her from my cross-legged position on the floor.

"Look at how cute your room looks already," Scarlett says, glancing around.

Her gaze sticks to the one poster on my wall: *The Lady of Shalott* by John William Waterhouse. I couldn't hang it in the attic in Mirror House, because the walls were slanted on one side and rough and unfinished on the other. But I tacked it up here and it's refreshing to see her again, the despairing, redheaded woman in a canoe who has been with me since high school.

"You know that painting?" I ask.

"No. But she kinda looks like me. Giving me goosebumps."

"She does kind of look like you." I notice this for the first time. "It's *The Lady of Shalott*. Famous painting about a famous poem by Alfred Tennyson."

I could go on about how I discovered the poem because it was in *Anne of Green Gables* and I adored that series when I was a child, how I memorized the entire poem and recited it at a sixth-grade talent show and everyone thought I was weird because what twelve-year-old memorizes long odes to suicide? But I stop myself.

"You'll have to read it to me sometime," Scarlett says. "Anyway, just wanted to see how you're settling in."

I smile. "Good."

An awkward pause stretches. I like Scarlett a lot, but she's never spent much time in my room. I'm not sure why she's in here.

"Thanks for talking to me earlier." She starts toward the bathroom door again, then turns back. "And oh—can we keep it all private, what we discussed?"

"Sure," I say with surprise, not even sure what it is she wants me to keep private.

"I'm *really* happy to be here," she emphasizes.

"Me too."

"Scarlett," Simon's voice sings from the bottom of the stairs. "We're returning the truck, you ready?"

"Yep!" she chirps back.

She goes her way and I go mine: downstairs, with an armload of flattened moving boxes. After putting them out on the back porch, I stand and shiver in the morning air and finally, finally, the fog parts. There's a cliff hanging over the ocean back there. The Pacific Ocean, love of my life. Sunshine peeks through and I breathe deeply. I imagine Grandma Jane saying, *Moving out here like this on a whim? You're crazy, child. And you know I love crazy!* If there's an afterlife, she's there cackling.

Back in the house, the living room is looking more like a place for the living. Lights on, curtains open. The furniture no longer has sheets on it and it's infinitely nicer than everything we left behind at old Mirror House. Out the front window, Simon climbs into the moving truck and guns the engine. Dakota and Scarlett head toward Dakota's car. I'm about to turn upstairs when I freeze.

My jaw drops at what happens next.

Dakota pops open her trunk, points, and without a word, Scarlett hoists herself onto the bumper and climbs inside. She lies down in a fetal position, arms in a cross over her chest, eyes closed.

I repeat: Scarlett just tucked herself into the trunk like a human suitcase.

It must be a joke. She's joking, right?

Slam.

Dakota heads back to the driver's seat, gets in, and drives away without a visible passenger, following the box truck down the long driveway. All I can stare at is the closed trunk, where you would never guess a woman is lying down inside.

I stand here in sheer disbelief as the vehicles shrink and then vanish. Dizzied by everything, I turn toward the kitchen for a glass of water. All I can think is how bumpy and dark and awful it must be in Dakota's trunk. The image keeps repeating, a hellish brain GIF: Scarlett crawling in, crossing her arms, closing her eyes. *Slam.*

In the kitchen, Maude is unpacking pots and pans and singing along with Ozzy Osbourne. She stops when she sees me, wiping sweat from her brow.

"What's up?" she asks as I fill my glass. She turns the volume down on her phone. "You okay there, hon?"

"Scarlett just climbed into the trunk of Dakota's car."

Maude waits, cast iron pan in hand. "Uh-huh."

I can't believe I have to say this out loud. "That's dangerous."

"Well, it's … it's not your business, is what it is," Maude says. "You know?"

"It's illegal," I say, softer.

"You're not the judge of anyone's journey." She opens a cupboard and scoots the pan inside. "And no one else is the judge of yours. You shouldn't be questioning and gossiping, it's ugly."

"I wasn't gossiping—"

"You were, and I don't want any part of it. You're pissing me off."

I've seen Maude lose her shit before. She goes from zero to ten in a snap. So far, I've managed to steer clear of her wrath and I'm not about to break my lucky streak. I back out of the room, glass in hand.

"Sorry, forget it," I say.

Back upstairs in my new bedroom, I take out my phone. A sudden churn of homesickness overtakes me—but homesick for where, I couldn't even say. I slip my phone back into my pocket.

Doesn't matter anyway.

No reception bars.

34

OUR FIRST NIGHT at the new Mirror House, we party.

Maude brings cozy blankets, Kristin pours us mugs of wine, Simon lights the fireplace, Scarlett busts out her guitar, Dakota captures video for TikTok like a documentarian. Everyone's smiling and hugging and excited and the uneasiness disappears. It's just how it was before. The location changed, that's all.

"How are you, sweet Winona?" Simon asks, stealing me into a corner and slow dancing with me as Scarlett sings a Dolly Parton song and the others roast marshmallows over the fire.

"I'm good," I say, lighting up at his nearness.

"I've missed you, even when you're three feet away from me," he says into my ear. "Painfully. I can't stop thinking about you."

"I miss you too," I whisper back, pulling him tighter toward me.

The way he talks to me makes me think I'm the only one. That he and Dakota don't have anything going on.

"We'll have a session soon," he says.

I stiffen, thrilled by the promise in every sense of the word.

Thrilled as in, excited. Thrilled as in, terrified. That potent mix of both.

The moment is cut short. He pulls away because Kristin's yelling in the kitchen about not being able to find the corkscrew. Then Maude pulls Simon aside for some mini rant on the back porch.

It's surreal. I'm so giddy from what he whispered to me it's like I stepped off a merry-go-round. I sit down next to Scarlett as she sings "Coat of Many Colors" and savor the sweet fading taste of his affection. She bumps my knee with hers and grins. And see? Scarlett's happy too. She's a grown woman, if she wants to ride around in someone's trunk, that's her weird, fucked-up choice. Who am I to talk? I have a lightning bolt etched between my tits.

The corkscrew crisis is averted, Kristin returns to refill our cups. Now she's wearing a beer hat, the novelty kind with two beers on the sides and straws that go into her mouth. I don't ask. Therapy shit.

"How's this brand of wine?" she asks me as she fills the cup.

"Oaky," I say. "With hints of currants and blackberries."

"Look at this fancy ho," she says, impressed.

"Kidding, I don't know anything about wine."

She laughs. "Bitch, I'm with you. Who cares, gets you drunk, that's all you need to know."

"Exactly."

Seems strange, reveling in alcohol with a recovering alcoholic, but whatever. Nothing's wrong with strange.

Simon returns with Maude, claps his hands, and asks us if we can have a meeting. Everyone takes seats as Simon stands in front of the fireplace, backlit by the flames, his glasses gleaming.

"No cameras for this," Simon says to Dakota. "This isn't for the audience."

She nods and puts her phone away.

"Cheers," Simon says, holding his glass up. "To the new-and-improved Mirror House."

*Clink*s all around.

"Now that we're here …" Simon paces. "What the hell are we going to do?"

Everyone giggles, but he stops and scans our faces like he's earnestly looking for the answer.

"How are each one of us going to be the butterfly effect here?" he asks.

"I think we need house roles, Boss," Maude says. "Jobs and responsibilities list kind of thing."

"I like that, Maude," Simon says with a snap. "Winona, you have a notepad or something so you can take notes?"

"Absolutely," I say, excited to be useful.

I retrieve one of about ten thousand cute notebooks I bought over the years thinking I would journal at some point. Spoiler: I did not journal. Sitting back down, I open a fresh new page.

"Maude, what are you thinking?" Simon asks. "House manager? You supervise the kitchen, house needs, everything like that?"

"You got it," Maude says.

"Dakota, TikTok maven," he says, giving her a wink. "I think we should keep you there, what say you?"

"Thumbs up, dude," says Dakota from the corner.

She's eaten so many edibles she looks about ready to launch into outer space right now in a blob of blankets.

He grimaces. "Kristin … finance? You could take inventory, figure out what we need, order supplies for the house?"

"I was thinking I'd like gardening and animals," Kristin says. She puts a fist up and chants, "Guinea pigs! Guinea pigs!"

"I think it's important to go where we're needed right now. Don't you?" Simon asks her, gently.

"You can't even keep a fuckin' houseplant alive, Krissy," jokes Maude.

Kristin's smile slackens. "Fine, yeah, I'll take finance." She pulls one of the straws into her mouth and chews it.

"Then Scarlett ... I'm sorry, don't hate me, but it's your fault!" Simon wags a finger at her. "You said you came from a farming family. So don't we all think she should oversee the garden?"

We raise our glasses and Scarlett shakes her head, as if this isn't what she hoped.

Simon leans over and strums her guitar. "*Go where you're needed,*" he sings.

That makes her laugh. He gives her a kiss on the head and she lights up, her cheeks pink from the alcohol and attention.

"Okay," she says.

"And you, Winona ..." Simon stops and ponders me like I'm a sculpture in a museum, one whose shape he doesn't recognize.

"Resident librarian?" I try, remembering our conversation from earlier.

"Floater," he says. "You'll go wherever you're needed."

My pen's poised, my mouth open.

"You've been getting all this, right?" he asks. "Write it down. *Floater.*"

He pronounces the word as if I'm something you'd find in a toilet. I swallow and write it down, even though it wasn't what I hoped for. But ... go where I'm needed. Everything's temporary.

"This is all a big experiment," Simon says. "Moving here. Expanding. And it's lofty. I'm sure some of you have had your doubts. But *we* are the only things in our way. You understand?"

Nods all around. He points his gaze straight at me. Through me, more like.

"Dakota and I have a vision we want to share with you," Simon says. "Dakota, you have the floor."

Those three words *Dakota and I* ring in my ears. I swallow the jealousy and tell myself it doesn't mean anything.

Dakota stands up, clasping her hands. Despite how stoned she is, she's well-spoken—clearly her shadow work has paid off. "Simon and I have had this revelation about how to utilize our TikTok channel and spread our message in a real-life way."

I'm prickling at the wording again. *Simon and I.*

"A lot of people have responded positively to our videos and we get DMs," she goes on, "like, all day long with people asking, how can I do what you're doing? People with real problems, you know—family issues and addictions and phobias and all sorts of shit. And we want to, like, open this up to other people and make it accessible."

"Make it into a movement." Simon takes the reins of the conversation again. "Make it something bigger than just us, our house. And this is perfect, out here—we have all this land. We can literally invite people to come here and experience what we experience and have what we have. To transcend fear."

"What about the 'no visitors' policy?" Scarlett asks, brushing her tangled hair with her fingers. "What if another reporter came and wrote another hit piece or got you in trouble, Simon?"

"I'm going to be in charge of approving every person who comes here," Simon says. "It's a risk I'm willing to take, to make an impact. If it's not hard work, it's not worth doing."

"Fear to love," Maude says, fist in the air.

"Fear to love," Simon answers, bumping his fist to hers.

Fear to love, the rest of us agree.

"So we're turning the area on the other side of Hitchcock Road—which is part of our property—into what will essentially be a campsite for visitors." Simon resumes his pacing in front of the fire. "And we can run workshops or talks or coach people who come here."

"For *free?*" Kristin asks.

"Love is only love if you give it for free, Kristin," Simon says sharply. "We aren't your blood family; our love isn't transactional."

Kristin stares down at the pizza socks on her feet.

"What, you worried about what daddy's going to think if we expand?" he asks, as if he's really wondering.

"No, no. It's fine," Kristin reassures him. "He won't care. He's in Hong Kong for the next couple of months anyway."

"Psychology, counseling, self-help gurus—predatory nonsense. *This* is the answer. Ordinary people helping ordinary people. *This* is the kind of thing that actually changes the world." Simon puts his hands on his hips and studies us. "Are we on the same page with this? Haven't all our lives been improved exponentially because of what we have here? Doesn't everyone feel like you woke up from a lifelong dream since we all came together?"

Murmurs of yeses and nods all around.

"Well, why should we be the only ones?" he asks. "Don't other people deserve to wake up, too?"

Everyone agrees and the conversation moves along to logistics. How will we determine criteria for who comes? What will the rules be? A decision is made to move full steam ahead, but I can't pinpoint where it happened.

I roll this around in my head as I sip wine. What he's saying is true, I can't deny that everyone deserves to live a life without being smothered by fear. But the idea of inviting strangers here makes me uncomfortable. These are my friends, my best friends, and I don't want that to change. Then again, it's not my house. I'm not even paying rent. No one in this room is, so who are we to deny anyone?

"And it will require everyone to be a hundred percent on board," Simon says, stopping in front of me. "Which means no secretive talk. No gossip. No judging. Hear me, Winona?"

I nod slowly, stung by the callout.

He narrows his eyes at me. "Because Maude told me that you went to her questioning something you saw earlier with Scarlett. How you wanted to gossip with Maude about it and judge Scarlett for her decisions."

Wait. Am I in trouble? I can hardly breathe.

The heat pouring over me, the way my stomach caves in like I've been kicked—this goes beyond shame. I'm so stunned to be called out in front of everyone, for the entire group to be watching me with hurt and confusion, and this seemingly came from *nowhere*. Worst of all, Scarlett has this crumpled look on her face.

"I wasn't—" I start.

"Oh, hon, don't lie, that'll just make it worse." Maude shakes her head at me. "Own up."

"There is zero judgment in here," Simon says to me. "Understand?"

I nod. There's nothing I can say right now to make it better, so I bite my tongue. Hard.

"It's simple. You're either in, or you're not." Simon enunciates every word in a way that makes me want to flinch. "You're either awake or you're dreaming. What are you?"

"Awake," I whisper.

In a jolting transformation, Simon cheers like he's at a football game. "She's awake, everyone!"

The room echoes his cheer. As if he can tell I'm imploding in real time, the humiliation and the copious amounts of wine turning me into a puddle, he floats over and puts his arms around me. He begins humming. Soon, the warmth multiplies, everyone joins in, *mmmmmmm,* that familiar feeling of a group hug, a Resonance, the buzz of us, our little hive, and I close my teary eyes to soak it up. I'm loved. I'm cleansed. This is when it settles in—when I relax into the bones of this house.

I'm sorry for what I did. So sorry.

I vow never to do anything to hurt them or disappoint them again.

Excerpt from the documentary *The Mirror House Girls: One Year Later*

LOCATION: Interviewee's home, Raven's Landing, California

SCARLETT breathes a deep sigh, shaking her head.

SCARLETT: The oh-shit feeling hit as soon as we got to Bodega. You know when your gut's just whispering to you that you took a wrong turn? We hadn't even hopped off the moving truck and I was already feeling like everything was different. There was this seriousness in the air. The weather had changed, inside and outside.

After dinner that first night, Simon and Dakota presented us all with "The Plan." (Finger quotes) They wanted to build this utopia, right? This we knew. But turns out this utopia wasn't just for us. They wanted to open it up to other people.

It sounded insane, if I'm going to be honest. But none of it was presented to us like "you have to do this." It was decided as a group, us sitting around the fireplace with mugs of wine in hand, which made us all feel like we were doing this. *We* were deciding this, not Simon. But it was him. It was all him. He was so fucking good at planting an idea in your head and making you think it was yours. He could turn you so ass-backwards you thought you wanted something you never asked for.

It happened fast and it kept us so busy there wasn't time to stop for questions. None of us had jobs, so this was what we talked about all the time. "The Plan." We went into build mode. I'm sure Kristin's daddy was footing the bill for it. Bought all these fancy tents, built up the campsite area, got grills and these outdoor showers and porta-potties, Simon and Dakota "screening" people to invite.

(Interviewer asks an unintelligible question and Scarlett leans in to hear it)

SCARLETT: Looking back, it's so obvious this was going to end badly. I had a spidey sense even if I didn't let myself acknowledge it. Why'd I stay? Why didn't I just get out then? Is that what you're asking?

(She sits back and crosses her arms) I had three hundred dollars in the bank. No job, no car, internet service spotty as all hell. And Simon's work *had* helped us. At that point, I could crawl into a shed or a doghouse or car trunk, shut my eyes, turn my fear off like a faucet. Disassociate. No tears. No fear. He did what he promised, didn't he? I learned that I might be locked in a tight space at any moment and *I was okay with it*. He erased my fear. (She shakes her head and her expression hardens) And so much more than that.

35

IT'S NOT AS hectic as I expected it to be, having strangers stay here.

The first ones arrived yesterday. We set the campsite up at the end of our driveway and on the other side of the dirt road, under a stretch of Monterey pines. So far, it feels more like neighbors than guests. From our living room window, you can just barely make out the parked cars and tents and campfire smoke.

Four people are out there right now—Isabella, Sadie, Katrina, and Sophia. They blend together for me, untalkative girls with flowing hair who barely look eighteen. Simon's spent the day having one-on-ones with them in his room. Lingering in the hallway upstairs, I overhear the sound of him typing on his keyboard and asking, "Have you ever traveled outside the U.S.?" The memory comes back to me like a shock of ice water: that first session we ever had in his room. Him asking me questions, taking notes, studying me like an experiment. Sitting back and listening to my answers in fascination.

He never looks at me like that anymore.

In the backyard, I help Scarlett weed the garden beds and hammer their wood frames back into place. Ever since last week when Simon told the group I'd been "gossiping" about Scarlett, she's been distant with me. I apologized and she smiled and forgave with her words, but her attitude says otherwise. We're quiet as we rip plants from their boxes and I try to stay positive. I should be grateful for all this, but my mood matches the weather: a persistent, overcast gloom.

"What do you think of those girls?" Scarlett asks me, breaking the silence.

I shrug. "They seem nice. What do you think?"

"I think they're dumber than a bag of rocks."

I burst out laughing, I can't help it. The way she says it, delivered almost like a compliment in her sweet North Carolina accent.

"What?" she says, laughing too. "I mean, who the hell abandons their life to follow some weirdo she sees on TikTok?"

"Hate to tell you, Scarlett ..." I say with a grimace.

She looks down at herself. "Shit."

We break into laughter. And suddenly, for the first time since I was called out in front of everyone, I know Scarlett really did forgive me for gossiping about her. She gives me a long look, one full of sunshine. For a moment, it's summertime again.

"I hope you know I trust you." She rips a mound of dandelions from the soil and tosses them in our compost pile. "I wasn't mad at you. You didn't do anything wrong."

"Thanks for saying that."

"I'm sure my exposures look cuckoo from the outside. I'll bet yours do, too." Scarlett scours my face for a reaction.

I nod, humiliation a warm spill inside me. All the things I've done flash back at me. I'm supposed to be proud of my progress, and it *is* progress, I've changed, I've overcome a fear I never thought I would. Then why such shame every time I remember the images I've stared at, the taste of Simon's blood, the zigzag pain of the razor on my chest? And even more confusingly, why am I sad because my exposures seem to have come to a full stop since I got to Bodega?

"That's probably why we're not supposed to share them," Scarlett says. "No one would understand."

"Simon doesn't do sessions with me so much anymore," I say as I rip a bag of soil open.

"Don't worry. You're on the outs but just lay low and behave. You'll be back in soon."

I look up at her, surprised. Part of me thought it was all in my head, that Simon was just busy and not fed up with me.

"Though who knows, with these pretty young things that just arrived," Scarlett says. "Maybe we'll be making room for them in the house soon."

My pulse skyrockets in a mini panic attack. I never considered until now that I could be kicked out. I gave up everything to be here; I've been so proud of being part of this group.

"Gardener! Floater!" Simon's voice yells.

We whip around. He's on the back porch with two of the girls. They're all waving and smiling.

"I'm giving you some extra hands!" he shouts. "Going to have Sophia and Isabella join you in backyard duties today."

"Goody!" Scarlett says.

She gives me a pained smile. The girls hurry through the grass to join us. One of them has a plastic butterfly in her hair, the other has a chipped front tooth. They look radiant, young, with faces open like flowers turning toward the sun. And I don't know why my heart sinks at the sight of their hope, but it does.

Because here in this house, nothing can be fixed until it's broken first.

36

OF COURSE, we throw a party for the new girls.

We gather around their campfire, bundled up, Kristin passing out full mugs of wine. Simon goes on a tangent about Prometheus, Dakota doles the edibles, Scarlett plays her guitar, Maude sings "Sweet Child of Mine" in a screech so loud my ears ring, and there's laughter and togetherness and that magic, warm feeling that I'm part of something greater than myself washes away my worries. We make s'mores. Then Simon suggests we play Truth and the group cheers and suddenly the grin on my face aches.

We haven't played the Truth game since the night I told them about my dad. This time I'm on the other side, about to watch it happen to someone else.

I huff out a breath, a puff of air visible in the firelight, and glance back at the house. Scarlett's beside me on another camping chair and she reaches out without even looking at me and squeezes my gloved hand.

"Since you're our guests of honor, ladies," Simon says, playfully, from his spot perched up on the picnic bench, "you need to go first tonight. Isabella?"

"Mmm?" Isabella asks with an apple-cheeked smile. She's so wasted she's swaying as she sits cross-legged in the mouth of her tent. "What's up?"

Everyone laughs at her adorably wasted response.

"Tell us something you've never told anyone before," Simon says.

Déjà vu grows legs and creeps like a spider in my chest. A shiver crawls slowly up my spine. It settles into a numbness that makes my ears ring. As Isabella dredges up her trauma in a slurry confession, publicly reliving being molested as a child, I hurt for her somewhere, but I don't feel it. That numbness, the alcohol, it's a painkiller. But I'm witnessing something right now in the sacred, holy quiet of the campfire. This is the moment. This is the moment Isabella's passing a threshold and she doesn't even know it. And I can predict what's coming next. Simon comes over and holds her and begins to hum. He gestures for the rest of us. Soon everyone is joining in, arms around arms, humming and vibrating and shuddering with human electricity. I'm the last one to join.

But I'm part of it.

37

As a "Floater," I've spent my days doing all the jobs no one else wants to do. Cleaned the toilets. Took out the garbage. Weeded, swept, did laundry. Worked with Kristin to assemble her new three-foot halfpipe in the side yard for skating. And today's random project: converting the chicken coop to her new guinea pig coop outside.

I don't know if I've ever seen Kristin this happy. We close the cage and watch her four furry little friends run up and down a ramp, making weird squeaky sounds and sniffing the hay on the floor. Kristin squeals and claps. Back in Santa Cruz, her nails were always impeccable gel manicures with glossy, vibrant colors, but now they're chipped and growing out.

"Aren't they so fucking cute you just want to bash your head in?" Kristin asks.

"That's one way of putting it," I say.

Scarlett stops pushing the wheelbarrow to peer at them with us.

"Y'all have some dopey little faces," she says to them.

Kristin pushes Scarlett playfully. "Watch out or I'm going to sic 'em on you."

My pocket trembles and I have no idea what's going on for a second until I realize my phone is buzzing. It's a shock, because my phone hasn't rung in weeks here—the only reception I get is when we drive a few minutes away. My mom's name flashes on the screen and zaps me like static electricity.

"Your phone's working?" Kristin says, amazed. "Shit. Who's your provider?"

"Hello?" I say, putting the phone to my ear and walking a few feet away.

My mom's voice is breaking up. "Noni?"

"Hey." I don't know what to say, it's been so long. My stomach is full of lead. I stare out at the trees and wait for the words to come. "Long time no talk."

"I kept hoping you'd call. I can't believe how long I've waited."

"Well, you could have called, too," I remind her.

"Noni, I'm worried about you."

The line breaks and all I hear is her voice coming in and out like a bad radio channel.

"I have no reception here, Mom."

Her voice comes back. "Where are you?" It breaks up again and I sigh. "—watching to figure out what happened—"

"Bodega. Up north. We moved." There's a long pause. "Hello?"

I strain to hear her. She sounds a thousand miles away.

"Mom, I can't hear you. I'll call you next time I go into town, okay?"

Silence. When her voice buzzes back for a moment, it sounds urgent. For the first time it strikes me that maybe something's wrong. Maybe my mom has cancer. She's in the hospital. She needs me to come.

"Is everything okay?" I ask, tentatively taking a step toward the house and hoping that clears the signal.

It does. She comes in loud and clear.

"I've been following everything on TikTok. I know everything. I've seen everything."

"What are you talking about?" I ask, so confused.

"It's a cult, Winona," she says loudly. "Open your eyes. You're in a cult."

So *that's* what she's trying to say. I burst out laughing, it's so ridiculous.

"You've been brainwashed," she says.

"Oh my god, Mom," I say. "Give me a break. Seriously. You are so overdramatic."

"I'm telling you—"

"I'm *fine*. I'll call you back soon, okay? I can barely hear you, it's too hard to have a conversation. It's a miracle I even got this call."

"Love you," my mom says weakly.

"Love you, too."

I hang up and shake my head at my phone. I realize suddenly that my entire adult relationship with my mom has felt like a call with bad reception. *A cult.* Please. I can't imagine living in the constant emergency state that is my mother's mind.

Scarlett and Kristin have disappeared into the house. I stand alone out here under a gray sky, always gray skies now. I used to miss the sun, but now I'm growing used to the mysterious creep of fog. An Emily Dickinson line blows through my mind in a whisper: "*We grow accustomed to the dark/ when light is put away.*" I let those lines echo, the way great poetry deserves.

I press the secret lightning bolt scar on my chest and glance at the beady-eyed, curious guinea pigs in their new pen.

They look so happy.

38

FINALLY, *finally,* I get a session with Simon.

He's been in high demand these days, juggling extra time with the new girls, filming content with Dakota. I've only seen him in passing and have lived in secret fear he hates me ever since he called me out in front of everyone. But out of the blue this morning, he tapped me on the shoulder while I sat at the breakfast table reading and whispered in my ear, "Session at ten."

So here I am: showered, perfumed, in the sexy shirt he likes, wearing red lipstick. My hands tremble as I sit in a chair opposite him. The room is set up the same way as his other room with the guru poster over the king bed. In the silence between us, as he turns his chair to me and his attention is mine, all mine, I could burst with joy. And at the same time, I'm sick to my stomach. I don't know what to expect.

"Winona," he says. "Here we are again."

"I've missed you," I say, instantly regretting how gushy I get with him. I clear my throat. "You've been busy, haven't you?"

"We're building something truly amazing." He makes his hands into a finger tent and observes me as he spins absent-mindedly back and forth in his office chair. "My conundrum at the moment is figuring out what to do with you."

It's as if a sinkhole opened and swallowed me whole. I blink back at him. "What do you mean?"

He gets up and paces the wood floor in his bare feet. Simon probably walks ten miles a day pacing and thinking, pacing and thinking, pacing and thinking. "I don't know where you belong in my vision of what we're building here. I can't figure out your role." He shakes his head. "I've almost given up on you."

"Why?" My throat tightens. "What did I do? I don't understand."

The room seems to get smaller. My lungs shrink, too. He's going to kick me out of Mirror House. He can't forgive me for talking to Maude about Scarlett, that was the last straw.

"Simon, this house and you and everyone in it mean everything to me." I use all my will to keep my tears from springing. "Why would you give up on me?"

"I'll be blunt with you, Winona." He sits back down in his chair. "I'm incredibly attracted to you. At one point, I thought there might be a real romantic connection between us. But I've come to realize that I just don't trust you."

A slap across the face would have felt better.

"Why?" I ask.

"There's this push-pull energy with you that's frenetic. You worked hard in our sessions, then you backed off, you would cry, get upset. Then it turns out that you've been judging my techniques behind my back—"

"I said I was sorry about that!" I say, eyes spilling.

He shakes his head. "Don't try to manipulate me by weaponizing your tears."

"I'm not trying to weaponize—"

"You want to be here?" His voice hardens, his eyes narrow. He leans in. "Then stop sniveling like a baby."

I nod, clenching every muscle in my face to stop the tears. I must be turning red.

"Do you trust me?" he asks, softer, reaching out and grabbing my hand. Rubbing my palm with his fingers.

His touch. How I missed it.

"Of course," I say.

"And you trust my methods? You trust I would never want to hurt you, or Scarlett, or Maude, or anyone in this house, or anyone in this whole wide world?"

"I do, Simon, I promise."

"Then prove it to me."

"How?" I ask after a loaded moment passes. "How do I do that?"

He gets up from his chair and goes to his closet, sliding open the door. On one of his shelves, next to neat rows of worn sneakers and Birkenstocks, there is a box. He picks it up and sits back down with it on his lap.

It's a blender.

The picture on the front is bright and happy, a smiling woman filling it with fresh fruit. *Chop, slice, dice, blend, or crush!*

My first reaction is a nervous laugh because ... why? I don't know what I was expecting, but it wasn't this. He's utterly still, watching me take it in. His face has no expression. And suddenly nothing feels funny. Just bizarre.

And frightening.

"What do you want?" I ask in a small voice.

"What do you think I want?"

"I don't know." I swallow, suddenly feeling as if the temperature dropped twenty degrees. "Can you just tell me?"

"I want to plug this in and see you stick your hand in it," he says.

His tone is so friendly, as if he's asking me a simple favor. He's joking. He has to be joking. He ... doesn't really expect me to put my hand in a blender right now, does he?

"I told you, you don't trust me," he says sadly.

"I do, Simon, but ... I—"

"If you trusted me, you would say yes."

There are degrees of imagination. Some things you think of head-on, in colorful detail. Others you think of in some peripheral place inside yourself, a place you're trying not to look. In that horrible place, that underworld of my imagination, I am seeing blood and bone and torn-up fingers twirling around in a blender.

I suppress a dry heave.

"I will ask one last time," he says. "One more chance, Winona. Do. You. Trust. Me?"

"Yes," I whisper, my vision sparkling.

I hope I faint. I really do, I hope I faint.

Simon gets up and removes the blender from the box, leaning over and plugging it into the wall. He sits back in his chair and presses a button to test it out with a single pulse.

I jump and flinch at the sound of it, a horrid mechanical scream.

It whirrs and slows to a stop again as he lifts his finger off the button.

"Come and reach inside," he says. "Right now. Prove it to me."

I cannot breathe. I know right now, whatever I decide to do is going to change my life forever. Either way, I'm losing something dear to me—my best friends, my found family, or my hand. But I can't hesitate. He's ready to give up on me. His finger hovers over the button and even though I want to scream and run away, I have to trust him. I have to believe he's doing this for a reason and I'm going to learn something from it. I have to. I have to, because this place is all I have.

I put my hand in the blender.

His fingertip hovers over the button.

I close my eyes and brace myself for the unthinkable.

39

I can feel the blades on my fingertips, chilly, waiting to rip me to shreds. I'm biting the side of my tongue so hard I've broken the skin. I don't care. I'm trying to go away from here, leave my body, astral project, anything, *anything* to not feel what is coming. I stand here for a long time, barely able to breathe, my entire body shaking in sheer terror. I'm imploding with antici-pation. A personalized horror movie flashes before my eyes: a stump of dripping flesh on the end of my arm; a bandaged mess; a prosthetic hand; a robotic claw. I imagine having to explain this to people: *yeah, I tried to prove my loyalty to this guy once by putting my hand in a blender.*

It makes no sense.

And yet, here I am.

Finally, the moment grows wings and flies away. The fear lifts in the quiet here. I open my eyes. Simon's finger is no longer poised over the button. He's watching me, hands on his knees. There's a glow in his gaze I've missed—like I suddenly became interesting to him again, with my hand in the blender.

"You did it!" He smacks his thighs victoriously and stands

207

up. Wrapping his arms around me, he kisses the top of my head. "You did it, Winona!"

My fingers are still caressing the blades inside the blender. My teeth are chattering and I'm trying not to show it.

"Take your hand out, it's over," he laughs, pulling my hand out. "It was a test, Winona."

"I passed?" I ask, a tsunami of relief buckling my knees.

"With flying colors," he says, running a finger along my jawline.

I pull my hand out. My intact, gorgeous hand. My unbloodied, unmutilated hand. I rub it lovingly. I've never appreciated my hand so much in all my life. He takes the hand and turns it, palm up, and kisses it, right in the center. I can't help a sob from rocketing through me. I'm so confused and rattled and overwhelmed. He pulls me in close.

"Shhh, it's okay, it's okay, sweet Winona," he says, his hand in my hair.

I bury my face in his shoulder, not wanting him to see me cry.

"It's okay. It's okay. That's it. That was all I needed from you. You passed," he whispers in my ear. "You passed. You belong here. You belong with me."

Simon pulls back to observe me. He plants a tender kiss on my forehead, uses his thumbs to wipe my cheekbones, where some traitorous tears have escaped despite me trying so hard to keep the sobs at bay. I use every ounce of willpower to hold them in, but they keep coming.

"I'm sorry," I whisper. "I'm all—all spun around."

"You graduated," he says to me. "You're done. You're awake now. You hear me? Your therapy is finished. You're no longer held hostage by the fear that brought you here. You're one of the *Woken*."

"What do you mean?"

"Here in the house, we're the *Woken*. I'm wrapping up exposures for you OG Mirror House girls this week. The new girls out there, they're the *Waking*. Their exposures are only beginning. And everyone else out in the world, they're Dreamers. Understand?"

I nod. I'm trying to hold onto his words. They're not quite sinking in.

"What are you thinking?" he asks.

"I'm—just taking it in," I say, my voice hoarse.

He tilts his head and dips it toward me, his lips suddenly on my lips, his tongue in my mouth. I'm still stunned and even though this is what I want—I've fantasized about this endlessly, about us being together again since the other time we hooked up—it's so different from how I imagined it that I have a hard time relaxing and enjoying it. He pulls me to his bed and rolls on top of me, kissing me, our bodies warm and pushing together. My body wants this. My nipples harden under my shirt, a warmth blooms in between my legs, but my mind? It's too dizzy.

My mind can't enjoy this moment.

I try to be here. Be here, enjoy this special moment that's everything I've wanted. He's pulling my shirt off. He's unsnapping my bra and telling me how perfect I look. He's tracing the outline of the lightning bolt with his index finger, raised pink and healed between my breasts. And I'm just ... I can't explain it. I'm an inanimate object. I'm numb.

The whole thing happens so fast, as if Simon's been pent up. In a flash, our pants are down and he's inside me, rolling back and forth, groaning. I whisper the appropriate responses and trace my fingernails along his back. But why am I not enjoying this? Why? Who knows how long it will be before this happens again. I've spent weeks pining for him and now he's inside me and I feel absolutely nothing.

He moans and pulls off me, out of breath, lying on his back. "Oh, Winona, how do you do this to me?" he asks. "How?"

I offer a tight smile. Glancing at his floor, in the corner of the room, there's a thong that doesn't belong to me. It's lacy and black. The sight of it makes my stomach flop. I turn the other way again.

"I want you to be in charge of the Floaters," he says, still catching his breath, buttoning his pants. "You can delegate to them, figure out where they're needed, keep them in line. Queen of the Floaters."

Such a left turn into business again that at first, I don't know what he's saying. Finally, I nod and answer, "Sure, yeah. I'll do that."

I go back to my room. Curl up in the fetal position on my bed, staring at my hand. Opening it and closing it, opening, closing, over and over. Trying to make sense of what just happened.

I should be relieved.

I should feel lucky.

I should be a lot of things I am not.

40

I DREAM I'm in Mirror House again.

The other Mirror House. Walking around from room to room with an anvil in my belly. No one is home. Everyone's bedroom doors are ajar, but their rooms are empty. The house is clean—the clean of the unliving. Not even a twinkle of dust in the air. A haunting and ghostly silence stretches in the stillness. I've never seen Mirror House without people inside. This doesn't feel right. Something bad happened here. It's solemn as a cemetery. I rush to the front door and there's no doorknob. There's no way out, the windows replaced by mirrors. Banging the floral wallpaper with my hands, I call out my housemates' names but hear no reply. When that doesn't work, I cry out for my mother and grandmother. A river of grief pours out of me when I realize I'm alone, I'm forever alone. Everyone I love has left me.

Then I'm torn back to the real world.

I wake up, drenched in snot and tears with my head on my pillow. Gasping for air and gutted by my own unconscious. Someone is rubbing my back. It's dark and I'm having trouble catching my breath. It takes a moment for my eyes to adjust, for me to center myself in my room as I make out the shape of *The Lady of Shalott* on my wall. I recognize the voice now. The person rubbing my back and whispering to me is Scarlett.

"It's okay, it's okay, I'm here," Scarlett says.

I sit up, blinking at her and wiping my face. I was sobbing in my sleep.

"I was having a nightmare," I say, the pain of the dream beginning to fade, the details drifting away like sailing ships.

"Yeah, I heard you calling out from the other room." Her hand rests on my back. "Want to talk about it?"

I shake my head, embarrassed by my overreaction. The dream wasn't *that* tragic. As far as nightmares go, pretty tame.

"I have nightmares too," she says. "I understand."

Scarlett's backlit by my window now, a halo of blue moonlight around her wild hair and catching the shine of her eyes. She could be a painting.

"Was I so loud that I woke you up?" I ask.

"Nah. I was tossing and turning myself. It was only because the bathroom doors were open, I think. No one else heard."

I listen to the silence of the house. Everyone is sleeping.

"Sure you don't want to talk about it?" she asks gently, tilting her head.

"That's okay. It doesn't make sense now."

"Funny how that works, right? Seems to matter so much at the time and doesn't make a lick of sense later."

"Like the rest of my life," I joke.

In the dark, the gleam of her smile lights up and then disappears. "Well," she says, standing up. "You need anything, I'm right there on the other side."

"Stay with me."

My mouth moved before my brain did. I didn't realize until

I spoke how much I don't want her to go, how the dream still has a ghostly grip on me even though it passed.

"Would you?" I ask.

"Course."

She sits down on my bed. I move over to the other side, making room for her. My pulse quickens as she pulls down my duvet and climbs in next to me and we lie down. She smells like vanilla and her hair is everywhere. We face each other, only a foot apart.

"Been a long time since I've been in someone else's bed," Scarlett says. "Forgive me if I kick you in my sleep."

"I've been told I snore."

"Well, this'll be fun."

We giggle. She utters a tired sigh. For a moment, she closes her eyes, angelic and peaceful. She opens them again.

"Wanna cuddle?" she asks.

A beat passes and the elevator where my heart lives goes up ten floors. "Sure."

"You want to be the big spoon or the little spoon?"

"Little spoon."

I turn my back toward her and her warm arms encircle my waist. She pulls me close and I sparkle from head to toe. My brain begins whispering worries to me, ones I haven't heard in a long time. *Are you gay? Why does this feel so good?*

"I knew it," she says into my neck.

My heart hammers in my chest. "Knew what?"

"That you were the little spoon."

I snort.

"What?" she asks. "You have LSE. Little Spoon Energy."

"You think I'm passive."

"No. I think you like to be held."

She kisses the top of my back, so softly I shiver. And then we just lie here for a long time. I hear pipes running in the house and an owl hoot outside. Someone treks down and back up the stairs again and a door shuts. I don't dare move a muscle because this—Scarlett's body, the way it fits into mine, the way our temperatures match—it's so perfect I could live here forever. This is the best I've felt in a long, long time. Skin tingling, soul soothed. Maybe a cuddle is better than sex. It's a tranquilizer, because before I know it, it's morning and the sun is slanting through my window.

I sit up. Scarlett's beside me, lying here patiently with her hair spread all over my pillow, bright-eyed and smiling.

The word *beautiful* is too weak to describe her. She is a masterpiece.

"Thanks for staying with me," I say. "Sorry I woke you."

She props herself up on an elbow. "I should thank *you*. Slept better than I have in a long time."

We lock eyes and there's something here between us, a delicious desire bubbling under the surface. It's not lusty and volatile like it is with Simon. It's a placid comfort. She brings me peace. And yet—I don't know how to put what is happening into words. Is this romantic? Are we just friends? I'm not sure how we got here.

Scarlett stretches and gets out of bed. She heads toward the bathroom door, then hesitates, her hand on the door frame.

"You're a pretty sight to wake up to in the morning, Little Spoon," she says with a special smile.

And then she's gone.

41

Simon gathers everyone together in the living room after lunch.

It's cozy and wonderful, this togetherness, this moment of respite in the middle of a day filled with work—cleaning sinks and hauling recycling and taking inventory in the kitchen. Finding odd jobs for the other Floaters to do. The new girls curl up in beanbag chairs on the floor at his feet, Scarlett and I share an overstuffed chair, Maude, Kristin, and Dakota on the couch. Outside the wide windows, the rain pours down in sheets.

"A few house announcements," Simon says. "Dakota, maybe grab some of this for content."

"Absolutely," Dakota says, pulling her phone from the pocket of her railroad overalls.

"Make sure you get my good side," he jokes.

"They're all good sides." Dakota gives him a dimpled smile. She crouches on the ground with her phone, filming Simon in front of the fire.

"All right. Today I want to have a group discussion." He rubs his hands together. "Fear is at the root of every negative emotion. Every single one. We know that. But what is the purpose of fear?"

The Floaters on the beanbag chairs whisper to one another. I'm trying to be open about them being here, but quite honestly, it's like someone invited a clique of high schoolers to come live with us and I've had a hard time fully embracing them. I can't help but stare at their happy faces and wonder about their shadow selves. The parts of them that will climb into a car trunk or suck the blood off someone else's finger. One of them was up on the roof the other day, crying for hours. Another has been walking around with a jar full of spiders. What other horrid things does Simon have them doing?

"Hey Floaters, zip your lips and listen up," Maude barks from the couch.

The Floaters freeze, united in shame, and turn their attention to Simon.

"What is the purpose of fear?" Simon asks again.

"To warn us of danger?" one of the Floaters tries.

"Yes, and yet—ninety-nine times out of a hundred, there's no actual danger at play," he says. "Humanity tops the food chain! We don't have a lot of tangible reasons for these danger signals ... and so we're left with this *fear* response that has nowhere to go." He paces and speaks as if he's thinking through this in real time. "Life is duality. Light and darkness; man and woman; good and evil. Fear and love." He stops and looks at us, as if marveling. "Or just fear and the absence of fear. Is that all love is? A true absence of fear?"

"Mmm," Kristin says, stirred by what he said.

"You do the sessions. You put in the hard work, because if it's not hard work, it's not worth doing. No pain, no gain. Ready to step into the shadows? You really do see results. I'm not making this up. The Woken in this house have all transcended their fears." Simon points at us, one by one. "Scarlett here. Maude. Dakota. Kristin. Even Winona."

I smile, but my insides tense up. *Even Winona.* What does that mean? As if she detects my worry, Scarlett squeezes my hand.

"You're next." Simon addresses the four girls in beanbag chairs. "You're going to be next."

They nod, rapt. Simon keeps talking about everything we've transcended. He talks about the importance of confronting fears through exposures. And for the first time at Mirror House, my mind drifts. I'm having a hard time holding onto his lecture.

It's the first time I've ever been bored by Simon.

He leads us in a meditation exercise. We've been doing more of these lately. It involves repetition, sometimes holding hands and sometimes not. We chant together: *Fear to love. Fear to love. Fear to love.* We go on like this for five, ten minutes. Our voices bleed together, become one thing. Our eyes glaze over.

Repetition is a fascinating thing. *Fear to love.* My lips shaping the words and the voice streams from my throat. *Fear to love.* Three simple monosyllabic words. *Fear to love.* But when I say them enough times, the words themselves lose their meaning. *Fear to love.* They feel foreign and new. *Fear to love.* I can't distinguish my own voice from anyone else's. *Fear to love.* I can't think of anything else but those three words holding my mind captive. *Fear to love. Fear to love. Fear to love.*

We end with a Resonance. Dakota films the purring group hug. As I hum and envelop myself in the warmth of our huddle, I imagine my mother somewhere, watching this on her phone and shaking her head. *It's a cult, Winona. Open your eyes.*

We're not a cult, of course. We're just a group of friends with a lifestyle she doesn't understand. But I must admit, I can see why she thinks so sometimes.

Excerpt from the documentary *The Mirror House Girls: One Year Later*

LOCATION: Interviewee's home, Raven's Landing, California

Perched forward in her seat, SCARLETT tilts her head, listening as the interviewer asks an off-camera question.

SCARLETT: You're asking when I knew it was a cult? (Sits back, contemplates) There wasn't one lightning-strike moment, you know? It happens gradually. Subtle cracks in the armor. But definitely once we moved to Bodega, once the new people started arriving, I could sense things were taking a turn.

Simon was on his own trip once we got up there. He'd always been someone who spun in brain circles talking and philosophizing. I liked that about him, it was charming, and the things he said were interesting. But then in Bodega, it was like—we weren't having conversations anymore, you know? He was monologuing. He had an audience. And we started doing these meditations together and it involved chanting. At that point I was like, okay, this is … what the hell is this, anyway?

I remember one night at a "party" I brought my guitar out and played a song. It was called "You Are the One."

CLIP of Scarlett playing guitar in her living room. (Singing)

> You're your audience
> your biggest fan
> your truest love
> When your life flashes
> you are the one
> you're thinking of
> If you were to lose yourself
> then you would soon forget
> all the lovers and the
>   strangers
> and the fakers and heart-
>   breakers
> and the bosses and the losers
> that you ever met
>
> You are the one,
> you are the one…

CUT back to interview.

SCARLETT: So I was playing this for everyone and suddenly Simon stands up and cuts me off and says to the group, "A round of applause for the most narcissistic singer-songwriter of all time!" And I froze. He said it so *meanly* and everyone laughed and applauded and then he went on about how all my songs are just me crying "Me! Me! Me! I'm so special! Look at me!" I was so hurt and humiliated to be mocked like that, to be torn down for something I created. He looked so *happy* while he tore me down, like he was having such *fun*. He looked … almost evil.

I know people watching, y'all are thinking, well, why didn't you leave, dumbass? No one was holding me hostage there, I could have walked away at any time. I don't know. I still felt like these were my people, this was my place. I believed that Simon cured everyone. And suddenly, my sessions and exposures were done, since we were "Woken" (finger quotes) and had "graduated" (finger quotes). In that way, our time in Bodega was better, an improvement from before. Once those new girls arrived, no more getting locked up in boxes and all that shit.

But you want to know the real reason I stayed? I fell deeply, stupidly, utterly in love.

42

DECEMBER IS COLD AND RAINY. December is a broken furnace and scarves in the house. December is enormous pots of soup on the stove and warm bread in the oven. December is a dead guinea pig and a funeral where Kristin is crying. December is Kristin drinking a mug of wine because she's graduated and transcended her fears. December is Kristin getting so drunk she takes a spill on her half-pipe and twists her ankle. December is Scarlett coming into bed with me every night and putting her arms around me and singing me Carter Family songs. December is more tents, a new cohort arriving, another welcome party. December is more drunken, tearful confessions and humming hugs. December is the sound of a headboard banging the wall in Simon's room. December is meandering walks through the fog and the gorgeous, everlasting ocean. December is meetings every afternoon and more chanting, *fear is love, fear is love, fear is love.* December is the neighbors coming to complain about the noise. December is the Floaters moving into our house and taking over Maude's room, Maude moving in with Kristin, Dakota sleeping on the couch downstairs among a scattering of ring lights and TikTok props. December is strangers in and out of our house all day. December is me wondering, is this even my house? Was it ever my house? Is this me anymore?

The only person I talk to about any of these doubts is Scarlett. And I say it in the dark, as if somehow, it's easier to talk about secrets here. We face each other as we lie in my bed, our legs drawn up, knees touching.

"You ever look around and ask yourself, 'what the fuck has this become?'" Scarlett asks.

"What do you mean?"

She weaves her fingers in mine and I get belly butterflies. Every time Scarlett touches me, it's like that. We've never kissed or anything. We've never talked about whatever this is. I tell myself we're best friends, that's all. Everyone in this house is more affectionate than most people are out in the world.

"Mirror House 2.0," she says. "All these new people coming. Simon preaching all the time. The chanting and—just everything."

"It's different than I thought it would be."

"I'm worried about Kristin. I don't think she transcended jack shit."

"Yeah," I say with a sigh as I remember the sound of Kristin's crushing fall in the half-pipe the other night—that smack of plastic wheels and concrete on bone, howls of pain. "That was scary."

"And Maude ... Between us? I think she's a psychopath."

I sputter a laugh.

"I'm not kidding. She killed her fuckin' snake, remember?"

"She says it jumped."

"Winona, how in hell does a snake jump?"

"You have a point."

"And she swaggers around like the town deputy these days. Always looking to tattle on people. Every time she gets someone in trouble with Simon, swear to god, she gets a dopamine rush like she just snorted a line of coke."

I have noticed what she's talking about. In fact, Maude bought a whistle this week and has wandered around blowing it at the Floaters like a drill sergeant.

"Simon's different too," Scarlett says. "His head seems a million miles away even when he's talking straight to your face."

I bite my lip. I agree with her, but something about this feels wrong. I shouldn't be gossiping about Simon. He's done so much for everyone. He never charged anyone a penny for his work. He's been nothing but kind and welcoming.

"How do you feel about Simon?" Scarlett asks.

"He's amazing."

"Yes," Scarlett says quietly. "But I don't think he's perfect."

"He hasn't claimed to be perfect."

"No, he hasn't, you're right. Just claims to have the answers."

I relax my grip on her fingers. "I don't even think he claims that."

A silence thickens between us.

"Look, I'm just shooting my mouth, please don't tell anybody I said that," Scarlett says.

"I won't."

"This is just pillow talk."

"I know."

She looks at our hands. "You think anybody knows I've been sneaking into your bed?"

"No," I say, kind of horrified at the thought.

"I almost feel guilty leaving an empty room each night. Poor Dakota down there on the couch and that dank little room with four Floaters in it."

It's true. I had been jealous of Dakota sharing Simon's room, but as soon as the new girls arrived, Dakota moved downstairs to the living room. Now she doesn't have her own space at all.

"Better than a tent outside," I say.

"You're right."

"What do you think of this new cohort?"

"Same as it ever was. Young, beautiful ladies. With long hair."

I snicker.

"He definitely has a type," Scarlett says.

I don't agree or disagree. I have noticed, but I squashed down the noticing. Simon is like god: if I say a bad word about him, he'll somehow know. Now that I'm back in with him, I don't want to give him any reason to push me out again.

"Once I told him I was going to cut my hair and he threatened to kick me out of the house if I did," she says.

"Oh, come on," I say. "He's not that bad."

"You don't believe me," she says flatly. "You think I'd just make that up."

I don't say anything. I can't win right now: either I'm betraying Scarlett by not believing her, or betraying Simon by believing her. Despite all his quirks, I have a hard time imagining Simon giving a shit about someone's haircut to that degree.

"He has a thing about control," she says. "He likes to control people."

Annoyed, I pull my hand away from Scarlett's. "If it's all so terrible, why are you here?"

She pulls my hand back, with a warm grip. "You know it's not black and white like that."

I sigh.

"Sorry," she says quietly. "I feel like I can tell you anything."

"You can, but what's the point of the negativity? We're here, this is where we are. It's not all bad."

"You're right. It isn't. Some of it is fucking beautiful and gorgeous and perfect."

She's looking at me when she says it and fireworks light up inside me. My hand relaxes in hers again. Every time I look at my hand I'm thankful I still have it. In some ways, it's like I never truly appreciated that hand until Simon almost took it away from me.

"Can I ask you something, Little Spoon?" Scarlett says.

"Mmm-hmm."

She pauses and then asks, softer, "You ever kiss a woman before?"

My skin prickles with goosebumps. "Once, in college."

"Did you like it?"

I wait a second before replying, "Yeah."

"Well, then." She tucks a wayward curl behind my ear. "Want to do it again?"

Takes me a second to find my voice. "Yeah."

We lean in, noses touching first, then close our eyes. We come together and a supernova explodes. Scarlett's lips are the plumpest, warmest, softest lips I've ever kissed. Shakespeare could write sonnets to her lips. These lips could launch a thousand ships. As we push and pull, our hands in each other's hair, our bodies warm and tangled under the blankets, I'm not sure where she ends and I begin. I've never felt a love this soft, this slow and gentle. Never had someone stroke my cheeks and kiss my earlobes. As we breathe heavily and devour each other quietly under the blankets, her hand flutters to my belly.

"Is this okay?" she asks, stopping.

"Yes," I whisper.

She moves her hand up further, to the spot below my breasts. She traces a heart there with her finger. As if a dam has broken, I want her so badly right now I tremble under her touch.

"Keep going," I whisper.

She moves her hand up again, cupping my breast, and I let out a sharp breath of pleasure.

"You're fucking exquisite, you know that?" she whispers in my ear, sending a current of electricity all through me.

And then suddenly she stops. She freezes.

"What?" I whisper.

Her fingertips are reading my chest like braille in the space where my cleavage usually is. She gasps. Oh god—I'd forgotten.

My stomach sinks. I fall down a deep well of shame.

She's feeling my scar.

"Winona," she says in this disappointed voice, almost as if it's an admonishment.

I push her hand away and sit up. "It's nothing."

"It's not nothing," she says, sitting up. And I resent the moonlight right now, because it spotlights the disappointment on her face.

"It doesn't matter," I say, my eyes filling.

I don't know how, but my scar changed the mood. Everything is wrecked now.

"It does matter," she insists, in a hiss of a whisper. "It very much matters."

I look away at the wall, at the shadows of dancing tree branches. My eyes burn with tears.

"Winona," she says, putting her hand on arm, but I don't want her pity.

I shake her hand off.

"Hey," she says. "Look at me."

Finally, I turn, expecting some sorrowful look. Some judgmental expression that tells me how fucked up I am. But instead, Scarlett's unbuttoned her own pajama top and what I see makes my jaw drop.

She has an identical lightning bolt carved between her perfect breasts.

43

I'M SHOCKED at the sight, the wind stolen from me.

"He did the same thing to me," she says, buttoning her shirt, flushed and tearful. "Did he tell you that?"

I shake my head, mirror tears in my eyes.

"Why?" she asks. "Why would he do that?"

There's so much I could say but it's all knotted up inside me. I can't get it out. It doesn't make any sense.

"It was my exposure," I say numbly. "Because I have hemophobia. But you don't have hemophobia, so why would *you* have one?"

"A month or two after I moved in, we had a session. He asked if I'd be willing to prove I was all in. A trust exercise."

I'm trying to understand. I'm really trying.

"What has he done to us?" she asks in a wavering voice.

I rub my temples and close my eyes, trying to breathe through the confusion. Even though it's not fair, a wildfire of rage directed at Scarlett spreads through me. As if she somehow ruined everything and this is her fault. I wish I could rewind and go back five minutes, unsee what I saw. Take back the kiss. Make different choices. The weird thing is that before now, the lightning bolt between my breasts never really bothered me. It was a secret badge of honor, a scar that commemorated me overcoming one of my greatest fears. It was also this perverse but special mark of Simon's affection. But my cheeks burn as I sit here staring at the wall, unable to speak. The illusion that I'm somehow special has been shattered. And part of me can't forgive Scarlett for shattering it.

"Winona?" Scarlett asks, her hand on my shoulder.

I shake her hand off.

"What? What'd I do?" she asks, her voice full.

"Can you just go back to your room?" I ask. "Please?"

The bed doesn't move. She sniffs. "Don't shut me out—"

"Give me some space."

"This *matters*," she says, and I don't know if she's talking about the scar or the two of us but suddenly I think if she doesn't get out of here I'm going to have a nuclear meltdown.

"Leave me alone!" I yell.

She scrambles up before I've even finished my outburst and scurries toward the bathroom. I've frightened her, her expression quivering and broken. And of course, I care about her and don't want to hurt her. But I can't explain it—an arctic wind blows a door shut somewhere inside me and I have no feelings anymore.

The door to my room bursts open and Maude pokes her head in. She wears a towel turban and a wide-eyed expression.

"Someone just yell?" she asks.

"I did." I clear my throat. "Sorry."

"Everything okay? Need me to break any heads?"

"Yes. I mean, no." I sigh and try again. "Everything's okay."

The weirdness in the air must have a scent because Maude seems to smell it suddenly, her nose wrinkling as she looks from me to Scarlett back to me again.

"Well," she says, as if she just realized something. "Good *night*."

She closes the door.

"Sorry I yelled," I say, turning to Scarlett, but all I see is a glimpse of her red hair before the bathroom door closes behind her.

I should get up and go to her room. I should talk to her about this, listen to her side of the story, try to make this right. But I don't want to. What I want is to forget this ever happened. I lie in the dark throbbing with thoughts. I dissect it logically, the way Simon would. He would say this stems from my fear of not being special, which, in part, it does. This pain boiling me from inside out as I lie in the dark and watch shadows on my ceiling? Unmask it; it's fear. If I wasn't so afraid, I could get through this. If I was stronger, it wouldn't matter.

Simon will have the answer if I ask him. I'll meet with him tomorrow, confront him about it. He'll make this make sense. He always does.

44

THE DINING ROOM has become chaotic as a cafeteria lately with so many people coming through. To complete the comparison, Maude's even started wearing hairnets and industrial aprons. I swear we have soup for breakfast, lunch, and dinner. Soup and bread. Between the Woken and the Waking, there are now sixteen people and a few new tents have popped up closer to the house. Last week, Simon had to tell a woman to turn back and go home because she tried to show up with a toddler.

"We're in such high demand we're turning people away now," Simon joked at the time.

Somehow, I manage to peel Simon away from his breakfast entourage this morning. He's at the head of the table talking about "the great men of history" like Jesus, Buddha, and Napoleon and how what made them great was the fact they transcended fear. But when I whisper and tell him it's important and I need his help, Simon immediately excuses himself and leaves his granola half-eaten to come take a walk with me. I'm so grateful for his warm response. Even though he's in charge and everyone wants his attention, he's still here for me when I need him.

"What's wrong, sweet Winona?" he asks, holding my hand as we bound down the steps, out into the salty wind that leaves a misty kiss on the tip of my nose.

I savor the warmth of his hand in mine, his compassionate stare. We take the path around the back of the house past the languid winter gardens that Scarlett planted. The wind blows Simon's hair as he smiles out at the sea. He stops to point out the ice plants, *carpobrotus edulis,* an invasive species with edible flowers. He picks a few and puts them in his pocket. I love that about him—that everything in his world seems to have a use.

Ahead, there's the rocky cliff and the sleepy blur of a slate-blue ocean coming into focus behind it. We stop at the edge and he turns the sunshine of his focus my way. It's as if, to Simon, there is no ocean. There is no cliff. There's only me in front of him.

"Get the words out," he says, putting a finger to my chattering chin.

"You did the same thing to Scarlett," I finally say in a shaky voice.

"Did what?"

I search his face and all I see is kindness.

"I can't understand what this is about unless you use your words," he says, with the patience of a parent dealing with a five-year-old. "Aren't you a poet? Use your words."

"What you carved, right here," I say, pointing to my chest and pantomiming a zigzag. "You did it to both of us."

"Ah," he says, the light bulb going on. He blinks, unfazed. "Indeed. I did."

A beat passes, a seagull screams.

"Why the fuck did you do that, Simon?" I manage.

He puts a hand to his chin and studies me. "How did you see it?"

"Answer my question."

"If you'll answer mine."

Even though I can barely feel my face from the whipping sea wind, I'm sure it's turning red. The way he's watching me—flirtatious. Mischievous. Like he's got X-ray vision and he can see me without my clothes. He reaches out and pulls me in for a hug. I stiffen up, not placated in the least. I want answers, not his arms around me. But he tightens his embrace.

"Winona," he murmurs, the buzz of his words in my ear sending shivers all through me. "What I do in other sessions and the reasons I do them isn't your business. Haven't you been warned about gossiping?"

"We weren't gossiping," I say.

"What were you doing then? Comparing your tits? Fucking quietly in your room?"

I don't answer, closing my eyes.

"You think I'm not aware of what happens under the roof of this house?" he asks.

Shame heats my cheeks. Somehow, I'd thought everything between Scarlett and me was this sacred thing, an unspoken secret, something that blooms in the dark. But Simon knows everything.

"I didn't know you had a thing for women, Winona. You never disclosed that to me."

"Just tell me why," I say. "I want to know."

He pulls away, putting a hand on my cheek and wiping a runaway tear from my eye. "I'm sorry that it felt like a betrayal to see that. If you don't want to see things that disturb you, keep your eyes shut from now on." He puts his forehead to mine, his intense gaze only inches away from me. "Why can't you trust me?"

My body relaxes slowly into his.

"I give and I give and I give," he says, laughing tiredly into my hair. "My time. My energy, my love, my *life*. Never asking you for anything except your trust. And you can't even give me that."

"I'm sorry."

He pulls a flower from his pocket and gives it to me. "Do you want to be here?"

I nod, taking it. I put it to my nose. It smells like nothing.

"Do you love me? Because I love you so much, Winona."

"Of course I love you."

He smiles. "Don't tell anyone, but you'll always be my favorite."

I flutter a little, unable to help my lips from curling up.

"Even if I can never quite win your trust," he adds.

"I trust you. Come on."

"Then show, don't tell." He adjusts his glasses, his hair blowing all around him. "Fundamental writing advice. Fundamental life advice."

I nod. He's right. And yet, for a single second, as he stands here in his puffy jacket and scruffy beard and serene simper like he has all the answers, I get this from-nowhere urge to shove him off the cliff.

It's horrifying. I jolt with guilt and push it from my mind.

I can't believe I just thought that.

"It was simply a mark of identity, like a tribal tattoo." Simon unzips his jacket and pulls up his T-shirt beneath. He, too, has a lightning bolt scar there in the middle of his hairy chest, razor-thin and healed pink. He pulls his shirt down, zips up his jacket again. "You're not alone. We all have them."

What hits me first is an odd sense of relief. What hits next is the realization that I've slept with him twice and yet have never seen him with his shirt off.

"Everyone here at Mirror House?" I ask.

"Not everyone. Just the Woken. Just us who've been here since the old Mirror House."

My mind's scrambling to make sense of this, because we weren't even "Woken" yet when I got mine.

"You got your answer. Happy now?" he asks, an edge to his voice.

I nod, unsure how to feel. I guess it makes sense. If all the Woken have them then it can't be bad, right?

He links our arms and we head back toward the house, windows lit up with a golden glow. Behind it rise the triangles of tents and campfire smoke. I can't believe I thought about pushing Simon off the cliff. What was that? I'm not a violent person, it's not like me. And what if—somehow—he heard my thoughts? I swallow hard and push the idea from my mind. Focus on my boots crunching the ground.

"You and Scarlett," he says, shaking his head. "Didn't see that one coming."

"We're not anything," I tell him.

He squeezes my arm. "Mmm."

Sometimes I think Simon knows me better than I know myself.

45

THAT NIGHT, as Scarlett and I brush our teeth together in the bathroom, Simon pokes his head in. He's wearing his pajamas, hair wild. He has a devilish grin on his face.

"Hey," he whispers. "Slumber party in my room tonight."

Our mouths are full of minty foam, but the suggestion shocks me so much I spit it out in the sink. He doesn't wait for our answer. He's gone by the time my mouth is empty.

I'm filled with disgust but can't pinpoint why. I've never been the lucky one chosen to sleep in his bed—that was Dakota at first, and since then it's been a rotation of Waking girls. I don't know what I'm in for. I don't want to have a threesome and I'm terrified that's what he wants. Scarlett says nothing. She won't even meet my eyes. I apologized to her earlier, told her about my conversation with Simon, tried to make everything okay again. She nodded and said it was all right, but she's been quiet ever since.

When we get into his room, he's waiting in his bed in the middle, wearing nothing but his boxers.

"I feel like we've drifted apart," he says. "I'd like you both to sleep in here from now on."

Scarlett and I exchange a look, mouths full of glue. He pats the bed and we sit. My stomach turns like a rusted wheel. I should be happy. I should feel lucky. Why do I feel so sick?

"Show me what you two do when you think no one sees," he says, lying back, putting his arms behind his head.

Scarlett and I scoot closer. She has impossibly bright, amber eyes, but I see the lights go out. We pet each other's hair, stroke each other's cheeks, and tilt our heads.

And it's so strange, so very strange, to feel my heart break while I kiss someone I love.

46

On Christmas, Maude drives me down the road so I can get reception and call my mom. We've drifted apart, she thinks I've been brainwashed, but it's still Christmas and I'm her only kid. I figure it's my turn to reach out. Maude blasts the car radio as I walk a few feet down a barbed wire fence, shivering.

"Finally I get a call from you," my mother says when she picks up.

"And Merry Christmas to you, too."

We exchange pleasantries until she tries to get me to admit I'm in a cult.

"Mom, if I were in a cult, I wouldn't be allowed to call you. I wouldn't be allowed to do anything. We're just friends who live communally."

An argument about semantics ensues and then I say so sorry, call's breaking up, talk soon. My phone tells me we spoke for just four minutes and some change.

"Your family giving you shit?" Maude asks as we drive the mile back home. She's steering the wheel with one hand and smoking a joint with the other, wearing a Santa hat and sunglasses even though it's overcast.

"Always."

"Fuck 'em," Maude says. "Who needs 'em."

When we pull back up to the house, everyone's gathered around a short pine tree that Simon is hacking down with an ax. I hear cheering. I love these weird people. I love this weird house. Even if I can't explain it to my mother and if I don't know exactly who lives here anymore. Even despite certain discomforts like our new sleeping arrangement and how distant Scarlett seems. I've made peace with it all. These are small prices to pay to live in this wonderland.

I'm having trouble keeping track of the people coming and going at Mirror House these days. A whole gaggle of people arrived in a pink-painted minibus the other day, hippies from a commune in Oregon or something. Drama ensued because Simon only wanted some to stay ("the females," Scarlett whispered in my ear) and some to leave because they weren't a "good fit" ("because they're men," Scarlett whispered). They called Simon a fascist and a gatekeeper and someone pulled a knife and then Maude came out with a baseball bat and the pink bus drove away.

At this point, we have the original four Floaters downstairs. They're basically Maude's house help—they clean, cook, do laundry. Then there's the cohort outside, more TikTok recruits. They come in and out of the house to eat or do yoga in the living room or whatever, but mostly they live outside and keep to themselves. Except Robin—this bespectacled girl who journals all the time and walks around asking questions.

"God, that girl is like a barnacle," Kristin whispers to me one day when we're hanging out near the guinea pig cage. "Simon keeps passing her off on me. She yaps all day long."

"She needs a job."

"I feel like we're running out of jobs." She does a tough-guy voice. "We're gonna need a bigger boat."

The guinea pigs are bumbling around. They have fashionable, long fur that reminds me of emo-kid bangs and they're all named after South Park characters.

"Shit," Kristin says, stooping. "I think Cartman is pregnant."

"I thought Cartman was male?"

She stands up. "So did I."

There's a long pause where Kristin chews her cheek. "We're gonna need a bigger boat," she says again, in a more dispirited tough-guy voice than a minute ago.

"Merry Christmas," I say.

It's good to spend time with Kristin. She's seemed off in her own world lately, always wrapped up in buying things and fixing things around the house and replacing things. The decision to move her in with Maude seems iffy, because they're prone to screaming matches. Then there's the drinking. She doesn't drink all day every day, but whenever she does drink, she goes overboard. And I can't help but question whether Simon's therapy did anything, because it looks to me like she's headed right back to where she started. But she doesn't think so. She says her relationship with alcohol has changed because the fear has been removed.

"Merry Christmas," she echoes, cheersing her mug in the air.

Out on the horizon, Scarlett's sitting by herself with her acoustic guitar, the breeze rustling her hair. It could be an album cover. She's been so quiet since we started sleeping in Simon's room a few nights ago. She walks around with her head in the clouds and her hands in her pockets or sits in her room playing guitar all day long. It's as if someone blew her fire out. While Kristin runs to tell the group (*Cartman's going to be a mommy!*), I walk out to join Scarlett. She's sitting on a flat rock on the edge of the cliff. When she sees me, she smiles and keeps strumming softly.

The view of the glassy sea is majestic, except for the billow of storm clouds creeping in.

"Just the lovely lady I wanted to see," she says. "Have a seat. I've got a present for you."

"What?" I scoot next to her. "I didn't know we were doing the whole gift exchange thing."

"Just shut up and listen," she says, then puts the fingers that hold her guitar pick on my cheek. "Pretty please."

The way she looks at me as she begins to strum soft chords with steel strings—I swear, this must be what it feels like to be a bird taking flight. Her voice is sweet and the song so simple it pangs my heart.

> There's a way that the bobbing boat feels
>   about the sea
> There's a way that the sleeping flower
>   opens for the bee
> There's a way a lizard sits as it basks in the
>   warm sun
> Well, that's the way that I feel about you
>
> There's a way cherry pie tastes just right
>   with black coffee
> There's a way that the heart feels when we
>   hear a symphony
> There's a way that a shoe must feel about
>   the other shoe
> Well, that's the way that I feel about you
>
> I'm sure you think this song is cheesy

All the chords are just too easy
And the lyrics are too cute
But sometimes cheesy is the truth

I could go on and on and on
'Cause we go on and on and on

There's a way that a spoon feels about
    another spoon
There's a way that we all feel when we're
    looking at the moon
There are sun and moon and stars wher-
    ever you are
Well, that's the way that I feel about you

The last chord rings out and she watches me closely.

I'm dumbstruck, so overwhelmed that I don't know what to say.

No one has ever done something so profound for me. This exquisite woman with a soul full of fireflies just took four chords and two minutes and was able to perfectly express feelings I couldn't begin to articulate myself. I'm a reader, a poetry lover, I eat words for breakfast—but this is the first thing anyone has ever written for me. It's the greatest gift I've ever received and it speaks so deeply that I'm not even sure how to respond.

"You okay?" she asks. "You have an aneurysm or something?"

I wipe my eyes. Finally, I manage to speak. "That is the nicest thing anyone has ever done for me."

"Oh, shoot, it's just a stupid little song. Don't cry or you're going to make me cry, too."

"Thank you so much, Scarlett," I say, reaching out for her hand. "I'm—stunned. It's the best song I've ever heard."

"Well, that was the good news." She sighs and puts her guitar down. Her face dims as she studies the waves. "Ready for the bad?"

My stomach pitches.

"What's going on?" I ask, reaching out for her hand.

"Keep a secret?"

"Always."

"I'm leaving." She turns to me. "Don't tell anyone."

If she had reached down and pulled a clump of dirt from the earth and thrown it in my face, I would have been less shocked than I am now. She can't have said what I think she said.

"No," I say.

"Yeah."

"Come on."

She nods, holding back emotion. "This is too much for me."

"This is my fault."

"It's not."

"Because I talked to Simon—"

Scarlett shakes her head. "Swear on my life, it's really not. You're why I stayed. I was planning on leaving and then ... I fell."

"Fell where?" I ask, so confused.

She gives me a look. "For *you*."

I sit up straighter. "Oh."

"That's why I stuck around."

"Then why would you go now?" I ask, but it's a stupid question. I've watched Scarlett deflate day by day since we got here. Since that first walk we took around the property. A humiliating montage plays in my head: Scarlett crawling into the car trunk; that night Simon berated her in front of the group for singing a pretty song; then, finally, Simon between us both in his bed.

I know why she's leaving. I'm almost envious. But to leave this impulsively seems like too rash a decision.

"Where will you go?" I try again.

"Have a cousin out in Riverwood, little town in the Sierras. I'm going out there for a while to sort out my head."

"You know Simon will never let you back here again."

"I do know."

"There has to be another option."

"Come with me," she says softly.

"I can't."

"Please? Don't shoot me down."

I roll my eyes. "It's ridiculous, come on."

"Why won't you just *think* about it?"

I start speaking and she puts a finger to my lips.

"Just *think* about it," she repeats.

Sighing, I do as she asks. The big-bellied clouds roll our way and I try to imagine what it would be like if I went with Scarlett. I see images of us dancing and drying dishes together, us laughing knee-deep in a river. As if we could live as a couple and be happy. It's a lovely fantasy, but that's all it is. Leaving here would mean losing an entire community and a special little world we've worked hard to create. We would never see anyone here again.

"We're building something," I remind her.

"What are we building?" She gestures back at the house. "What is all this?"

I don't answer, because there aren't words for what this is.

"It's toxic, abusive shit," she says. "Wake up."

"We are waking up!" I say, frustrated. "We're the Woken."

She blows a long sigh out of her plump, lovely lips—perhaps the loveliest lips I'll ever know.

"When you're ready, Little Spoon," she says. "I'll be waiting for you on the other side."

So this is what it feels like to be torn in two.

My world goes blurry. Distantly, thunder rumbles. I stay seated right here, shivering and stubborn from pain. The words *wish we were just getting started* throb in my mind in Grandma Jane's voice. Scarlett walks away with the guitar on her back. I try to take a picture with my eyeballs: her unruly copper hair, that trailing skirt covered in violet wildflowers, and that bounce in her step like she has a world to attend to.

Excerpt from the documentary *The Mirror House Girls: One Year Later*

LOCATION: Interviewee's home, Raven's Landing, California

SCARLETT is now seated on a couch in the opposite corner of her living room. Behind her, a guitar hangs on the wall next to a reprint of John Waterhouse's *The Lady of Shalott*. A black Labrador now sits beside her, asleep. She absentmindedly pets the dog.

SCARLETT: Leaving Mirror House was by far the hardest thing I'd ever done. Keep in mind, I had left behind (counts on fingers) my family, my church, my community, the state I grew up in. (Nods at camera) Leaving Mirror House was harder.

When I told Simon, we had this one-on-one. I was honest. I said, you know, this doesn't feel right anymore. This feels … bizarre. It's getting bizarre. And I told him I was getting Manson-family vibes and he said, *are you actually comparing me to Charles Manson?* And I looked straight at him and I said, *yes, Simon, I am.*

I had never seen the look that came over his face. It was like … he transformed into somebody else in front of my eyes. And he said to me, *I know things about you that nobody else in this world knows.* He was talking about the Truth game and the sessions. He'd taken a couple of pictures of me and Winona, too, that were—um—salacious, I guess you would say. So yes, he had a mountain of dirt on me. He said, *if you leave, it's all fair game. It's all coming out.*

I said, *go ahead, motherfucker. You're the one who taught me not to be afraid.* And he. Turned. *Red.* I mean, I thought I was about to watch a coronary happen in real time. He said to me, *if I ever see your face again, I'll kill you.* And know what? I think he would have, if I'd given him the chance. But I got my ass out of there.

47

IT's mind-boggling how someone's absence can take up so much space. For days after Scarlett leaves, I find myself weighed down by thoughts of her. I replay our last conversation in my mind and wonder if I could have done a better job trying to convince her to stay. I try to picture where she is now. I hear little lines from her songs echoing in my ears. And then, over and over again, I just have to let the thought of her go.

The new year thrusts itself upon us with a stretch of storms. They turn the property—the trails and golden grasses, the shady forest and its encampment—into a sludgy mess. Our creek overflows and the porta-potty is overturned. Walk outside and there's no escaping the stench of it. Trash has blown all over the front of our property and onto Hitchcock Road. The neighbors threaten to call the police if we don't clean the encampment up. Inside the house, it's stuffy and loud and there are people everywhere. Mud is tracked all over the house and Maude yells about it so often that I snicker and think she should change her name to Mud but I have no one to snark with anymore now that Scarlett is gone, so the snicker dies on my lips. Outside my window, the garden beds are flooded and full and all the work Scarlett and I did is washed away. Behind it, an indifferent sea that could swallow us if it cared to.

My lights dimmed when Scarlett left. I've been trying to be productive, help out, clean up, make the world better each day, be the butterfly effect. I've repeated "fear to love" so many times it becomes one word—*feartolove, feartolovefeartolovefeartolove*—but I can't help it. There's a weight I've been carrying that I don't have a name for. I'm angry with her for leaving us and abandoning what we were all building together. I'm shocked she did it so suddenly, with no real warning. And I mourn her as if she's dead, because she's not the person I thought she was.

"Scarlett wasn't truly Woken," Simon tells the group as we gather in the living room.

He stands in front of the fireplace. Everyone else is nestled on furniture or beanbags. A few people just sit on the hardwood floor. I count twenty-one people. Man, no wonder Maude ran out of soup last night.

"And unfortunately, she had a toxic energy. A perpetual victim. You know people like this. Some of you have *been* these people. If you're astute, you'll spot them from a mile away. Every story in their life has them playing the victim. Scarlett abandoned her friends and family back in North Carolina *on her own accord* and came to California sobbing about—" Simon's voice drops to a mocking snivel "'—Poor me! I'm queer, I'm so rejected!'"

Everyone laughs. I feel my mouth smile along with them, but the smile doesn't reach my soul.

"She wrote whiny, narcissistic songs about it," he goes on, shaking his head.

I fly through memories of Scarlett's sweet, simple folk

songs. Did she ever write one like that? I don't remember any. But Simon knew her longer than I did.

"Perpetual victimhood's something you can capitalize on and monetize out there in the Dream World," Simon muses. "So many songs, movies, poems."

He looks straight at me with that one. I nod to show him I don't disagree.

"Oh yeah, you can make a lot of money off it if that's what you want. If you're greedy. And Scarlett was greedy. She was greedy for attention, for sympathy. For affection."

His gaze is still fixed on me. My cheeks burn. I'm afraid he's criticizing me, too.

"Scarlett was an imposter," he says, softer. "But *you* are the true Woken."

I swear he's speaking solely to me. I nod at him, relieved.

"We don't need Dreamers here trying to wake us up. Scarlett can go live her dream and play her 'me me me' music, but we're going to stay here, aren't we?"

"Fear to fuckin' love," Kristin says, fist in the air.

I cannot tell if she's drunk anymore these days. Next to her, that Robin girl is taking notes as if she's in class. She's earnest and hardworking to an almost irritating degree. But I'm sure that's just some underlying fear of mine—maybe fear that I'm not working hard enough, like her. Fear that she'll supersede me somehow.

"Are you saying all art has an inherent narcissism to it?" Robin asks Simon, as if he's teaching a class.

Simon ignores her, continuing to pace and spin his theory aloud. "If you are still married to the dream of perpetual victimhood, if you want to walk around making excuses for yourself, if you want to keep living a lie, please, go on ahead. There's a whole Dream World out there for you." He points to the window, where the wind is beating raindrops against the glass.

"I'm not keeping anyone here against their will. All I'm offering is a free place to live and coexist. It's up to you if you want to wake up."

He's talking directly to me. I always feel that way, he's that kind of charismatic speaker, but he's been going after Scarlett in his speeches constantly since she left. It's been about two weeks and this is maybe the fourth or fifth time he's circled back to criticizing her. What Simon is saying is true. He's not holding us hostage. The only reason I'm torn is because I cared about Scarlett and her decision to leave suddenly means one of two things: either she's not who I thought she was, or even worse, this place isn't what I think it is. But that can't be so. If it were as bad as Scarlett tried to say it was, people would be abandoning Mirror House in droves. Even right now, looking around the lamplit room, there's a joy and a warmth that binds us all together. Harsh as Simon's words are, he has a point. We're still here and we're happy. It's Scarlett who was the problem, not the group.

"So who's ready to wake up with me?" Simon asks the room.

Everyone raises their hands and cheers. Simon makes a heart shape with his hands and Dakota sidles up to him with her phone, capturing the cheer and his gesture for social media. The meeting is over and I'm not even sure what the purpose of it was besides roasting Scarlett's memory over an open fire of shame, but I guess that's not for me to know. Maude blows a whistle and gets up to bark some housekeeping announcements, mostly about mud. It's so loud in here, four or five people coming up to Simon to ask him something, footsteps clobbering down the front porch.

I get up and go to my room, close the door, and read a book. That's another thing that's changed with Scarlett leaving: I've been sleeping in my own room again.

I should be grateful for the refuge—many other people here

don't have their own room. It's a privilege, one I know could go away at any moment. But even this room feels different, my bed bigger, my silence sadder. Everything has a muted filter on it now that Scarlett's gone.

Simon has explained that Scarlett manipulated me. That she was trying to control me. That when you seduce someone, you're trying to exert control over them.

"Like you seduced me?" I said, half-jokingly.

"You seduced *me*, Winona. Like Scarlett seduced you." He gave me a look that was sharp as a jackknife. "Don't get it backwards."

Backwards, forwards, I don't even know anymore. My brain is working to believe him. My heart just wants her back.

Kristin lives in Scarlett's room now, so she's my new bathroom buddy. I'm glad she's out of the room with Maude because the yelling was annoying as hell. And I like Kristin a lot. She's funny and loud and generous. We've gotten closer since Scarlett left, probably because we were the two people who loved her best. And us original Mirror House crew have a special bond.

"Hey, nerd," Kristin says from the bathroom doorway. "You going to help us sandbag the place?"

I glance up from Edgar Allan Poe. I'm curled on my bed like a cat and plan to stay here until the house quiets down. Lunchtime is so hectic that I usually just steal downstairs between meals to grab leftovers these days.

"I might sit this one out," I say.

"You know, you can't mope around forever."

I sit up. "I'm not moping."

"Um, yeah ya are. You're walking around with this butthurt look on your face all the time. You should feel free, you know? Freed from Scar's negative energy. Come on. She was dragging everybody down."

But I love her, a little voice whispers.

Hush now.

"I know," I say, closing my book.

"She's out in the Dream World now," Kristin says. "And it sucks, I know. It sucks that we can't take everyone with us on this journey, but … we're Woken. And that's what matters."

I nod.

"I love you," Kristin says. "You know that, right? We all love you."

"I love you, too."

"So come haul some sandbags with me, then," Kristin says. "The rain's supposed to get worse tonight."

I groan.

"Come on, bitch. If you don't do it with me, I'm going to have to ask Robin and I'm so sick of her. She's a fucking pest. It's like hanging out with a five-year-old. 'Why is this like this?' 'Why is that like that?' All. Day. Long."

I stretch. "Fine."

Kristin comes and gives me a hi-five. "Atta girl."

I'm lighter when I get up off the bed, like maybe it's okay Scarlett is gone. She needs to go her way and I need to go mine. I'm Woken, we're Woken, and that's what matters.

48

AFTER SCARLETT LEFT and Simon stopped inviting me to sleep with him, I wasn't offended. Actually, I was relieved. Everyone wants to sleep with Simon. If you sleep with Simon, you're lucky. And I love Simon. He's passionate and sensual. But ever since Scarlett and I slept with him together, I don't feel the same way about him. That desire was snuffed out and I can't quite say why. I used to want him so badly. Not even that long ago, I had this idea that he and I might get together, which seems so ludicrous now. Simon's on another level. He's untouchable.

But even if I don't necessarily want to sleep with him, I still crave his attention and advice. And when he asks me if I want to take a walk with him, I put a bookmark in *Paradise Lost*, spring up from my bed, and grab my coat.

"Sweet Winona," he says, putting an arm around me. He kisses my temple. "I have a secret to show you."

I glow as we descend the stairs together. An animated discussion is happening in the living room right now. Someone shouts, "That's racist!"

"Hey, hey, hey," Simon says, waving his arms like a referee. "What's this? Racist?"

Janae is a woman who arrived in the second wave. She's still in a tent outside and sometimes uses my shower. I don't know what her exact background is, but she looks multiracial.

"Simon, come on," Janae says. "Juliet's sitting here trying to say Black people don't tip well."

White-blond Juliet looks like she's been slapped. "I am *not* racist. I prefaced what I said by specifically saying this was just based on my experience."

"Racism! Waah! Waah!" Simon says, coming closer to the group.

Everyone laughs at his unexpected response.

"How's that perpetual victimhood working out for you, Janae?" he asks with a grin.

Now Janae looks like someone slapped her. She sits up straighter, jaw unhinged. The others on the couch—I couldn't even tell you all their names, one of them arrived only yesterday —watch Janae for a response.

"Cries of racism, sexism, classism, ism, ism, ism. Any-isms— they're all just illusions from the Dream World out there. They're not real, tangible things. Once you've truly Woken you see through it all. You transcend it. What's the fear under racism? How can you move it to love?"

Janae flares her nostrils.

"You feel the anger, don't you?" Simon asks. "You feel the fear."

It's so quiet, all I hear are the sparks in the fireplace. The fire reflects in the shine of Janae's eyes. She nods slowly.

"Fear to love," someone says.

"Fear to love," others echo, making the heart-hand gesture.

Simon bows to the room and we head outside.

49

I'm surprised to see Kristin, Maude, and Dakota waiting for us at the bottom of the front steps, kicking pebbles around the dirt. I balk at the sight of them. It seems sinister—as if an intervention is about to happen. My mind whirls with awful possibilities. They're going to kick me out of the house. They're taking my room away from me, giving it to some of the Waking. Even though the sun's peeking through the clouds and the meadow is flushed with green after the spell of rain, a paranoia chills me from head to toe. I shove my hands in my jacket pockets and paste a smile on my face.

"What's this, an OG Mirror House reunion?" I joke.

"Of sorts," Simon says. "I've got a huge secret, ladies. Come with me."

"So mysterious," Dakota says, squealing.

"This better be good, Boss, because I've got burritos to roll," Maude says.

"Why are you rolling burritos?" he asks, leading the way down the path. "You should be delegating at this point. You have so much help. You've got to think like an executive."

I blow out a small, warm breath, knowing that the other women seem just as in the dark as I am. If Maude doesn't know what this is about, then no one does.

"What the fuck is an executive?" Maude asks as we all walk alongside him.

"One who executes," Simon says.

"Like, the grim reaper?" Maude cackles at her own joke. "No, but seriously. What are you talking about?"

Simon's walking briskly, glancing back over his shoulder as we turn around the side of the house.

"I guess that segues into what I wanted to chat with you about today," Simon says, without answering her question. "I know I don't have to say this, but everything we discuss needs to stay between us."

"Absolutely," Dakota says.

"Always," Kristin says.

"Hundred percent," Maude says.

I nod.

Simon cranes his neck to look at me. "Winona?"

"Yes, I was nodding. Of course."

We pass the storm-wrecked garden beds, veering off the path and walking along the barbed-wire fence toward the ocean. Simon stops beneath a cluster of pine trees that grow along the edge of the property. I've passed this many times but never explored the brush like this.

Simon takes a deep breath. His beard has grown fully in, his hair to his shoulders. There are a few grays here and there in his beard. I love him, but I can't believe I used to find him so attractive. "What I'm about to show you is something so incredible that it has given me a spiritual revelation. It has made me a hundred percent sure that there is some kind of divine hand leading this group."

He squats and pushes a boulder aside. The ground is covered in dry pine needles. He brushes them away.

"Hidden treasure?" Maude tries.

"No. Even better. You know about this, Kristin?" he asks.

"I literally have no idea what the hell is going on," Kristin says.

"Isn't that true most of the time, Krissy?" Maude asks.

"Shut your piehole," Kristin says, raising her voice.

"Hey, hey, hey," Simon says. "Stop it right now. Keep your voices down." He shakes his head as he feels around for something in the dirt.

"Dude, you two bicker like sisters," Dakota says, blinking tiredly at them.

"Sisters?" Kristin says, crossing her arms. "Yeah right. Maude's old as shit."

"And I could still whoop your skinny little ass if I wanted to," Maude challenges.

Simon looks up at them blankly, which quiets them.

"Sorry, Boss," Maude mutters.

And then Simon pulls something and there's a noise, the scream of rusty hinges.

A door. A trap door. It opens with a gust of stale-smelling air.

We gasp.

He grins, whipping a flashlight from his pocket like a magician and pointing the light down there. There's a wood ladder leading into a space that can't be more than six-by-six feet. Concrete walls, concrete floor. I shiver. The first word flashing to mind is *dungeon*.

"Whoa," Dakota says.

"What's that for? Storage?" Maude asks.

"Damn, probably a secret bunker," Kristin says. "The previous owner was a prepper."

"I haven't tried the ladder yet." Simon puts a hand on my shoulder. "Why don't you do the honors?"

I almost laugh, thinking he's kidding. But his expression is deadpan, his hand still on my shoulder.

"What if it breaks?" I ask. "How do you know it's safe?"

"I don't. Hate to be the bearer of bad news, sweet Winona, but life is uncertain." Simon smiles. "That said, have I ever steered you wrong? Haven't I always protected you?"

"Yeah," I say, staring down into the darkness where ten thousand spiders probably live.

"Fear to love," Maude says.

Those words—I've heard them spoken so often recently that they ring hollow right now. Tell it to my gut, which is clenched at the thought of going down there.

Slowly, sickened, I slide my body down onto the ladder, tentatively landing my foot on a rung and testing it to decide if it can bear my weight. It can, so I put a second foot on it and there's a splintering sound. I freeze and give my friends a look conveying just how apprehensive I am.

"You're good," Kristin assures me. "You've got this."

I grip the ladder's sides with my hands and go down, one rung at a time. Each step there's a creaky, splintering sound like this wood is ready to fall to pieces at any moment. Who knows how long this has been here, how long it's been since someone was down here. A damp whiff of mold punches me in the nose. Finally, after six arduous, terrifying steps down the ladder, I land at the bottom.

I peer up at the faces peering back down at me.

So this is what it feels like to be in your own grave. I've always wondered.

For just a moment I can imagine their faces contorting into cruel laughter. I can picture them kicking the trap door shut and putting a boulder over it and walking away and leaving me here. And I feel so small and scared and helpless.

But then they all join me, one by one, gusts of dust every time someone comes down. It's a tight squeeze for five people. Might be for the best that Scarlett's gone now, because I don't see this being easy for someone with claustrophobia—or someone who used to have claustrophobia, I guess.

"Ladies, we've got something serious to discuss," Simon says, rubbing his hands like a football coach about to give his huddle a speech. He meets our eyes as if to convey how serious this is.

"What is it?" Kristin asks.

I'm quite sure I smell alcohol on her breath in these close quarters. I can also smell Dakota's BO, Simon's spicy aftershave, and I can tell that Maude ate peanut butter for lunch. I might appreciate fresh air in a new way after this.

Simon lowers his voice, clenching his jaw. "There's a rat in Mirror House."

50

A BEAT PASSES and we search each other's faces for some spark of recognition that isn't here. *A rat.* What exactly does he mean?

"I told that Ava girl to set the traps up out near the dumpster," Kristin says.

An *a-ha* lights up Maude's eyes. "He means a snitch."

"I'm so confused," Dakota says, furrowing her brow.

"Maude's got it. There are comments on our TikTok posts saying there's someone undercover here who wants to expose our group." Simon sighs, running his hands through his hair and making it wilder. "Can we sit? This will likely be a lengthy discussion."

"*Here?*" Kristin asks, casting a dubious look at the filthy concrete floor.

"We need absolute discretion," Simon says.

Not only is it gross in here, there are hairline cracks cobwebbing the concrete. I wouldn't be surprised if the walls caved in on us. But this sounds important. We all sit in a tight circle, cross-legged, knees touching. Now I'm positive it's better that Scarlett's gone. She wouldn't have even fit in here with us.

It's better that Scarlett's gone.

Really, it is.

"From here forward, this is my circle," Simon says. "This is as far as my trust reaches. You are my *imperial legates*. In the Roman army, that was a commander of the highest rank. That's you from now on. My A-team. My capos."

So many different languages and metaphors, my head spins, but I nod anyway.

He shares screenshots of the TikTok comments that have spun him into a tizzy. We read them silently, one by one.

100% CULT i know someone who snuck in there and they be exposing them soon 🙏

CULT CULT CULT my friend living there says its nuts 🤪

CULT i know for fact this dude be boning all these brainwashed ladies

yall better be ready...soon the worlds gonna find out all youre doing 👁

I digest these comments. Yes, I'm a little offended every time someone tries to call me and my friends cult members. And yes, it's unnerving to imagine someone in this house is gossiping about the house to outsiders, or "Dreamers" as Simon would say. But this is much milder than I was expecting. The comments came from an anonymous nobody with less than a hundred followers. Social media comment sections are always vomitous hellscapes. Why would ours be any different?

Kristin is the last to read them, brow wrinkled, lips moving. She hands the phone back to Simon with a sniff.

"Stupid fucker," Maude finally says, breaking the silence.

"How can we verify whether it's true?" I ask. "That could just be a troll for all we know."

Simon puts his hands together and glances up at the sky as if he's praying for my stupidity.

Dakota says, "Maybe we could try messaging the person and ask who they know—"

"This is an existential threat." Simon hits the ground to emphasize this to us. "If someone is leaking information about Mirror House, then next they're going to be leaking information about *me*, about my methods. Confidential information."

"Like what?" Kristin asks.

"Details about activities that go on behind closed doors, Kristin," he says. "Treatments. Sessions. Therapeutic techniques." He squeezes each of our hands, one at a time. "You know that my methods are atypical. Many people don't understand the kind of work I do. I could be ruined if certain things got out." His hazel eyes are pleading. "I don't talk about it much, but I'm a psychologist licensed in the state of California. Which means there are certain so-called 'ethics' I'm bound to from the corrupt Dream World. And I haven't been abiding by them."

"Why not just … give up your license, Boss?" Maude asks.

"A little late for that now," Simon says quietly. "Even if I did, everything up until this point would still put me in hot water."

Oh god. I remember my mom's threat to report him. Is this my mom, commenting on our TikTok posts? That would be mortifying. But my mom's always been a stickler for perfect punctuation and despises emojis. No, it can't be her.

Simon practices mindful breathing, as if he's barely holding himself under control, and I see, for the first time, a true vulnerability in him. He's always seemed superhuman to me. He doesn't cry. He rarely loses his temper. Fear wouldn't look right on him. But right now, he's shaken.

"You're not our psychologist," Kristin says. "So what does it matter?"

"Oh, believe me, it matters. In the eyes of the state of California, I'm a licensed psychologist practicing pro bono," Simon says. "I could not only lose my license, I could face significant legal action for what I've done. In civil court, I could be sued for everything I'm worth—which, admittedly, isn't much. But I could also face criminal charges."

"You've got to give up your license, then," Maude says.

"Maude," Simon says impatiently. "The board would retain jurisdiction over any misconduct that has already happened. In fact, if there *has* been anything reported, me surrendering my license right now could backfire and raise red flags to look even deeper into what I've been doing."

"Wouldn't you know if anything was already reported, though?" Kristin asks.

"I feel like you're not focusing on the very real threat this poses," Simon says, clenching his jaw. "I'm off the grid now. I haven't received mail since we moved from Santa Cruz. My focus has been on what we're building."

"This is so ridiculous!" Dakota says with an unusual fire. Dakota is usually lazy grins and giant clouds of weed smoke. She's not the type to get angry. But apparently, when it comes to Simon, different rules apply.

"Seriously. This much trouble? For giving free advice?" Kristin says. "That can't be true."

"Believe me, I'm the one who took these draconian ethics exams and classes to get licensed." He steeples his fingers and rests them on his chin. "I know what I'm talking about."

"That just seems so wrong!" Dakota says, her voice squeaky

with emotion. "You just—just did something out of the kind-ness of your heart. What, would they sue Gandhi too?"

"I'm sure they would if they could," Simon says, with a bitter snort. "The Dream World out there perceives the Woken as a threat. Doesn't want people to wake up. Doesn't want people improving each other's lives without the need for gate-keepers. Doesn't want enlightenment, because who can make money off enlightenment? And heaven forbid if people start peeling off society to make their own rules and live communally and unconventionally! People like me, we'll be stopped at any cost. Tale old as time." His voice cracks with emotion. "I'm stuck because I feel this—this higher power, this deep, reso-nant, universal gravity pulling me to help people. To grow this movement and make it into something bigger. But the bigger we grow, the more likely we are to be shut down."

I'm dizzied and fighting my own emotions. As we sit down here in this damp concrete hole, I'm faced with the thought that everything I love, everything I've based my life around, could be dismantled. Could just vanish, because of legalities I don't even quite understand. And that is terrifying.

"I need you all to help me figure this out," Simon says, reaching for us.

We grab his hands, two of our hands to each of his. Maude scoots even closer, enveloping Simon into a hug. Kristin joins next, then Dakota, then me. And soon we're in a group hug and we're humming, tingling together with Simon at the center. I squeeze my eyes shut and beam every ounce of positivity I can into this Resonance right now. I'm asking the universe to protect this group, to protect Simon.

"You need to help me find the rat," Simon says. "Because they're trying to put an end to us."

"Oh, I can find a rat, Boss," Maude says, nostrils flaring.

"And, unfortunately, because of this mess, we're going to

need to shut down any new recruits for the time being. Close our borders." He shakes his head, as if this next part makes him sorriest of all. "I want to stop broadcasting on TikTok, kill our internet service, and—unfortunately—I want to instate a policy that no one in this house has a phone."

"No!" Dakota wails, as if he just told her he was going to kill a kitten. "Our channel though, we have so many followers—"

"I know," Simon says. "Right now, it just doesn't matter."

Dakota's actually going to cry right now, about TikTok. Come *on*. I fight the urge to tell her to get a grip.

"Dakota, social media isn't real, it's—it's a dream within a dream," Simon says. "Maybe this is a divine hand guiding us back to our original path, which was to move off the grid. Now we'll truly be off the grid."

Everyone's phones barely work anyway and our internet service is so slow it's like 1996 up in here. Still, the idea of cutting off everything is unsettling.

"What about emergencies?" I ask.

"Run to the neighbors," Simon says. "Use their phone."

The neighbors—same ones who aren't even there most of the time because it's a vacation home. Same ones who label us a nuisance and threaten to call the authorities on us. I'm sure they'll love that.

"Makes complete sense," Maude says. "I'll be happy to enforce it. I can do random searches, make sure no one's sneaking any contraband."

"Thank you, Maude. That might be necessary." Simon strokes his beard. "You are all my protectors now. You hear that? You're my inner circle. In the coming weeks, months, we might invite others to join the inner circle, my *legates*, but for now, this is it."

We nod in agreement.

"Think about it. Talk to people. Sniff it out. We'll throw a party tonight—mill around, get some intel. I'll make an announcement about the changes and we'll instate them right then and there. People don't like it, they can fuck themselves." A vein bulges on Simon's neck as he gains steam. "We're going to come back here tomorrow morning at seven so we can put our heads together, see if we can tease out who it is. This is our new meeting spot. I want this mission to be a hundred percent sealed off from the Waking."

We murmur a round of yeses. And even though we're facing an existential threat and my fear response is activated, I'm fortified by this mission. I remember how much I love these people all the more now that it's just us again. They're my friends and they're my family. This togetherness—I needed this. I need them. I need to know I'm needed.

As we stand up and stretch, I'm a little blinded. The sky above us has never looked brighter. Simon tells us how much he loves us, his "OG Mirror House girls." He winks at me and I get that flutter I haven't had in a while.

"Oh, and one more thing," he says, finger to his lips. "This is going to sound silly, so bear with me." He laughs at himself. "I'd like you all to wear your hair in a braid from now on."

It does sound silly, which is why we snicker. But Simon's smile remains cemented as he studies each of our faces.

"I mean it," he says. "It's a symbol of unity. It's a way I can see you've committed to this, that this group, here, we're the Woken. We're in our own league." He reaches out and touches Kristin's blond ponytail she's pulled through the hole in the back of her baseball cap. Then he squeezes Maude's silver-streaked auburn topknot. Next, Dakota's head, hidden by a bandanna. Then he runs his fingers through my brown waves. "No hats. No bandannas. No hiding. Just a single braid for my secret favorites."

I watch the other girls for a reaction, because I don't know how I'm feeling about this request. But he's given me so much, Mirror House has given me so much, and I love that we're his "secret favorites." I nod along with them. Then I turn to the ladder, but Maude grabs my arm.

"Hey, hey, hey," she says. "Where are you going, hon? You heard the boss."

I glance back at them. Maude's loosening her bun, Dakota pulls off her bandanna, and Kristin shakes her hair free from its ponytail. Now? Really? We're doing this now? Okay, then.

Simon watches proudly, arms crossed. I finger-brush my hair and divide it into three sections. My arms are goosebumping. Scarlett's voice echoes in my head, saying, *Once I told him I was going to cut my hair and he threatened to kick me out of the house if I did.*

Oh, come on, I said at the time. *He's not that bad.*

You don't believe me, she said flatly. *You think I'd just make that up.*

"Look at us," Dakota says with a laugh, yanking our braids like she's blowing a series of train whistles.

I laugh too, ignoring the goosebumps.

We emerge from the hole one by one, fully aware that there's some new secret glue keeping us all together. Despite how sinister a situation we're facing with a rat somewhere to sniff out, there's a certain joy I haven't felt since Santa Cruz. We're giggling and pushing each other and everything's fun and games again—until Maude spots a garter snake in the grass.

"Fucking shit!" she screams, her face turning white.

She jumps back from the group and runs up to the house in such a flash it's like she was never here. Kristin, Dakota, and Simon double over with laughter. But for the first time, I ask myself, does Simon's therapy even work?

And then a boot of guilt kicks my gut.

How dare I think that, after all his sacrifice?

Excerpt from the documentary *The Mirror House Girls: One Year Later*

LOCATION: Interviewee's home, Raven's Landing, California

SCARLETT is on the couch now, scratching her dog's head.

SCARLETT: I hightailed out of there right before shit hit the fan. And whatever happened after that must have happened fast. Because when I still lived at Mirror House, the TikTok was still up, people had their phones, there was no bizarro hair-braiding rules, and certainly no mention of suicide. Not *one*.

When I heard the news, all this front-page, every-channel coverage—it just didn't compute. (Tears) They kept showing the severed braids and the shoes, you know this … horrible image that I will never be able to erase from my brain.

I was in denial for the longest time, thinking, it's a lie. They didn't all jump into the ocean. They fled. They left. They cut their hair and, you know, ran away together somewhere. Because why? Why would they do that? These people who had so much to live for. I had no warning when I was leaving that they were heading for mass destruction. These were rational people. Young, beautiful, wonderful people and I loved them all so much and this wasn't how it was supposed to end.

(Wipes eyes, stares off distantly) Then they started finding body parts washing up on beaches all along the coast. They used DNA and identified some of them. And I realized, holy shit. This is real. They jumped off the edge of the world. They're all dead.

51

TIME FOR A PARTY.

The living room is so crowded we push the couches against the walls for extra space. Out comes the beat-up boombox, up goes the music, everyone jiving and singing along with Prince. We dim the lights and decorate the dining room table with booze, so much booze, and a cookie sheet with mini homemade burritos.

In the corner near the blacklight and the lava lamp, Simon is gesticulating and preaching to the newest additions of the house, who arrived here sometime around when Scarlett left. It's all mixed up in my head, so many people coming and going. One has bright blue hair, another black, and there are two brunettes. I can't help but notice all the long-haired women in this dark room right now and how alike they look in the shadows, young and pretty and similar as a pile of paper dolls.

He definitely has a type, whispers Scarlett's ghost.

I run my hand along the rope of my new braid.

"Heyo," Kristin says in my ear, jolting me back to the

moment. She holds her mug. "Cheers. To the poison and the antidote."

Her words strike me as a bit unsettling, considering her history with alcohol. I worry about her. I try to trust the process, Simon knows what he's doing, but last time I peeked in her room the empty vodka bottles on her windowsill winked back at me.

"So poetic, Kristin," I say.

"I'm a goddamn Sophia Plath."

"Sylvia."

"Whatever."

We clink glasses. The party's just started and her lids are already at half-mast. Now that Kristin drinks again, her barmaid days are over. Instead, she saunters around with a mug missing its handle, a purple-lipped smile, and her volume knob turned up to eleven.

"Got any leads?" she practically screams over the music. "Don't forget, we're on a mission."

I flinch at her enthusiasm and merlot-sour breath. "Nothing yet."

She points her chin toward Robin, who's leaning on a wall in a corner, scrolling through her phone. Next to her is the corner where Scarlett's guitar used to rest. Gut punch.

"My money's on her," Kristin says.

"I have no money, but if I did, it would be on her too," I agree.

Robin arrived after the first cohort wave in this tiny yellow Honda Accord older than Maude. Robin sleeps in it alone every night. Walks around and kind of tries to join in conversations, an appendage always on the outskirts. Constantly journaling, writing inspired notes in her phone, raising her hand when Simon speaks to the group as if this is school. Very socially awkward. She does not laugh at my jokes. Her long, curly blond-brown hair frames a lazy eye hidden behind giant red glasses.

Earlier today, Simon had the Floaters build an eighteen-inch-high wooden platform in the living room he jokingly called his soapbox. The Floaters relished the assignment so much they painted it with psychedelic daisies and hearts. He stands on it now, getting everyone's attention by raising his hands in the air. It's stunning how he can quiet an entire room that way, as if we're his orchestra and he's the conductor. Even the boombox goes silent.

"This is my first time standing up on this thing," he says, kind of sheepishly. "Feels ... strange to be so tall. Can everybody hear me?"

We affirm with nods and yeses.

"Great. I guess those two years of theater classes where I was taught to *project to my audience*—" he booms these words teasingly and the crowd laughs "—paid off." He smiles. From here, you'd never know he's a man grappling with paranoia. I empathize with him. He created this spirited group, teaching others to overcome their worst fears—and now he's facing the possibility of repercussions he doesn't deserve.

But a little part of me wishes it didn't have to come to this. We had a good thing going. Will these new rules change everything?

"The time has come, everyone," he says. "Bold, tenacious moves. Are you ready to walk with me into the unknown?"

"Fuck yeah we are, Boss," Maude hoots from somewhere across the room.

"When we first came to Mirror House, the Woken had this vision." He sweeps his hand across the air, as if he's painting a picture. "This golden utopia we imagined we would build together. We would grow our own food, live off the grid, bid farewell to the Dream World." His grin melts. "But instead

we've become slaves to our own social media account. *TikTok*."
He says the word as if it's a silly word, a frivolous toy, which I
suppose it is. "A dream within a dream. Texts and phone calls
and videos—you know these things aren't real, right? You know
that *this* is what's real. The now. This moment. The person next
to you—they're real. Reach out and touch them. Do it."

People giggle and turn to their neighbor, tentatively
reaching out to push them playfully, sling an arm around them,
or press their skin like a button.

"Reality," he says. "*That* is reality. This?" He holds his phone
up in the air. "This isn't reality."

As if she's an actor who has been waiting for her cue, Maude
steps up to him with our kitchen garbage can in her hand. He
throws his phone in it.

"Fuck the Dream World," he shouts. "Fuck the dream
within a dream. Wake up!"

Simon's the most eloquent person I've ever met and he
doesn't swear often, so when he does, there's this sharpness to it
that cuts deep. The room begins buzzing with whispers.

"Moving forward, the Woken have decided we're fully
committing to our original vision of going off the grid," he says,
smiling widely. "Of being the butterfly effect. We're cutting the
internet. We're killing the TikTok account. We're giving up our
phones. And we're asking you to do the same."

A choir of gasps and conversations.

"I know it seems extreme, but—why are you here? Why are
we here?" He asks this softer, his gentle tone seeming to calm
the energy in the room along with it. "Are you here to live the
same life you lived in the Dream World? Or are you here to
learn a spiritual lesson? To find a deeper understanding? Sometimes you have to disconnect to reconnect."

"What about staying in touch with our families?" someone
asks.

"There's a lovely café on the interstate about a mile and a half up the road," he says. "They have a payphone outside. There's a library a few miles beyond that with computers and the internet. And you know what else there is? There's a whole Dream World out there if that's what you want! I say this with the utmost kindness, people—if you want to keep living the dream, scrolling your phones all day long, I'm not stopping you. But if you want to *stay*, this is mandatory. And I know it's a big ask, but I'm asking you to do it right now."

"Are you in or not?" Maude yells with the gusto of a pro wrestler, reaching into her pocket and *thunk*ing her own phone into the trash can while she mills around the room.

"Disconnect to reconnect," Simon says, cupping his hands to shout into them over the rising noise of the crowd. "Fear to love. Fear to love. Fear to love."

Some join him in the chant. Others turn to one another with furrowed brows, frantic and confused exchanges. The cluster of starry-eyed cohort girls Simon was preaching to before his speech all immediately run to the front to show their loyalty. And a few other random folks hurry out the door like they're having none of this. Like they're about to get in their vehicles and hightail it out of here.

In short, it's mayhem.

There are too many bodies, too much talking, too much movement as people try to make their way up to the front of the room or out the door. At first, when the shouting starts, I think people are angry, but I quickly realize the Floaters and Dakota are chanting along with Simon saying "Fear to love, fear to love, fear to love ..." Dakota looks so bare there without her ring light and phone, hugging her arms and chanting. I'm so used to her being in a corner, standing on a chair and playing documentarian. Maude comes over to Kristin and me and we pitch our phones in the can.

It's okay, I tell myself as the room spins with frenetic energy around me. Party energy. Drunk energy. Argument energy. Emotional energy. I already memorized the only two phone numbers that matter anyway: my mother's and Scarlett's. My pictures and memories live in a cloud somewhere. If I ever return to the Dream World, I can have them back.

Did I just think that? It rings so hollow as I stand here dizzy in the eye of the hurricane.

One word. Two letters. *If.*

Like I might never go back there.

52

THE NEXT MORNING, I'm up bright and early for our Woken bunker meeting. We whisper-laugh as we scurry outside while the rest of Mirror House sleeps. There are probably half as many cars as there were last night. Honestly, it's a relief. Our breath fogs in the air and we're bundled up and carrying mugs of coffee and tea that we soon realize we probably aren't deft enough to bring down into the bunker with us. We leave the mugs in the grass and climb down one by one.

"Pee-yew," Kristin says, waving her hand in front of her face as we sit on the floor. "Maude, your dragon breath is lethal."

Maude purposefully breathes on Kristin. "Aww, too bad it's not," she says sadly. "You're still alive."

Dakota blinks her little pink eyes from inside her jacket's puffy hood. "I am so fucking tired."

As early as it is, we still managed to braid our hair this morning. Simon reaches out and touches each of them with a grateful smile. It tickles me.

"Okay," Simon says. "My Woken women. My *legates*. Any idea who the rat is?"

"Whoever it is, they're either *hasta la vista*, or if they're still here, they have no phone for snitching anymore," Maude says.

"I saw Robin's car was still here," Kristin says. "I just know it's her, guys."

"Did you get her phone last night?" I ask Maude.

Maude blinks, clearly trying to remember.

"Robin's an odd duck," Simon says. "But she's been ... quite eager with her sessions." A sly half-smile creeps to his lips as he replays some memory I'm glad I'm not seeing. "It would be something if she were that deep undercover." His brow crinkles. "I wouldn't be surprised. I really wouldn't. They'll go to any length to take us down."

"She didn't give me her phone," Maude says abruptly, as if she's just realizing this. "I'm about ninety-eight-point-five percent sure."

"Very exact," I say.

"You know what we'll do?" Simon says with a snap of the fingers. "We'll have Winona go around and take attendance of who's still here and Maude will double-check that every one of those people gave us their devices."

"Roger," says Maude, bumping his fist.

"And ladies, please," Simon says, squeezing his hands into balls so tight they whiten. "Your number one job is figuring out who this person is. Existential threat. Everything depends on this."

I don't barrage him with the questions cannonballing through my brain. Why does this matter to this degree? Are four mysterious TikTok comments from a random person worth all this? Can't we instead focus on what I thought was happening, which was getting this utopia back on track? What about the garden beds back there that we should tend to? Or the garbage that still hasn't been properly removed from the encampment area? What about the overpopulated guinea pig situation? I don't want to hear any more stories about Cartman eating one of her babies. That freaked me out when Kristin told me about it.

Instead, I chirp a "You got it" along with everyone else.

A pause stretches its long arms around our small group. Simon's eyes are bloodshot. He looks older to me today and so much more exhausted. We did all drink a small sea's worth of wine last night. "I've had trouble sleeping the last few nights," he mumbles, almost to himself. "These dreams ..."

His eyes seem to well up as he trails off; there it is again, that peek of heartbreaking vulnerability in him. That shakiness, like he too doesn't know what to do, where to lead us, where we go next. It pains me to see him this way and yet it reminds me that he's as human as the rest of us. I'd do anything to restore his confidence and make him feel better.

"What's going on?" Kristin asks.

"In my dreams lately, I've been visited by the great men of history," he says quietly. "Martin Luther King Jr., Saint Francis, Abraham Lincoln. Jesus Christ. Julius Caesar. All coming to me, all telling me it's okay. It's going to be okay."

His confession is so raw, I suck in a breath.

Dakota reaches out her hand to squeeze his. "It *is* going to be okay."

"Don't you understand?" he asks, looking at each of us with glassy eyes. "All those men were assassinated for what they believed in."

"Boss." Maude chuckles uncomfortably. "Nobody's going to murder you."

"It's just a dream, Simon," Kristin says. "You can't read too much into it."

After a long beat, one where Simon seems to be completely lost in the wilderness of his own thoughts, he meets our eyes again. "Just a dream. Right."

We climb back up the ladder, one by one. I'm the last and get a shiver as I wait, watching a centipede slithering up the wall with its eyelash-thin legs. My skin crawls, the damp chill and stink of rain suddenly oppressive. As if the walls are about to close. As if the earth is widening its jaws, ready to swallow my skeleton. Truly feels like I'm standing in a grave.

And when I glance up and grip the ladder with both hands to begin my ascent, Simon's staring back with a dark look in his unblinking eyes—like he could close the door on me and never look back if he decided it was for my benefit.

I shiver and scurry up the ladder with a heart full of fireworks.

53

Over the next week, the inner circle tightens.

Maude conducts searches and checks that every phone has been confiscated. Good. Phew. The internet router is ripped from the wall and thrown out near the overflowing dumpster. Several NO TRESPASSING and CLOSED signs are put up at the entrance to our driveway, our "borders are sealed." After the chaos, a calmness sparkles the air and the tension seems to dissipate.

My days are full of morning meditations with Simon in the living room and chanting *feartolove* until my mind goes numb. Delicious pots of soup and fresh bread. Tiring afternoons weeding and gardening and cleaning up broken glass and trash that people left behind. Evenings drinking mugs of wine and reading books by candlelight. Long, quiet nights where the wind rattles the windows. Since Simon drew his line in the sand, shut down the TikTok account and asked people to give up their phones, the group shrank to half its size, from nearly thirty to fifteen. A calm has come over the house. Simon hasn't even been sleeping with anyone, as far as I can tell. It's a true breath of fresh air compared to the past few months.

"The self is the greatest lie ever sold," Simon tells us as he leads us on a foraging walk along Hitchcock Road, in front of our property. He has a tall, crooked walking stick that reminds me of a shepherd, the wind blowing his hair and his bright red parka. We follow behind him. "The self is the reason we're lonely. The reason we're jealous, the reason we hurt other people. Our true obsession. We're all guilty of it. The *self*. And what happens when we shed the self? When we come together for a group hug, when we, for one brief, shining moment, forget ourselves, lose ourselves in each other—what happens?"

He stops in the middle of the dirt road, turning back to us for a response.

"We, like, connect with a higher power and stuff?" tries one of the Floaters.

"Essentially, yes," Simon says, excitement lighting up his face. "We connect with the Infinite Divine. Only by transcending these lies we call our 'selves' can we spiritually evolve. This Simon suit I've been wearing all my life—it's a lovely suit, you know? But that's all it is; a suit." He points to me. "And you in your Winona suit." He points to Kristin. "You there in your Kristin suit."

"Mmm," Kristin says with a sigh, as if this is a comfort.

Simon points his chin at Robin, who is writing down what Simon is saying like a stenographer. She does this whenever he opens his mouth. Despite the fact she did hand over her phone after all, I remain suspicious of her. "Robin in her Robin suit." He watches us all with a sadness glinting in his eyes. "They're only suits. They're not real. You know that, right?"

Everyone nods, including me.

"Do you want to connect with the Infinite Divine or do you want to keep the suit on and live in a dream?"

"Infinite Divine," we all mumble.

As soon as Simon turns and leads us toward a patch of mushrooms, though, I feel this itch in me. This rebellious thought: I'm not just a suit. I'm a person. And, from nowhere, I hear my grandmother's voice saying, *Noni, if a man ever promises you forever, turn and run the other way.*

I get goosebumps. Her voice is so clear it's as if she spoke it straight into my ear.

She said that about Dean. Dean—haven't thought of him in so long. The name is a bell and it's a knife. It's not just the jolting memory of what a disaster that relationship was, if you could even call it a relationship. It's a reminder of my life before this, of how different things were only a little more than a year ago. Living in a guest bedroom in Grandma Jane's Escondido condo. Doctor appointments and errands and lying on the couch with Grandma, frozen dinners and quiet chats and movie marathons. Dating a handsome fraud. It's like I was a completely different person living a totally separate life.

"Anyone familiar with decimation?" Simon asks as he plucks a cartoonishly large mushroom from the ground. He looks at it thoughtfully, brushing the dirt from it, and we watch him in fascination. "It was an infamous loyalty test for Roman soldiers. If a unit was guilty of cowardice or disobedience, one tenth of the cohort would be executed by their fellow soldiers." Simon holds the mushroom up to the light, examining it, turning it in his hand. "It might strike you as barbaric, and indeed it is, but nature is barbaric, isn't it?"

I nod even though I'll be quite honest: He lost me. Sometimes Simon falls down a rabbit hole in his sermons and zigzags from one thought to another and I have a hard time following. Usually I blame myself, he's far more intelligent than I am and his brain moves quicker, but this time it seems as if he's a bit disjointed, as if I'm listening to someone else's stream of consciousness that might not make complete sense.

"I will be giving you loyalty tests," Simon says, handing Maude the mushroom. "I don't want to, but I must. I'm putting myself at great risk being here now. There are people who would like to see me ruined, who see me as a threat. And I have to be sure you're not one of them. The mushroom—I picked it from the earth. It could be poisonous. It could be edible. Do you trust me to know the difference? Maude, take a bite."

Maude holds the mushroom in her fingers and looks at it dubiously.

"You of all people, Maude," he scolds.

"Okay, Boss, okay. It's just ... dirty. But okay." She sinks her teeth delicately into the cap.

"Leave some for the rest of them," he says to her. "Take a nibble and pass it on."

Déjà vu, remembering the day I first met Simon, when he gave me the mushroom on our first foraging walk. How far we've come since then, how deep the roots of my trust have grown.

One of the Floaters tries the mushroom next. Then Kristin, who has her lip upturned like she might puke. A few hesitate, but none refuse. I know Simon. He wouldn't poison us or hurt us. This loyalty test is an easy one to ace. Despite the grit of the soil, I chew the mushroom and swallow it. Soon, we've eaten the whole thing.

"*Boletas edulis grandedulis,*" shouts Simon, almost like a preacher, his hands in the air in a hallelujah gesture. "Porcini mushroom. Wild and edible. They grow everywhere. Fear to love, fear to love, fear to love!"

He repeats this and we swarm in for a group hug, humming for a minute and becoming one. It's a happy drug every time we come together like this. A warm shiver shimmies up my spine.

And then, as we stand here, I spot the neighbors in their driveway just twenty or thirty feet up the road. They're frozen, groceries in arms, watching us with bewilderment and maybe even a little fear. Like we're aliens.

I catch a glimpse of cheese puffs sticking out of their bag and it makes me so hungry my mouth waters. I recognize that bag. I used to eat them all the time, but it's been a while. We eat stuff like bread and giant salads and soup now, not junk food. In a flash, I wish I was on their side of the picture—two feet in the real world. Then I'm horrified at myself for thinking such a thing.

Those people aren't real, I remind myself. *They're dreaming.* This *is what's real.*

54

WE ARE WINE-DRUNK AT NOON, under a silvery sky, and I remember that I love my life.

Maude pedals her rusty pedicab around the property with Kristin and me in the back. A boombox buzzes between us, blasting Bon Jovi. We whip by misty cypresses slung with hammocks. A few girls do yoga in the meadow. Another few shiver as they wash Simon's van in the driveway. We pass Kristin's half-pipe and the guinea pig coop. The secret bunker spot. And, finally, the flat rock where Scarlett once sang me the best song I've ever heard. Usually that memory comes with a pinch, but right now, I've drowned it out with cabernet sauvignon and it's glorious. I remember joy, what it is to be free. That these people, not Scarlett, are my best friends. This is my home. Life is an adventure. Maude pedals toward the bluffs and stops for the epic view and we all belt the chorus of "Livin' on a Prayer" together as if the ocean is our audience.

When we turn back around, I lock eyes with the house and wonder ... do they see it too?

Do they see Simon staring down at us from his bedroom window, jaundiced from the yellow light? Still as a mannequin?

Are they wondering if he's been up there all morning like that?

Have they noticed how withdrawn he's been? How he whispers to himself?

"Fear to love," Maude says as she pedals back toward the house, fist in the air.

"Fear to love!" Kristin and I shout back.

Kristin reaches over the boombox and engulfs me in a clumsy hug with a squeal. She's all bones ("liquid diet" is her running joke, delivered with a *cheers*). Her jerky, manic energy always comes as a surprise and my wine sloshes everywhere all over us. Splattered on her Snuggie. Spattered on my skirt. We burst into giggles.

Maude glances over her shoulder and shouts, "You wino bitches better not fuck up my pedicab."

"We look like murder victims," Kristin says, laughing uncontrollably.

I don't know if it's the mention of murder or if it's the glimpse of a black car pulling down Hitchcock Road that bothers me first, but they both hit at the same time and turn my stomach. Maude, too, must notice, because she slows her pedaling as we round the house to the front porch. As it creeps closer, I notice it's not just a black car. It's a Rolls Royce.

"Who is that?" Juliet, one of the girls carefully polishing the mirrors on Simon's van, asks us.

"I don't know, but I'm about to tell them they can get the hell off our property," Maude says, jumping off her pedicab and thrusting her chest out.

Cracking her knuckles and strutting into the center of the dirt driveway, Maude blocks the car from being able to drive all the way to the house. She raises her arms up like she's either in church or trying to stop traffic. With her bike helmet still on, the image strikes me as kind of funny, though I don't feel much like laughing.

The black car rolling slowly up the driveway is sinister as a hearse. The windows are tinted. This shiny luxury vehicle doesn't belong here. I'm loaded and dizzy sitting here in the back of the pedicab and I don't know why, the first thing I think is that it's the FBI, which is absurd.

"Fuck," Kristin whispers next to me.

She clutches my hand, her grip so tight and icy that I shiver.

"What is going *on?*" I whisper back.

The car stops in front of where Maude stands. A door in the back opens and a man gets out. He's in a sharp suit, graying hair coiffed, sunglasses. His skin has the orange glow of a tanning salon regular. Jaw clenched, fists clenched—the stress emanates off of him like a stink.

"That's my dad," Kristin whispers.

Pop. She deflates like a human balloon. I've never seen her crumple this way, slouching in her seat beside me.

"What's he doing here?" I ask.

"I don't know. I thought he was in Hong Kong until spring. Maybe it has something to do with his work, maybe he got pulled back into headquarters. You know Jolvix?"

Do I know *Jolvix?* It's only the largest tech company in the world. "Um, yeah."

"He's Director of Global Partnerships."

I have no idea what that title means, but I gather this guy's a pretty big deal.

"Kris," he barks, pointing at Kristin beside me.

"Excuse me, sir, but who the fuck are you?" Maude asks, stepping in front of him.

The man flicks his sharp-blue eyes over her as if she's about as intimidating to him as a sparrow. "I'm the fucking owner of this house. And who the fuck are you?"

"Maude, sir," Maude says, softening her tone and holding out her hand. "Pleasure to meet you. I'm the house manager—"

He walks past her, waving her away, and makes a beeline for the pedicab. He points at Kristin.

"What the fuck is going on?" he asks in a quieter tone, coming closer.

"Hi, Daddy," Kristin says with a forced smile.

He shakes his head at us as if we're a damn shame. "Kris."

I get it. We're soaked in wine. Kristin's wearing a Snuggie and, for some reason, a paper crown. There's a 1.5-liter bottle of wine on her lap and the boombox now plays "School's Out" by Alice Cooper. I can't imagine he's terribly impressed with what we've done to the property, either—the trash blown over the road, the porta-potty still lying on its side, the pirate flag flapping at the entrance, the random car seat and broken lamp and inflatable dinosaur in the meadow.

"What are you doing here?" Kristin asks. "I thought you were in Hong Kong."

"I'm back in Palo Alto. Flew in yesterday. Your fuckin' phone isn't working now?"

"We're off the grid."

"You're off the grid." He looks at the sky, as if it might help him out. "Jesus Christ."

A uniformed chauffer gets out of the car's driver's seat and stretches his legs. He surveys the property with a smile, like this is hilarious to him. And as I watch him, it hits me that I haven't spoken to a man besides Simon in longer than I can even remember. Their sudden presence shifts the energy.

"I thought you were dead in a ditch, Kris," he says in a low voice. "You don't answer your phone, your voicemail box is full,

I can't reach you, you're off social media, my mind goes to awful places. The shit you put me through, I swear to god."

"Look, sorry, Daddy," she says in a childish voice, "but I'm *fine*."

He gestures toward the property. "This is not fine." As if he just noticed I exist, and as if I'm some kind of cancerous growth, he glances at me for one disgusted second before addressing Kristin again. "Who the fuck are all these people?"

"My friends."

"I got a complaint from the neighbors. Saying some ... religious group has taken over the property. What the fuck is going on?"

"They're just my friends."

"And you're drinking again." He shakes his head. "I can't even *begin*."

"Daddy, it's different now. I've transcended my addiction."

The crestfallen expression that passes over his face like a shadow is one of the saddest things I've ever seen. I detect a history, a tiredness, a despair shaped from years of disappointment. Underneath his businessman attire and his shield of extreme wealth, he's just a dad. A dad who apparently loves his kid enough to come out here to make sure she's still living and breathing.

"You look like shit," he says. "You look like you did before I booked you into Recovery Haven."

"It's not like that."

He looks at me, puffing out an exasperated breath. "You think she looks okay? You think she looks healthy?"

"I don't know."

"Why am I asking you?" he says, swatting the side of the pedicab. "You're as much a zombie as she is."

I'm offended, but don't know how to respond. "We're

Woken," is what I manage. It sounds stupider than I thought it would.

"Uh-huh," he says.

Kristin's dad spends the next five minutes trying to convince her that she should go back to rehab, then gives up and hugs her for a long time, whispering in her ear. She is as limp and unanimated as a doll.

"Excuse me," Simon says from the porch.

Everyone turns to him. He's wearing a sweater and linen pants and his beard is trimmed and his hair is brushed. He looks wholesome and together, in comparison to us.

"Can I help you?" he asks, folding his hands.

"I own this property," Kristin's dad says, walking to Simon.

Kristin and I get out of the pedicab and join the group that forms around Simon—the Waking and Woken, all deferring to him as he lords over the porch stairs.

"Ah, Kevin Park! Of course. Nice to meet you." Simon grins amiably. "Now, you do realize California tenant laws require at least twenty-four hours and just cause for you to enter the property?"

"Nobody here is paying me rent. You're not my tenants. Technically, you're guests. So you can take your tenant law and shove it where the sun don't shine, buddy." Kevin points a finger at him. "You're standing on my property. You're sleeping in my house. And don't you forget it."

"Mmm, the dream of property." Simon sweeps his hand through the air. "With all due respect?" Simon pauses and a breeze blows through his hair. "You're dreaming, sir. Ownership is an illusion."

"What will it be when I kick your asses out to the curb and call the cops to remove you from my property?" Kevin asks, hands on hips. "Will that be an illusion?"

Simon has a look on his face like he's been kneed in the groin. He opens his mouth, then shuts it again.

"Look, I'm coming back here in the next week or two," Kevin says. "If this place isn't cleaned up, everyone is out of here. Including you, Kris." He gestures to the meadow. "Everything needs to be hauled and the place needs to look the way it was before. Understand?"

Everyone murmurs, some in agreement, some in protest. Simon doesn't respond, heading inside, leaving us to look at one another with lost expressions.

"Better start cleaning this shit up," Kevin yells at everyone as he heads back to his car.

He and his chauffer climb into his beetle-black Rolls Royce and they glide away, leaving dust clouds behind. Everyone buzzes around me. Two of the Floaters are crying and holding each other like they've been given a death sentence. Maude picks up a hoe and beats the ground with it. Kristin sits in the pedicab and drinks straight from the bottle with a far-off expression. Janae drops to a child's pose on the ground and hums and soon a few others join her in a Resonance.

I think of the way the neighbors have looked at us. The way Kevin looked at me today and called me a "zombie."

My eyes glaze over as the wine churns in my stomach. The wind blows the pirate flag in the air and the trash through the grass. I wonder if, perhaps, the end for us is near—and feel an odd, secret flutter of relief.

In a flash, an imaginary Scarlett smiles at me and my heart skips a beat. But then I remind myself I'm still here. I'm still a Mirror House girl. And we've apparently got some work to do if we're going to keep this place.

55

EVERYTHING IS CONTAGIOUS. Not just microorganisms that make us ill, but all of life's invisible magic tricks: laughter. Rage. Sadness. Trends. Speech patterns. Habits. Loves. Inclinations. Aversions. Beliefs.

And fear: the heart of everything.

Fear spreads through us like a wildfire.

Mirror House erupts in noise and desperation as soon as that black car drives away. The Woken and the Waking turn to one another with wide eyes asking, "What now? What do we do?" We tug our braids nervously. We're not sure if we should start dismantling the changes we've made to the property. When everyone keeps asking Kristin, she just yells, "The fuck do I know?" and trudges upstairs with the bottle. Maude stomps inside and begins rage-baking. Simon is locked in his room and not answering. He has a sign hanging from his door-knob that says "MEDITATION IN PROGRESS: PLEASE DO NOT DISTURB."

The house is abuzz in a heightened state of awareness, waiting for orders, next steps. If we begin cleaning up the property the way Kevin demanded, Simon might get upset. We don't want to upset Simon. A Waking throng in the living room are group-hugging and humming and I almost join in, but I'm not in the mood. For a fleeting second, I think, *I don't even know these people.* I go upstairs and pass Dakota in the fetal position on her tiny bed in the annex, go to my room, and shut the door. I try to read but can't. The words are slippery. Nothing makes sense and something is unraveling and I'm deeply unsettled. Scarlett's song rings in my head, her low voice echoey and singing, *My home's my home, it lives with me, it does not carry, it is carried* ...

I don't know where it came from, but oh how it makes me miss her.

After dinner we gather in the living room. It's raining, so we're stuck inside. Someone lights incense that stinks like burning feet and everyone is already a bit drunk because we're collectively confused and drowning our feelings. Despair is in the air. Even the music choice is somber: Elliott Smith. Kristin is sitting beside me, mascara rivers under her eyes, telling me for the fortieth time that she refuses to go back to rehab.

You ever look around and ask yourself, "what the fuck has this become?" Scarlett's ghost whispers to me.

I bat the memory of her away.

Finally, Simon descends the stairs and the whole room sighs in relief. He's been locked in his room since Kevin left. The Waking and the Woken hush each other and the music gets turned down as he approaches. He has a sober look on his face, fingers tented.

"We have some things to discuss," he says. "Everyone grab a seat."

We do as we're told, some plopping on beanbags, others on the floor. The Woken lounge on the couches, as if there's an unspoken hierarchy. Simon pushes his "soapbox" in front of the fireplace and mounts it. The tension in the room is suffocating. All fourteen of us girls share a pained expression and sparkling eyes. It's as if there's a giant rusty screw in my stomach tightening, tightening. I might have felt a secret twinge of relief after Kevin threatened to kick us out earlier, but that was a moment of weakness and not how I really feel. I can't imagine losing this place, what comes next. We're dangling off the edge of a cliff and we need Simon to save us.

"I'm in a very dangerous and precarious position here," he says, brows furrowed. "I've sacrificed so much. I've risked my life and reputation to help you all."

"We love you, Simon," someone says tearfully.

"Fear to love," Maude says.

"*Fear to love*," the group chants back.

"They want to crucify me the way they crucify every great prophet or saint," he says. "This is a movie we've seen before. We know how it ends, don't we?"

"We won't let them, Simon!" yells one of the Floaters.

"Fear to love," Maude says, fist in the air.

"*Fear to love!*" the group booms, louder. A chill crawls up my spine as I say it with them.

"I need your protection," Simon says, impassioned. "And your trust. I need to trust you, too. To know I can count on you. We need to wake up and realize we're one thing. One. There is no you, no me, there is no self—the self is an illusion. Identity is a dream. Do you all know that? Do you *truly* know that?"

Everyone nods and yells yes, yes, we are enthusiastically all in agreement that we are one. *Fear to love!*

"This is it." He balls his fists. "We are the Infinite Divine, here, this is it. Moving forward, you're either Woken or you're still asleep and you need to go back to the Dream World. It's time to root out the weak."

A few gasps and whispers. A shudder squirms through me. My brain is trying so hard to make sense of what he's saying, like I'm interpreting another language I barely speak. Is it the endless wine I've drunk, is it the weird mood of this party, am I too dense to understand what he's saying?

Or ... does it make no sense?

"Everyone lives in this house now. Everyone is Woken." There is sweat on his brow, a trickle running down his temple. "They can't take us down if we're united. If we're all the Infinite Divine, we are untouchable. And everyone is going to need to sacrifice. I can't be the only one. Complete trust. Are you with me?"

The house roars with agreement and Simon's eyes blaze.

"Then show me!" he shouts. "You want to be one of the Woken? Prove it! I want to *see* your sacrifice! Find a material item you love, something important to you that means something to you. Throw it in the fireplace!"

No one moves as we do a collective double-take, making sure we heard correctly, side-eyeing one another to see what everyone else is doing.

"Now!" he yells urgently, spinning his hand like a wheel. "We're rooting out the weak. Now, now, now!"

We shift and scramble up from our seats, dispersing in all directions as we scour the room for something valuable. A few women go right up to the fireplace, throwing rings or earrings or necklaces into the flames as Simon nods approvingly. My mind flounders—a material item I love, that means something to me. What would that be at this point? Everything that mattered, I already sacrificed.

But I'm wary of Simon's energy right now. I don't want to make him angry. I hurry upstairs and into my room, grabbing the first thing my eye catches on my bookshelf—my worn copy of the

Rubaiyat. The same copy I read to my new friends at Mirror House only months ago, a lifetime ago. An invisible hand clutches my throat as I hurry back downstairs into the living room where everyone is chucking items into the fire before taking their seats again. It smells rank. Plasticky suffocating smoke fills the air.

Simon nods on encouragingly and points at each person as if he's a priest doling out communion. "You're Woken. You're Woken. You're Woken."

I toss the *Rubiyaat* in, watching the pages crumple to ash. Maude and Dakota and Kristin cheer for me. Someone else tosses in a dress that shrinks and melts.

Robin approaches Simon near the fireplace, holding her notebook and raising her hand. "Simon?"

"Toss it in!" he says, trying to grab the notebook from her hand.

She pulls the notebook against her chest. "No, I—I wanted to ask a question."

"This is not a time for questions," Simon says, wiping sweat from his forehead. "It's a time for sacrifice."

"I already threw in a bracelet—"

"Throw in what *matters* to you," he shouts in her face. "Prove your loyalty. Or are you a rat? Writing down everything we say and do?"

Robin winces, blinking hard behind her red plastic glasses. "No, I—"

"Throw the notebook in, *rat*," Maude parrots, pushing Robin from behind.

"I don't want to—"

Simon explodes, completely, as if she just pulled a pin from his grenade. "I asked for trust! Complete trust! And this is what you give me?"

Robin's face reddens. "I was—"

"Wake the fuck up, Robin!" he screams at her, getting down near her face.

She cowers. My hand flies to my mouth. The whole room goes still. Simon watches us for reaction, his eyes wide.

"Yell it with me," he says, beckoning us to come closer. "Come on, come on!"

Everyone scrambles from our places on the couch, the bean-bags, the floor to surround Robin as she crouches, her hung head with two braids. She ducks and covers as if she's trying to disappear into herself.

"Wake the fuck up, Robin!" we all yell at her, our voices overlapping.

"Again, again!" Simon screams, raising his arms over the symphony of our voices.

"Wake the fuck up, Robin!"

A frenzy stirs, as if someone took Mirror House and spun it like a top. *Wake the fuck up, Robin! Wake the fuck up!* Someone's hand reaches down and smacks the back of Robin's head. *Wake the fuck up!* The room is humid with everyone's wet breath and chanting and yelling. The irritation I've had for Robin swells in my chest. The confusion about our future. *Wake the fuck up!* The aimless desperation. It's all being taken out on her. Someone pulls her hair. Someone pushes her, hard, and she stumbles onto all fours. *Wake the fuck up!* I realize suddenly that I'm crying, my face is wet, and I don't know what I'm feeling. *Wake the fuck up!* It's infectious. Girls around me are spitting and screaming at Robin on the ground. Maude looks so enraged her eyes might pop out of her skull, like all the suspicion she had for Robin is boiling up from nowhere. She smacks the back of Robin's head with her hand.

"Wake her up, then! Wake her up!" Simon roars, holding his arms out and shaking them, as if he controls the electricity in the room.

The energy is spiraling out of control. I might as well be in a room with fifteen hundred people and not fifteen. It's so dark in here except for the fire and the rain pelts the windows louder, louder, and then the screaming turns to pushing and the pushing turns to hitting. Maude kicks Robin with her giant boot. Robin spills to the ground, on her side, trying to protect her head. Everyone's wailing on her now. It's too much. The momentum has swallowed everyone. By the time I realize we've gone too far, it's too late.

I freeze and stop screaming along with everyone.

"Wake her up! Wake her up!" cheers Simon from his soapbox.

Wake her up! Kristin yells, bending over and pulling Robin's hair so hard her neck yanks back and face wrenches in pain.

Wake her up! Dakota grabs an empty wine bottle. She looks at Simon and he pantomimes a *thwack.*

"Don't!" I yell, but no one hears me.

Without a second thought, Dakota steps toward the commotion and whacks Robin on the back of the head with the wine bottle.

Robin jerks, her face contorted as she tries to get up and is kicked down again. Her scream is inaudible over the noise. Someone grabs a mug and throws it toward her, shattering it on the hardwood floor. Someone pushes her into the mess of it.

Wake her up! Wake her up! Wake her up!

Everyone has lost their goddamn minds. It's happening so fast I can't wrap my mind around it. Chaos. A vicious mosh pit. A living room riot. Arms flailing and pushing one another until it's hard to breathe and there are fingernails scratching and braid pulling and it's like no one even knows who the target is anymore.

"Stop!" I yell, my body crushed between bodies as I try to pull the wine bottle out of Dakota's hands. She's sobbing like she doesn't have control of herself and hits Robin with it again from below, like she's playing miniature golf and not bludgeoning someone's cheekbone.

It's no use. I get elbowed in the gut from nowhere and suddenly, I think I'm going to throw up. I'm going to turn inside out. *Things fall apart; the center cannot hold.*

My god, what is going on?

Is the world ending?

It's a Mirror House apocalypse.

Squinting through the whirlpool of bodies and shadows, I spot a smear of blood on the floor, and Robin's hair in it, and a tooth, maybe, and she's limp and everyone's still screaming and chanting *Wake her up! Wake her up!*

I turn and stumble toward the front door, mouth full of bile. Hand on the knob, I open it and the fresh air rushes over me as I gape at the sweet nothingness of the rainy, starless night. I turn behind me, so stunned that I have to check—is this really happening?

Is this real life, or a dream?

Simon stares back at me with a void in his eyes. A vein throbs on his forehead. Who is this man? I hardly recognize him. He waves at me, a little cute curl of a wave, smile slithering to his lips, and I can't move. Robin's ballet-slippered feet are splayed on the floor, her legs jolting as someone stomps on her. A violent dance surrounds him, and Simon is nothing but utterly pleased.

"They're killing her!" I scream.

Simon gives me a little shrug, like *what are you going to do?*

And suddenly, I hate him like I've never hated anyone in my life. This is sick. This is wrong. This is not normal. This is criminal. He did this. He made this. He lied to us. He promised us paradise. I scream and no one even hears me. I want to stop this, but how? How can I compete with the fever and the roar of them all? I turn and run away, toward the trees where the encampment used to be, toward the road, as fast as my legs can carry me.

This is toxic, abusive shit, I hear Scarlett saying. *Wake up.*

And for the first time since I arrived at Mirror House, I am now *truly* woken.

Excerpt from the documentary *The Mirror House Girls: One Year Later*

LOCATION: Interviewee's home, Raven's Landing, California

SCARLETT sits on her couch, shaking her head sadly as she studies a picture of ROBIN RILEY smiling in her high school senior portrait. SCARLETT sighs heavily and puts the flier down, gathering her thoughts for a moment before speaking.

SCARLETT: I saw the news about Robin and I recognized her, yes, but I'd never really talked to her when she was there. And you know, drifters blew through that property like tumbleweeds. (Shakes her head) Thirteen broken bones and twenty-three skull frac- tures, I mean ... I can't even begin to imagine what he did to make that happen. But you know it was him. Even if he didn't lay a finger on that girl, it was *him*.

56

I RUN until my lungs burn. Until my legs ache and my slippers are heavy with mud. Every step is a slip, a squelch. The rain pours down. It soaks my sweater and my hair and runs down the back of my neck in any icy river. I'm sniveling, lost in the dark, the darkest dark—the sky moonless, not a streetlamp in sight, not a light on in the neighbor's house. No cars in their driveway. This is their vacation home and they're only here on occasional weekends, so it's not like they can help me now. No phone. No bars. No one.

It's so desolate and hopeless out here.

An owl hoots and distantly, unintelligible shouting and chanting bleed from Mirror House.

I make a left turn into a thicket of cypresses. Catching my breath, my eyes adjust. Suddenly I can see the glitter of the rain up in the black web of branches above me, the trees gnarled and looming. Beyond the meadow across the road, the yellow lights of Mirror House are lit up like demon eyes. I collapse on a log with a hand on my chest and glance up Hitchcock Road: a spooky, unlit void. It's over a mile walk to the highway. I glance back at Mirror House, which is only a three-minute walk from here. Illuminated. Watching. Waiting.

My home.

"Why?" I whisper to the air, shivering.

Here I am, breaking open, spilling everywhere. That question throbs through me. Why did they all erupt like that? Why did Simon incite them to hurt Robin? Why am I here, wet and lost as a baby bird in the woods? Up in the sky, no stars are visible behind the curtain of clouds. The rain lightens to mist.

I'm paralyzed.

My inner compass is broken.

The desperation I experienced, fleeing from Mirror House, settles into a vague ache. My breath steadies and my fingers and toes are so cold I can't feel them. I don't know how long I sit here on the log, how long I close my eyes and wait for some kind of sign. The images of everyone attacking Robin run in a horrid loop in my brain. A plan is what I need, a plan, how to move forward, but I'm just so tired, drunk, emotional. I don't know where I end and the world begins anymore. The sound of a branch breaking makes me gasp and jump, my adrenaline gone haywire. I lie down to try to calm myself, stop the world from spinning. Shut my eyes and make it all disappear.

The sound of a buzzsaw jolts my eyelids open.

Wait, did I fall asleep?

My cheek is stuck to the log. Everything is sideways and I'm soaked. I push myself up weakly and the scenery tips right-side up. Yes, I fell asleep here. Car lights blink on in front of Mirror House and a vehicle makes its way down the driveway. Robin's yellow car. Oh thank god, that means she survived. She's getting out of here. It turns onto Hitchcock Road, about twenty feet in front of me, and drives by, headlights blinding me, splashing muddy water as it zooms out of sight. I stand up and a deluge of relief washes over me.

"Robin!" I yell after the car, but it turns down the road and accelerates out of sight.

I exhale a sigh that could blow a house down.

She's okay. She's speeding away from this madness.

There are people milling around outside of Mirror House, but I can't make out who they are or what they're doing through the fog. The tiny figures are so far away, ants on a hill, lit up only by the glow of the windows and a few bobbing flashlights.

I start questioning what really happened, what I really saw.

It probably looked a lot worse than it was. I couldn't see what was happening in exact detail there at the end—they might not have been stomping on her after all. Robin was conscious when I last saw her. She must have got out of it okay. I blew it out of proportion. My fear response took over and I fled and now I'm so confused. Like a child who ran away from home and walked into the jaws of the big, bad world, I don't know where to turn now. I'm paralyzed.

I'm overwhelmed with homesickness. But for what home? For the Mirror House I'm looking at right now? For the old Mirror House, or for my life before it? Or maybe I'm not even homesick, but worldsick, missing everything that exists outside this place. There's a magnet in my heart, and it's pulling me— but which direction, I couldn't tell you. I ache with grief, though I'm not quite sure what I've lost. All I know is nothing is what I thought it was. I'm sick to my stomach from what I saw tonight. But I don't know what to do except go back to the one place I still call home.

Numbly, soaked head to toe, I walk back to Mirror House. In the distance, near the side of the fence on the way to the cliffs, flashlights dance like fireflies. I stop in the middle of the driveway. Simon is standing on the stairs of the porch with his hands on his hips and a hard look on his face, like he's been waiting for me all this time.

"Look who's crawled back," he says as I come closer.

I swallow hard. I can barely make eye contact with him. For the first time in my life, I'm scared of Simon. I remember that triumphant smile he gave me in the middle of the chaos when he encouraged everyone to beat Robin. He could encourage everyone to beat me next if he decided I deserved it.

I hang my head, and even though I'm not quite sure what I'm apologizing for, I tell him what I know he wants to hear. "I'm sorry."

"It's you, isn't it?" He shakes his head. "*You're* the rat."

Rat. The word stabs me with terror. I get a flashback of Robin on the ground, the crowd swarming her.

"What?" My mouth goes dry. "Come on, I'm not a rat!"

"How am I supposed to trust a single thing you say?"

I swallow. There's nothing I can offer that will ease his anger, his suspicion. I just need to let it pass.

"Is Robin okay?" I ask.

He stares at me. "She's fine. Everyone's fine."

I nod and start up the stairs, but he blocks me. "You deserted us."

The emotional and physical exhaustion of the night is wearing me down. All I want is to go to bed and forget this night ever happened. What does he want me to say right now?

"I was afraid," I say, my voice shaking. "It was my fear response."

He crosses his arms, his expression hollow and vacant. I smell wine on his breath.

"Simon, it was a simple mistake," I say, as gently as I can, hoping to soften his expression. "Can we talk about it tomorrow?"

As if I'm beyond reproach, he shakes his head.

"I'm so tired," I beg him, tears pricking my eyes. "Please, Simon. Let me go to my room."

"You're pathetic," he says in a whisper. "The most pathetic, vacuous, worthless woman I've ever met."

These insults sting so badly it's like he threw a vial of acid in my face. He's been cold to me before, he's frozen me out, but he's never been outright mean. Warm rivers stream down my cheeks.

"You are *no one*. You are *nothing*. You belong *nowhere*."

I don't know how to respond. I don't know what he wants to hear, what the magic word is that can let me back into the house. All I can manage is a whispered "Okay."

His nostrils flare. He takes off his glasses in a flash and pinches between his eyes. "Go inside. Clean up the mess in the living room. And then you're not allowed in the house until I think you're ready to come back."

If he had thrust a machete in my spleen, it would have hurt less than this.

"Where am I supposed to go?" I croak.

"There are still tents out near the forest."

The abandoned encampment. Tents that have blown on their sides and filled with dirty rainwater. Next to the toppled porta-potty.

"Can I go upstairs for some of my things?"

"Not until I think you're ready. You're not ready."

"Can I sleep on the couch?" I wipe my nose, trying to control myself. "Please?"

"Clean up the mess," he says, enunciating every word. "And then get out of my sight. You sicken me."

Simon pushes past me with such force, I nearly topple over. I stand here, dripping and muddy and shivering. It's surreal. So surreal. I go inside and find the paper towels and the cleaner and the buckets. The house is so quiet, I hear the ticking of a clock I've never noticed before.

Where is everyone?

Uneasily, I crouch on the floor and fight the urge to dry heave. There are three puddles of blood the size of dinner plates. One of them drying already. I spray pine-scented cleaner on them, let it soak in. Take a paper towel and pick up a clump of Robin's hair. I remind myself she left in one piece, I saw her car drive away, it looked worse than it was. I scrub it, sickly. *Progress,* I tell myself, trying to spin it in a positive light. *I've come so far from the girl who couldn't handle a paper cut.* But the thought is empty, void of any pride. I wipe up the blood until all the paper towels are sopping red. I clean the blood up so well it's like it was never there.

After I finish, I sit on the porch steps numbly and wait for everyone to come back. When they do, no one says a single word to me. They have muddy shoes, faraway looks, wet braids. They don't even make eye contact. They go straight inside with Simon and shut the door. A pang tightens in my chest. I don't know if I've ever felt this lonely in all my life.

Fear to love, I hear them chanting.

"Fear to love," I whisper, lying on the top step.

The world spins as I close my eyes. They chant and chant, *fear to love, fear to love, fear to love,* lulling me to sleep.

When I wake up, the world is golden with sunshine, the meadow sparkles with last night's rain, the trees burst with birdsong—and I'm shivering so intensely my teeth chatter. The terror of last night rumbles through me like an aftershock. The people I thought I knew turning into a violent mob. Robin's narrow escape. The puddles of blood I made disappear. And now Simon won't let me back in the house. I can't even go eat breakfast or change my clothes.

I'm so fucked. I'm trapped here with no way out. Something has to change drastically, and soon. I just don't know what or how.

57

"You sicken me."

Simon's words echo in my head.

I sit on the porch steps, stunned, trying to find the way out of this. My head pounds and sobriety hits with an avalanche of anxiety. The insanity of last night becomes more detailed, a horror-movie montage that won't stop looping: Robin cowering on the floor. The metallic stink of her blood. Her yellow car tearing off into the night. Running drunkenly through the mud and rain. Bobbing flashlights in the distance. Sopping up the rusty mess of her blood like spilled wine. It's as if we all went on some nightmare drug trip together and now I'm emerging from it and I don't know what's real anymore.

It was awful, what I saw happening to Robin, but maybe I should have trusted they had reasons for what they did. As bloody as the floor was, as wrong as it felt to sweep her glasses and hair and hoop earring into a dustpan, she drove away and left. She's gone. A part of me wishes I could have gone with her. But then what? Leave here a muddy mess, no phone, no wallet, with none of my things? And go where? I imagine finding Scarlett and telling her what happened last night, her shock and disgust at me for being a part of it.

I don't know what my future looks like, but one thing's for sure: the next thing I need to do is to get back inside.

The smell of fresh coffee and toasted bagels waft from the cracked windows and make my stomach grumble as I wait on the porch. Their voices through the wall, the laughter—I'm a ghost. When the Floaters come out to sip coffee and admire the sunshine, or Janae and Juliet lay out their yoga mats and begin stretching, no one acknowledges me sitting here. I say "good morning!" over and over again and no one even turns their head.

Kristin comes out and heads down the stairs. She's in her cargo shorts and Santa Cruz Skateboards sweatshirt and a pair of aviator sunglasses. In the light of the day, all the bruises on her legs she's gotten from drunk skating are glaringly obvious and quite alarming. She's carrying her bucket of guinea pig food out to the yard. I can tell she notices me and then clamps her mouth shut and keeps moving, turning around the side of the house.

"Kristin!" I say, springing to my feet and catching up with her.

She doesn't respond. Doesn't even flick her gaze my way.

"Kristin, please talk to me," I beg, the words hurting as they leave my throat. "Don't shut me out."

She swallows and unlatches the coop.

"Hi, babies." Kristin pushes her sunglasses up on her head. She steps inside the cage and hitches the door shut again. She has to duck so her head doesn't hit the ceiling. The guinea pigs squeak and run around her ankles. There are so many in there, it's seething with guinea pigs—the babies have grown up and there are even more babies. The sight is weirdly nauseating. "How are we? You have a rough night too?"

She scoops the food and puts it in their bowl. The guinea pigs swarm the dish, one on top of another, a mob of fur and squeaks, pushing each other out of the way.

"Yeah, it was a weird night, wasn't it?" she asks, reaching down and petting their backs. "But that's okay. Everything's going to be okay. Just living in the present moment, right? Fear to love, little babies. Fear to sacrificial love."

"Kristin?" I ask through the chicken wire.

"If you can't sacrifice, it isn't really love," Kristin says sadly, glancing at me. "If you can't sacrifice, you're still rooted in fear."

I nod. "Last night—was a lot. But Robin's okay, right? We can all move on from it?"

Kristin's bloodshot eyes linger on me for just a moment. "Go away," she says pleadingly. "You'll get me in trouble."

She turns back to the guinea pigs, cleaning their water bowl, and my eyes prickle. I back away from the cage.

I'm stunned. Dizzy with exhaustion. My stomach screams with hunger and I don't know where to go from here. I walk to the edge of the property and cross Hitchcock Road to where the abandoned encampment is. I cross paths with Maude, who is walking back to the property seemingly from nowhere. Her pajama pant legs are brown from ankles to thighs, as if she was wading in mud.

"Don't even look at me, bitch," she says, narrowing her eyes.

I scurry to the encampment. Two blown-over tents puddled with water; a picnic bench sinking in mud; a barbecue knocked on its side. It used to be so full and vibrant, a shantytown with a chaotic rotation of guests. And now it's just me here.

Suddenly, I remember that this was where Scarlett sang that song and Simon made fun of her for being "the most narcissistic singer-songwriter of all time." *You're your audience, your biggest fan, your truest love.* Remember? *You are the one...*

I loved her music. I'm so lucky to remember it, like I

somehow snatched a little piece of her and tucked it in a pocket in my heart.

There's a hose spigot here. I get on my knees and drink from the faucet, feeling like an animal. I'm still damp from being out in the storm last night. My sleeves and pant legs are so caked with dirt they're stiff. Drinking water helps, though, even if it's gritty and metallic. I breathe in deeply and repeat *fear to love, fear to love, fear to love*. Then I get to work trying to fix one of the tents up. If I do what Simon says, I can get into my room again. I can take a shower again and change my clothes and eat a meal. Then maybe I can figure out the bigger picture. I manage to turn one tent inside out and hang it to dry in the sun. In an hour or so, I pitch the tent again.

Through the veil of cypress branches, I spy my Mirror House family in the distance. They're gathered in a circle. Feeling like some kind of swamp creature that lurks in the woods, I emerge from the trees and slowly approach the group, hoping they might let me back in. I walk through the meadow. The brush sighs with wind. Everyone is seated with their eyes closed, holding hands, Simon in the middle of the circle in a meditation position. I take a seat on the outside near Maude and Dakota. Maude sniffs performatively in my direction.

"Geez, something stinks like chickenshit," she says.

No one dares to look my way.

"If you are truly Woken," Simon says, continuing his speech. "If you have truly shed your fear, then you transcend this earthly realm. You realize that all this—this world, these people, everything you hold so dear—are but a dream. The Dreamers, they don't want that. They really don't. They are terrified of what we represent. They don't want people to be Woken, because that means the dream is over."

"Fear to love," Dakota says.

I hold my hands in a prayer position and try to listen, really listen. Dedicate myself wholly to this. Be in this moment. But all I can think is, this is how far I've sunk. This is all I have—a hollow mantra and a community that now hates me. I don't have possessions. I severed my ties to the outside world. The worst part is that I did it to myself. I volunteered for this.

And now I have nothing.

"This is revolutionary, what we're doing," he says. "We are spiritual revolutionaries. That's why the world wants us destroyed. They want to break us apart, imprison us. Take our freedom away. Enslave us. That's what they're trying to do. That's what they *will* do, if we let them."

My heart beats faster. I imagine myself stuck in a prison cell. Could that really happen? Or is he exaggerating?

"We will not let them," he says.

"Fear to love," someone says in agreement.

"Fear to sacrificial love. Love requires sacrifice. We're reaching the end of our journey here. But for our Woken spirits, it's only the beginning."

Simon talks like this for hours upon hours. Everyone is quieter than usual as they listen—ragged, dazed, and tired. It's the longest talk he's ever given the group; I don't even know what the point of it is. He talks in circles until everyone seems hypnotized. When it's lunchtime, they head inside, and I know without asking I'm not invited. Maude gets up and spits deliberately right next to me. No one acknowledges my existence. But Simon saw me here listening to his every word. Maybe he'll let me back inside later today and we can make up and move on. Even though a part of me feels trapped, this place, these people, everything we believe and built—it's all I have.

I just want to forget any of this ever happened.

58

THREE DAYS GO on like this.

Mornings and afternoons in the meadows with the group chanting and talking. I'm never allowed in the circle; I'm only allowed to watch from the outside. *Fear to sacrificial love,* everyone chants. *Fear to sacrificial love.* We repeat it so many times our minds go numb. Everyone lies on their backs in the grass and meditates for hours. We visualize transcending our bodies. Simon tells us that ancient Romans believed that the truly virtuous went to a paradise called the Elysian Fields, the "Islands of the Blessed" filled with music and shady trees. I let my mind drift there on a mental vacation and it's the best part of my day.

Reality is shivers. Loneliness. Silent treatment. Pissing in the forest. Twitching at every sound, scared of snakes and coyotes. Hunger pangs. That flat rock overlooking the ocean reminds me of Scarlett singing to me and I shake the memory from my mind because it's pretty and it's gone and it hurts.

My clothes are glued to me with dirt. I haunt the property

like a ghost, take a walk to the garden and notice the Floaters have taken my job. There's a fresh patch of earth where they planted a lemon tree. I get a flashback of cleaning up Robin's blood and have to hurry my steps and keep walking to push the thoughts from my mind.

The doubt I'm battling is wearing me down. I'm being tested and I don't know how much longer I can do this. When I consider all that I sacrificed to be here—when I think about the possibility that Scarlett was right about this place being toxic and abusive—it's like the ground disappears beneath my feet and I'm in freefall. That would mean everyone I love, everything I've believed, everything I've done, the person I thought I was, has all been lies. My reality would be shattered. I can't see a future. All roads that lead out of this place look like dead ends from here. Who am I at this point without Mirror House?

On the third night, I'm shivering in my tent when I'm star-tled by a noise. My first terrified thought is *oh god it's a mountain lion, come to devour me in my sleep*—but when the tent unzips, I can make out Kristin's shape. She hands me a mug of wine and crawls inside. The plastic tarp crackles beneath us as she sits next to me.

"Hey," she says.

"Kristin!" I say, flooded with relief to have company. I give her a side hug and squeeze tight.

"I shouldn't be here, but I ... just wanted to see you."

"I've missed everyone so much." My eyes burn. "You have no idea."

"It's fucking *cold* out here."

"I know."

"How are you okay without a sleeping bag?"

"I just kind of cuddle up. Curl up like a roly poly."

"Balls."

"Yeah."

"You shouldn't have run."

"I know." I swallow. I want to try to explain it, but words don't feel like they work the way they used to. "Fear took over."

"You have to be bigger than that. You're acting mortal."

"I didn't want Robin to get hurt."

"Well." She sighs, heavily, and then pauses so long it's like she doesn't know what to say.

"Kristin?"

"Let's not talk about it anymore."

"Okay."

"Let's drink instead." She clinks her mug to mine and her voice climbs, chipper and clipped. "To the poison and the antidote."

I gulp my wine down, grateful for anything besides water to fill my stomach. It relaxes me instantly. I close my eyes, soaking up the tingly joy rushing through my veins.

"I can't stay long," she says. "Just wanted to see you one more time."

Her last three words ring like an alarm bell. A doomed farewell.

"What do you mean by that?" I ask.

The tent is pure darkness. But somehow, after being here with my eyes open long enough, I begin to make out specifics. The shine of Kristin's eyes. The shape of the hood around her head and the roundness of the mug in her hands.

"We're going to be moving on soon," she says.

"Where?"

The sound of distant footsteps freezes Kristin. She's at attention, a deer in the woods. After a moment, she lets out a breath and turns to me again.

"Don't worry about it, okay? I just want to tell you I love you. In case we don't see each other again in this earthly realm."

I'm so stunned, I can't breathe for a second. Are they all going to leave me? Are they starting a new Mirror House, one I'm not invited to?

"Kristin—"

"We'll see each other soon though, okay? We all will. Because everything's going to change. The revolution's beginning. So be happy, okay? Be happy."

Her hand finds mine, a shocking warmth. What the hell is she saying? Suddenly, I wonder if she's talking about something so horrid that I can't even allow my brain to fully articulate it.

Don't drink the purple Kool-Aid.

"You're scaring me," I whisper. "What are you talking about? You're not going to do something stupid, are you?"

"No, not at all. Not at all."

I take a deep breath of relief. "Then where are you going? Just tell me."

"Sorry. I can't."

The dread is crushing. The past few days, I've been wondering what my future is here and now I'm finding out I have no future. No choice in the matter. They're abandoning me.

"Please don't leave me."

"It's okay, Winona. We'll see each other again. Just ... not here."

"I don't understand."

"That's because you're still dreaming," she says, squeezing my hand once and then letting go. "Fear to love, all right?"

Kristin unzips the tent, flashes me a peace sign, and steps back into the night. Then all I hear are boots crunching leaves as she walks away, leaving me cold and alone once again. The night air is too still as her words loop in my mind. Where are they going? Where's the new Mirror House? Are they going to hide somewhere? Will they just leave me behind? I lie awake as long as I can, stubbornly, needing answers and seething in silence.

But eventually, like always, I'm swallowed by the hungry jaws of sleep.

59

I PEEL myself from the plastic floor and wipe my eyes. Shivering, I emerge from the tent. My breath is a visible puff of air. Day, night, doesn't matter. I'm in California but I'm always freezing my ass off.

The air is so quiet. I drink water from the spigot on my hands and knees, find a place to squat and piss. Then I patiently wait on the picnic bench, watching the house for signs of life. Lights flickering on or the front door opening. Meditation circles, yoga groups. Peals of laughter or chanting. But it is eerily still.

Where is everybody?

My throat hurts when I swallow. I'm hollow, a husk of a person with a heart of mud. My hunger is a constant companion these days, a dull ache only quelled for a minute or two if I chug water. The sound of silence is interrupted by the distant cawing of ravens.

Uneasiness prickles all over my skin. Kristin's cryptic conversation in the dark last night—she didn't mean they were all leaving *today?* It already happened?

I thought I had time to figure this out. My head is swimming. If they up and left me here, I have no idea what to do next. I'm so shocked by the thought I can't move. I just keep studying the house in disbelief, hoping I'm wrong.

Dakota's car and Simon's van are still here. I try to steady my breath but there's this panic bursting in me, the childlike panic of being alone forever, of being left behind. I wait here, hands in my lap, for a long time. Staring at the still house. Willing someone to come out of it, for some sign of life. I hear Kristin saying, *The revolution's beginning.*

In a flash, I remember everyone lying in a circle in the grass, visualizing transcending their bodies.

... in case we don't see each other again in this earthly realm.

I stand, these thoughts clicking together like tragic puzzle pieces.

There it is again, that horrible, horrible sentence: *Don't drink the purple Kool-Aid.*

Oh no. No. She said they weren't—they wouldn't. It's not like that.

Right?

The world doesn't have enough oxygen for my lungs.

My panic morphs into dread.

And it doesn't matter how many times I whisper "fear to love" to myself as I walk quickly toward the house. As I begin jogging through the meadow where we shared a trance and chanted together for hours only yesterday. Fear to love, fear to love, fear to love—I could say it until my tongue lost all feeling, but it doesn't matter.

I am suddenly terrified of what I'm going to find.

As I approach Mirror House, a breeze whistles and the ocean sighs. There are birds and sunshine and clouds passing by like ships in the sky. But the air is way too still. It's wrong, how quiet it is. I walk up the stairs and knock on the door, hoping someone will answer it. Uncertain if I'm allowed inside.

Nothing. I peek through the living room window. Mugs sit on the end tables, someone's sweater draped on a chair. A paperback book is splayed on the couch next to a half-eaten muffin on a plate.

"Hello?" I ask, rapping the glass. "Anyone?"

I go back to the door, knocking again, louder this time. When no one comes, I hover my hand over the knob. What if this is a test? What if Simon is testing me and I'm failing? I wasn't supposed to come inside until he said I was ready, but—I have this jittery emergency gut feeling and I don't know what else to do except follow it, even though I know it's not what Simon would want. I push the door open.

"Hey," I say, softly. "Anybody home?"

It's unrecognizable, how silent it is. Dust sparkles the air and the clock ticks from the dining room and otherwise, there seems to be no movement, no life left in this house. I swallow, a chill rolling through me.

"Hello?" I whisper.

Every room I poke my head into, there's no one.

The kitchen is piled with dirty dishes and a loaf of bread sits out on the counter. In the Floaters' room, their four twin mattresses are made up neatly beneath the mural they painted that says *Fear to love*. In the dining room, it's as if everyone abandoned their breakfasts: half-eaten bowls of oatmeal, toast with one bite missing, cups of coffee nearly full.

Upstairs, the sight of my room gives me a wave of relief. I could cry. Just seeing my books there and my bedspread and my *Lady of Shalott* poster reminds me I'm not truly a ghost. I'm alive. My room is still here. I walk through the bathroom to Kristin's room, which is a disaster of empty bottles and dirty clothes and baseball caps and skateboard decks with no wheels. Maude's room—there's nothing in it but a mattress and a blanket. But that's Maude; the woman practices the minimalism of a serial killer. Simon's door is shut. I push it open and gasp when I see him.

In the flesh.

Alive.

Real.

Standing at the window. Staring out at the ocean.

I sigh with relief at the sight of him. They didn't all leave me behind after all. When he turns, he wears the strangest look on his face, as if he's a hundred miles away. As if he doesn't know who I am.

I smile at him, trying to meet his eyes and stir that familiar something he's always had for me. But he doesn't return the gesture.

Instead, he adjusts his glasses and squints at me. "I'd forgotten all about you."

My smile melts, arrow to heart. "This is still my home."

"Property is an illusion and so are you."

His words are so cold, his retort so automatic, I don't know what to say.

"Where is everyone?" I finally ask. "Where did they go?"

He turns, hands poised as if he's praying. His sorrow worries me. He resembles someone about to deliver very bad news. "*Alea iacta est.*"

"What does that mean?"

"'The die is cast.'"

"What die?" My brow wrinkles. "Where *is* everyone, Simon?"

"They did as they were told. They moved on."

His vague wording is so eerie, the hairs on my neck stand on end. "Moved on where?"

"They trusted me, wholly. That I know the truth. That I'm wise, that I'm chosen, that I have reasons. They transcended the illusion."

My breath gets shallow. There's no way. There's no way he's saying what I'm scared he's saying. "Illusion of what?"

"Of having a body. Of being in this earthly realm."

It's like I swallowed a jagged stone. I choke out the word, "What?"

"They're gone, Winona."

I hug my arms, barely able to speak. "What do you mean 'gone?'"

"They reached the end of the movie." He scratches his curls. "What a mess it ended up being. I don't understand how you all made such a mess of it."

"Made a ..."

He walks past me, as if lost in his thoughts, and heads out of his bedroom.

"No," I say from the doorway, my heart thundering in my chest.

It's not true. Absolutely not. Things aren't this bad. They wouldn't have done what he's implying they did. Simon is lying to me, playing a mind game. This is some kind of exposure.

"It's the end of their world, what is there to understand?" He heads downstairs, taking the steps two at a time. "They walked off the edge of the earth."

His statement swirls around my brain like smoke, nothing I can hold onto, sheer nonsense. My feet remain glued to the hardwood.

"Simon?" I say.

"You shouldn't be in the house," he calls over his shoulder.

He's out of sight now. I can hear that ticking clock again as I stand still, waiting for his response. *Tick-tick-tick-tick-tick-tick-tick.*

They walked off the edge of the earth.

No. Absolutely not.

They reached the end of the movie.

That's not what he means. Metaphor, metaphor.

My chest caves in. I push myself from his doorway and stumble down the stairs, unable to get a full breath.

Off the edge of the earth.

As if there is a spring inside me, I burst out the front door to the porch and run as fast as I can toward the cliff. When I see the guinea pig coop open, an empty mess of litter without a furry rodent in sight, my stomach pitches miserably.

"What happened?" I whisper, hurrying past it.

I fly past the garden beds flooded with rainwater. Leaping over rocks and garbage, trudging through mud, nearly tripping over a wheelbarrow. The ocean comes fully into view, so calm from here, an infinite blur of blue-green. The air stings with salt and something else—a damp rot. For a moment, as I stand here at the cliff's edge, I'm stunned by how beautiful and infinite and humbling it is ... until I look down.

Here, at my feet, there are twelve pairs of shoes and twelve braids laid upon the ground in a spiral like the sun. A rainbow of shorn braids. An array of worn shoes. They're perfectly spaced apart on the dried, cracked earth and I have never seen anything more haunting in all my life.

I know these braids: a silver one, two blond, five brunette, one blue, three black.

I know these shoes: Maude's boots, Kristin's checkered Vans, Dakota's Crocs, flats, sneakers, rubber rain boots with rainbows. All in neat pairs.

In the middle of them, a silver pair of scissors glints with light. The quiet is awful. Nothing but the wind in my ears and the distant roar of the surf.

The Mirror House Girls

I fall to my knees and wish the world would swallow me.

My brain can't comprehend the shock at first, but my chest is screaming. My heart knows. It lets ugly reality in.

Then it shatters into a million sharp little pieces.

60

GRIEF THROBS, a parade of unanswered questions.

How can I unwind time? What bargain with a divine hand will take me back to the way things were before? How *could* they? What was going through their heads as they fell to the ocean? How could they leave me all alone like this? We were a family, we were best friends, they were my entire world, so why didn't they want me to come with them?

The loss is so monstrous that I might as well jump in after them. The ocean below glistens. The waves beckon. There's no way to tell that it just swallowed twelve of my friends. I wonder how much it would hurt, how fast it would be over. I could end my life, too, if I just had the strength to stand up and walk a few extra steps.

This is real. This is not a dream. They're gone. Really, actually gone. There's nothing left to live for anymore.

Time has stopped, my knees here in the dirt at the cliff's edge, still stunned by this garden of horrors—the sunburst of braids, of empty shoes, a scene so silent not even the ghosts whisper.

"It happened hours ago now," Simon says from behind me. "There's nothing to be done."

I sob, the well of sorrow so deep I could spend all my life weeping.

"I know," Simon says, rubbing my back. "I know, sweet Winona. I know."

I am a bottomless hole of sadness. I can't even catch my breath. His hand moves in circles and then he reaches from behind me, wrapping his arms around me.

"Get off me!" I yell, thrashing.

He holds me tighter, calm, murmuring in my ear. "I know. Let it out. It's okay. I know."

"Why?" I scream, my throat raw.

"We've reached the end. You of all people know every story has an end."

"They're *dead!*" I yell, clawing at his arms, but he remains still.

"They've transcended this earthly realm," he says coolly, as if what he's saying is logical. "It was an act of self-sacrifice. The world will never forget us and our teachings now. We should be celebrating." His embrace tightens and it doesn't feel affectionate. It feels like a cage. "In ancient Rome, suicide was often revered as an expression of willpower, a choice to maintain your honor."

I try to wriggle out of his arms. "I don't fucking care about ancient Rome."

His grip tightens and his tone sharpens. "Rejoice. They're martyrs."

With every word he speaks, a pressure inside me is mounting.

"They will be remembered forever now," he goes on, his arms constricting tighter, tighter, like a python. I can't feel my fingertips. "The legacy they leave behind is more important than anything they would have accomplished otherwise. 'The greater part of those who had hated him most bitterly while he lived lauded him to the skies when he was dead.'"

It doesn't matter how much I writhe in his arms, he won't let me go. Simon and his quotes and his Roman history and his rational tone as if everything is a thought exercise. As if this is not the deepest tragedy but some kind of interesting lesson. I am quivering with contempt.

I enunciate every word as I say, "This wasn't supposed to happen."

"It's time to *really* wake up, Winona."

Suddenly, his tight hold on me relaxes. He pulls away from me. I turn to look back at him. His eyes are wide with wonder, a content half-smile on his face. He rises to his feet and I'm still crouched and cowering, my arms up defensively, thinking he's going to hurt me.

But he just holds his hands up and takes a step back. "It's your turn."

I inhale sharply and listen to the crashing waves. He takes another step back, a good few feet between us now, and relief fills me. Both of us watch a flock of geese in the shape of a V soar overhead. As I catch my breath, I consider his suggestion. I wonder if the impact of the fall would kill me first, or if I'd drown. I wonder how badly it would hurt, how soon it would be over.

"There's nothing left for us here," Simon says. "This is the only way we might all be together again."

Tears fall down my cheeks. The anguish is too big. I can't bear it. "Why did you do this?"

"Be brave," he says gently. "It won't hurt. I know you can do it, Winona."

Shock paralyzes me. We lock eyes. I'm so devastated, I don't know how to respond for a moment.

"I plan to join them after penning a short manifesto for us," he says, softer. "Something that will be published so my legacy and philosophy can live on."

I stay here, facing the ocean, sitting on my knees, for a little eternity. I have been electrocuted by such intense pain that I can't feel anything anymore. The wind blows my cheeks dry and there's just a dull throb where my heart supposedly lives.

"Don't you want to join us?" Simon asks. "You don't want to be the only one left behind."

This is the end, isn't it?

I spent my life longing to belong. Wanting that sacred closeness of being truly seen and known. I love infectious laughter and the boisterous energy of a party and teams and congregations and friends. Mirror House was the only family I ever invited into my life and now they're gone. For a flicker, there's no choice ahead of me except to jump after them. But then my despair grows wings. It whispers, *he did this*.

And I am overwhelmed with rage.

"Yes," I say, gritting my teeth.

I stand up, knees shaky.

"Become a part of history," he says, walking toward me, slowly. I tense up at his nearness. "Life is brief, but energy is timeless. The self is an illusion. It didn't hurt, I promise. They were smiling when they did it, Winona, I was here. It was the most remarkable thing I've ever seen in my life. They flew. They *flew*."

He reaches down to retrieve the scissors and hands them to me.

"Do what they did," he says.

I nod, barely able to breathe. I loathe how close he is to me, how I can smell him. I slip off my slippers and squeeze them into the circle.

"You'll be remembered forever. Like Virginia Woolf. Like Anne Sexton."

I put the jaws of the scissors to my braid and clench the steel handle, severing through it like rope.

Thwack.

My hair falls to the ground like a dead snake. It took me years to grow it and one second to cut it all off. Takes a lifetime to build a person and one second to end them. And all at once, I'm lighter than I've been in a long time, maybe ever.

I walk a few steps toward the end of the earth. I'm aware of Simon behind me every step of the way, stalking me like a shadow. My grip tightens on the scissors.

A boat glides along the glassy water. The breeze tickles my neck and gives me a shiver. Somewhere, my Grandma Jane's ashes are churning around that same sea that swallowed everyone I love. It's bound to swallow me too.

But not today.

I turn around, quicker than lightning, and stab Simon's smiling face with the scissors. For just one moment, with his nose askew and blood running down his chin, he looks scared—almost human—before the mask slips back into place.

61

"WINONA," Simon says, surprised. He feels his gashed cheek as he backs away from me a few steps, toward the house. He seems calm, unbothered, even though I've got the scissors poised and ready to do it again. He holds a hand out defensively. "Look at how much progress you've made. The little mouse who moved to Mirror House would never have been able to do such a thing."

Fire spreads throughout me from limb to limb. I could stab this motherfucker to death and he would still somehow take credit for it.

I breathe heavily, clutching the scissors, a metallic smell mixing with the salty tang of the beach. My ears ring and I fight the urge to faint at the sight of his wounded face. I'm frozen, bracing myself for him to charge at me and try to wrestle the scissors away. Instead, a gory grin is fixed on his maniacal face.

"Did you split it open?" he asks, licking his crimson lips. Then he begins applauding. "Well done. Not even blinking an eye. This is what it looks like to transcend your fear."

His words light me up like dynamite.

I lunge toward him and stab his throat this time. Blood spurts down his shirt. He stumbles but doesn't fall. Every one of my muscles is clenched. I keep expecting him to come for me, attack me back, defend himself somehow. Instead, he only peers down and examines his blood with wonder.

"Is this how it ends?" He turns to me as if he doesn't recognize me. "I always knew I'd be crucified—but I never guessed it would be by you."

I shudder with a sob, my hand grasping the scissors tighter. "Why aren't you fighting back, you coward?"

He puts his hands in a namaste gesture, glancing up at the sky as if sharing a secret moment with a higher power, and it only fuels my fury. This man is delusional. A monster who truly thinks he's some kind of messiah. I want to destroy him. But even that wouldn't be enough.

He needs to suffer.

I go for his eye with the scissors but end up breaking his glasses and splitting his forehead. He jerks back, glass glittering on his cheeks. Touching his neck, fingers covered in blood, he yanks the front of his shirt up to his throat to try to plug the bleeding. As red blooms all over the front of him, I spy the lightning bolt scar on his chest and burn with revulsion.

"Ironic, isn't it?" he says, with the calm self-assurance of a man in the middle of a philosophical discussion instead of a man bleeding out through his throat. He backs away from me toward the garden beds, feeling behind him, his glasses crooked and his eyes squeezed shut. His forehead wound looks like a bloody smile. "Without me, you'd never have been capable of such a thing."

I move toward him, slashing the scissors along his arms. *Snick snick snick* through his pale flesh, wrist to elbow. He winces and cries out. The punctures ooze violet-red. Harder. *Harder.*

"What are you afraid of, Simon?" I ask, quivering with

vengeance I've never felt before in my life. "Why are you protecting yourself? Transcend your fear."

He yelps as I gain momentum and the scissors meet his collarbone. Tripping backwards, he falls, his head smacking the edge of the garden bed. He rolls in the dirt, blood and soil spackled over his arms. His face and throat are raw and meaty, his eyes closed and sprinkled with broken glass. We're about twenty or thirty feet away from the cliff's edge now. Maybe I should drag him back and throw him over.

"Please," he begs. "I can't see. Winona, be rational. I understand your anger right now. Believe me. But you've gone too far."

"No, I haven't," I say, panting as I look down at him.

My anger is fire ants under my skin. My anger is a scream that never ends.

"Fine," he says, grimacing, his breathing labored. "Do what you will. I'll die a martyr like everyone else."

I catch my breath as I gaze down at Simon with a wave of déjà vu. The gruesome, gushing sight of his injuries reminds me those crime scene photos I stared at for so long. I shudder. It's as if the world stopped and I'm looking in a mirror. Everything suddenly seems so backwards, as if maybe it's not his face bleeding, but mine. Warmth trickles down my cheeks. But then I touch it and examine my fingers: tears, not blood. He's the one bleeding, not me.

I'll die a martyr like everyone else.

His voice is raspy. "What are you waiting for?"

I choke on a sob. I hadn't expected him to crumble, to not fight back, and all at once I'm so confused. Am I playing right into his hand? Is my killing him here giving him exactly what he wants? Is it turning him into a victim? Even now, even when I'm standing over his bloody body with a knife in my hand, I never feel like I have the power.

A breeze breathes over me with a chill and dries my tears. It hits me, the mountain of sheer tragedy that has happened today. The monumental loss. I can't fathom it. I don't know what to do. I glance past Simon, at the cliff's edge. I want to jump into the ocean with them. I want to kill him, to end him, to make him shut up, to stab him until he bleeds out in the clovers.

But all of that would just be giving Simon what he wants.

The sweet and horrid sound of the waves breaking. That abysmal ocean which gobbled the bones of everyone I love. It waits for me, patiently, turning and turning and turning.

And suddenly, I know exactly what Simon deserves.

I drop the scissors and stoop down to put my hand in his. He's shivering as he squeezes back. The gore is surreal. His entire shirt is crimson, the blood leaking slowly but steadily out of his throat. His face is the worst: that smile-slit on his forehead and a punctured cheek, his eyes full of glass.

"I'll help you up," I say, sprinkling sugar in my voice. "Come on. You're right. There's still a little time. You need to write your manifesto before we go."

He's still cowering at my shadow over him, but he sits up slowly, moaning in pain. I help him to his feet, pulling hard. Guiding his arm around my shoulders.

"I knew you'd be sensible," he says, a gurgle in his voice. "You're erratic, you're untrusting, but you always come around in the end. My loyal girl. My secret favorite."

Secret favorite, my ass, a voice in my head says. It's jarring to hear it. Who is that? Scarlett's voice? I hardly recognize it.

"Come on," I say quietly.

"'The tyrant dies and his rule is over. The martyr dies and his rule begins,'" Simon says. "Kierkegaard said that, I believe."

"Did he, now?"

We head back toward the house in my bare feet through the

brush. Slow steps. Baby steps. He begins talking about Jesus again. His face is bloody, his eyes squeezed shut in pain, and yet he's smiling and blathering on about the Bible.

Snake oil salesman, that sharp voice in my head says. *Mass murderer.*

Who is that? Who's saying that?

And then, in a sucker-punch lightbulb moment, I recognize who it is.

It's me.

Not Simon. Not Scarlett. Not my mother, not my grandmother, not a spirit speaking from beyond. Me.

I hate him.

Murder would be too kind.

"Much like me, with wounds all over his body before he was crucified ..." Simon is saying.

He thinks he's going to die a messiah.

My right hand that held the scissors is still clenched as we hobble together—one soaked creature, one bloody, tear-stained monster—alongside the garden beds that will never grow my vegetables and the pedicab that Maude will never drive again. The wind tickles the back of my bare neck. I spot that familiar pine tree, the one that marks where we had our secret bunker meetings. We will never have a secret bunker meeting again. It's all over, because of the man with his arm around me. Because of him.

I stop us in our tracks.

"Who knows?" he's saying. "Perhaps I too will rise again—"

"Wait a second."

I leave him standing, his butchered face wrenched in pain.

"Where are we?" he asks, feeling the air with his fingertips, lost without me there to prop him up.

"We're almost there," I call back to him, stooping in the shade of the pine tree. Dropping to my knees, I search for the spot, my fingers meeting the loop of rope. I tug it open slowly so he can't hear it creak. Darkness gapes back at me. The sweet, damp stink of earth and stale air.

"Winona?" he asks. "Don't leave me now."

"I wouldn't do that," I say, coming back to him.

My heart is pumping with thunder as I take his hand and lead him toward the hole in the ground. He seems resistant, his muscles stiffening, as if he can sense danger. He reaches out in front of him, grasping the air.

"Wait, where are we?"

It's as if he knows. I see the shadow pass over him as he grows still.

"Winona, don't do this. Can't we—"

I answer his question with a mighty push that plunges him into the suffocating darkness. His body lands with a thud and a crack of bones six feet below. His breath comes in ragged, shallow gasps. Then he howls wetly like a drowning dog. He tries to sit up, feeling around him in confusion as his fingertips meet nothing but the kiss of cold concrete.

"Winona!" he shouts.

"You don't get to die a martyr," I say as I look down at him one last time. "You'll die in a cold, dark hole and no one will remember you were even here."

His wounded face is contorted in pain and … something else, something almost unfamiliar, quivering and pleading.

Oh.

Fear. That's what I'm seeing.

Sheer, unadulterated fear.

I've finally discovered the only true punishment for a villain like him: not murder, not suicide—but complete irrelevance. Erasure.

The world will pay him no attention and forget he ever existed.

His lips tremble as reality spreads its dark wings.

I savor that image—the trembling, pitiful man beneath the grand façade—for just a single second before shutting the door with a *thump*.

As I push a boulder to cover it up, a weight shifts in me too. I breathe the deepest breath. Getting up, I retrace the path we walked and use my sneakers to kick our tracks, hide the evidence of him, smear his blood into the dirt. I find the scissors and pitch them into the ocean. I don't hear them hit the water over the song of the waves. I gaze at the horizon and weep for my friends. By the time I walk back toward the house, I don't hear the muffled, high-pitched sound of his screaming anymore, either. There's no sign of him now. Nothing there but a boulder.

Simon Spellmeyer will never see the light again.

62

A HALF HOUR later and one and a half miles up the road, the wind whips my face. I stand between the ocean and the highway. With shaking hands, I pick up the payphone's receiver, glancing at Simon's van, which I parked on the shoulder. I rub my neck, not used to how bare it is. The cold is numbing. My teeth chatter. I'm wearing Kristin's baseball cap, a scarf Maude knit, and a weed-leaf sweatshirt of Dakota's, but I'm chilled in a deep place that might never be warm again.

I dial 911 and close my eyes.

The dispatcher answers with the blasé, robotic voice of someone who eats crises for breakfast, lunch, and dinner.

"911, what is your emergency?"

I drop my voice to a lower register, trying to disguise myself by sounding like a man. Despite my best effort to control it, my voice shakes anyway. "I think they're all dead."

"What's your name, sir?"

"I—I just want to phone in an anonymous tip."

She answers with flat annoyance. "Can you please tell me what's happening?"

"There's a ... a group, living out at the property, 221 Hitchcock Road. I think there's been a mass suicide."

"Police and paramedics are on their way. Is anyone still breathing?"

"No." I squeeze my stinging eyes shut. "They're gone."

"Sir, can you—"

"They jumped." I can't help a sob from escaping. "They jumped, together. Every single one."

I hang up, pressing my forehead against the scratched glass of the booth, guilt grasping my throat with invisible fingers. Finally, I climb back into the van. I drive away, Bodega Bay fading in my rearview through blurry eyes. A place full of dreams and corpses, best friends, big loves—and the worst monster I've ever met.

Excerpt from the documentary *The Mirror House Girls: One Year Later*

LOCATION: Interviewee's home, Raven's Landing, California

SHOTS: SCARLETT's five deadbolts on her front door; the rifle hanging on a wall; the baseball bat resting in the corner.

SCARLETT shivers on her living room couch, tightening the sweater around her.

SCARLETT: Of course I wonder what happened to him. Doesn't everyone? Hell, I was in line at the supermarket the other day, and there was on a tabloid cover—some blurry picture they claimed was Simon hiking the Pacific Coast Trail. Isn't there a reward out for him? I mean, he fled the scene of a mass suicide he most certainly brainwashed everybody into, and then there's Robin. His van was found abandoned off Highway 1. Look at the fuckin' coward—too chicken to even kill himself.

Yeah, I won't lie to you. I can't sleep at night knowing he's out there. He's probably got a new haircut, a new name, and someone else to manipulate. Part of me will never rest until I know how his movie ends.

(Leaning in, listening to interviewer's question)

Do I think he's a sociopath? No, I actually don't. (Sinks into thought) I think the man was a narcissist, high off his own supply. He believed his own bullshit, and that's scarier to me than a con artist. Evil that thinks it's righteous and good … that's the scariest thing in the world.

If I could say one thing to Simon? (Waves her hand) I wouldn't say a goddamn thing. That's what he deserves. To be ignored. I would much rather say something to the girls he murdered with his ideas.

(Tearfully, looking straight at the camera) I would say, I love you. I'd march right back into that awful place just to see you one last time.

63

I'VE LIVED a year now as a dead woman.

After fleeing Mirror House, I drove up the coast and ditched Simon's van somewhere near Eureka. From there, I wandered, dazed and homeless. Days bled into weeks that bled into months. I was a ghost, watching humanity's movies playing out in shop windows. Simon was right; it was a Dream World. And I was in a walking coma. I wasn't in Mirror House anymore, but I didn't belong anywhere else, either.

I slept in parks and ate from dumpsters. I sought shelter in libraries when it rained. I begged for spare change, bought liquor, and forgot about my life a little while. Rinse, repeat.

In this fresh shock of the first few weeks, I thought about reaching out to Scarlett. She might understand. But then I looked her up online and saw her smiling face. Working as a barista, planting a garden, her arm around another girl. She was better off without me. I was afraid she would blame me for what happened at Mirror House. And I deserved it.

The thought of calling my mom was even worse. Facing her

judgment, admitting I was in a cult—the shame was a wall I couldn't climb. We had already parted ways. She didn't need me.

I wished I'd jumped with everyone else.

Time froze. Guilt rotted me from inside out. I watched the world dance around me and tried to forget I was Winona Hawthorne. I dreamed of suicide: razorblades or pills or a gun to my temple. I drank too much and ate too little. My cheeks hollowed. My eyes dulled. When I caught my own reflection, a stranger stared back. How do you keep going after something like that? My friends jumped off a cliff and I didn't stop them. I left Simon to die in the dark. Perhaps I was no better than him.

The library was my refuge. One day, months later, I searched the news. Just seeing the headlines splashed everywhere was like sticking my finger in an electrical socket. THIRTEEN DEAD IN MASS SUICIDE; POLICE IDENTIFY REMAINS OF 'MIRROR HOUSE' CULT; CULT LEADER STILL AT LARGE; NEW REMAINS DISCOVERED AT 'MIRROR HOUSE'.

They found Robin's remains buried beneath the lemon tree.

I wanted to die all over again, seeing that.

Because deep down in a place I wouldn't let myself dwell, I already knew that was true. They killed her that night. That wasn't her driving away. I cleaned up her blood and pretended not to see the truth. That made me an accessory to murder. I could never show my face again.

Remains belonging to Maude, Sadie, and Juliet washed up on beaches. Sometimes I imagined that somehow Kristin and Dakota escaped. But my heart knows.

And they never found Simon.

I spent a phantom year wandering the streets of small towns. Telling myself that anything nice that happened, I didn't deserve. The free meals I ate, served by perky college students in the park on Saturdays. The radiant blue skies, grinning yellow moons, or the wind hissing though the oak trees. A snatch of piano music that wafted from an open window or the happy trot of a passing housecat. I deserved none of it.

And I certainly don't deserve the job I was given two weeks ago, cleaning motel rooms in exchange for a warm place to sleep—even if it's the kind of place with nicotine-stained curtains and not enough hot water. It's more than I've had in a year: a bed, a shower, and a television.

And that's where I see Scarlett.

I turn on my television and there she is, talking in a documentary.

* * *

To see her onscreen, glowing and thriving—telling our sad, strange story in her own special way—I nearly short-circuit. I collapse on the edge of the motel bed for an hour, rapt and shiny-eyed, hardly able to breathe. I hang onto her words like they're water and I've been lost in the desert.

Scarlett holds up the mirror and reminds me of who I am.

Yes, there's infinite pain. Hearing it spoken aloud, the stark-naked madness we believed, is nearly unbearable. But there's something equally important that I forgot about: the beauty, inseparable from the pain. The hope before the tragedy; the way her hair lifted in the wind; her songs and her funny expressions; how our bodies fit together, like they were made that way. There was a time when we thought fear was surmountable, utopia was possible, and that we had a life-changing message to spread around the world.

I never knew true homesickness until I heard Scarlett's voice today.

And as the credits of this documentary roll, I know exactly what I need to do.

I've been hiding, fearing judgment, but the world deserves answers. Scarlett deserves answers. And I'm the only one who has them. Fear drove me this past year as I wandered lonely as a cloud, but maybe Simon was right about one thing: If it's not hard work, it's not worth doing.

64

IT TAKES one hour to find Scarlett's new address, six hours on three buses, and a mile walk through the countryside. Everything I own fits in my backpack. She'll hardly recognize me— I'm tanned and freckled from all my time outside. My hair is to my shoulders. I wear sweatpants and T-shirts and sensible shoes. I'm quiet, too. Smiles are so rare these days they feel like they might split my face. But right now, as I walk along this gravelly road beneath a sea-blue sky, I'm smiling.

Butterflies flutter through the wildflowers speckled through knee-high grass. Painted ladies and monarchs. Bees and hummingbirds. I smell cherry blossoms as I walk up the shade-speckled road, following my shadow up the hill to her little pink cottage. Somewhere, I can hear the tranquil babble of a creek. There are stone steps leading to her porch, flower boxes hanging from her windows. I take a deep breath to savor it all as I stand on her doorstep. It's so peaceful and lovely here. It's just what Scarlett deserves.

As I knock, there are so many things swimming around in

Faith Gardner

me. Aching, permanent guilt. Traumatic memories that make me flinch in the sunshine. Trepidation about what's to come, about what the world will do with me when they learn I've been alive and hiding. Something like relief at knowing no matter how sad this story ends, at least the end is near.

Here's the thing I've realized since I heard Scarlett tell her story: the very thing I fear is the thing I need most. I'm talking about human intimacy—the sweetness of belonging. Couples. Groups. Friends. Romance. Tribes. Teams. Identities. Churches. Community. Laughter we bring out of one another in choruses. Wars. Warm hands in mine. Murder. The harmony of overlapping voices; the noise of riotous shouting.

You can't have one without the other.

Have you ever truly pondered that expression? *You can't have one without the other.*

Togetherness is a violent mob, but it's also a loving family. It's behind the worst horrors and the most astonishing human accomplishments.

It's the poison and the antidote.

Scarlett opens the door. Her amber eyes widen and fill. She gasps with a croak. There's a pause so extended it stops time.

"How?" she whispers. "How? How? How?"

"I'm sorry, Scarlett. It's a long story."

Her breath snags and she can't even speak. But she drinks in the sight of me, like I'm a miracle. She reaches out and touches my arm. The look on her face could light up a whole city. She clamps her hands over her mouth and I worry she might faint, so I reach out to prop her up. When I do, she pulls me in for the world's longest hug.

She clutches me with such intensity, rocking back and forth. She smells like vanilla and summertime and mornings and hope.

"Hey," I whisper into her strawberry hair. "I'm home."

* * *

Want to know what happens next for Winona and Scarlett—and Simon, too? **Sign up for my newsletter and you can download the bonus epilogue, "Home."**

One more thing ...

IF YOU ENJOYED *The Mirror House Girls,* good news: I have other psychological thrillers I think you'll like, too.

Check out *Like It Never Was,* an unhinged psychological thriller about a female friendship plagued by paranoia and revenge.

Or maybe try *They Are the Hunters*, a psychological thriller about a family with some deep, dark secrets.

Or give *The Second Life of Ava Rivers* a read! It's a psychological thriller/mystery about a twin who comes back after twelve years missing with no memory of where she's been all this time.

I also have a collection of psychological thrillers all set in the same universe. They're called **The Jolvix Episodes**, and you can **grab the first three books in this discounted box set** or read them one by one.

NOTE: These standalone novels can be read in whatever order you want, but *Eve in Overdrive* is technically a prequel to *The Slaying Game.*

- **THE PREDICTION:** A newlywed woman's smart device begins offering chilling predictions about her husband.

- **VIOLET IS NOWHERE:** A kidnapped woman and a stranger on the end of a phone line have one week to figure out how they're connected or their lives are over.

- **WHAT JANUARY REMEMBERS:** A dysfunctional family and their sentient companion bot gather for the holidays for the first time since their last Christmas together—which ended in attempted murder.

- **PEARL IN DEEP:** The love of one woman's life turns out to be a psychopath with a disturbing talent for deepfake video.

- **EVE IN OVERDRIVE:** An outspoken journalist buys a cutting-edge car only to find herself at the mercy of a vengeful internet troll.

- **THE SLAYING GAME:** A former Jolvix employee ends up at the center of a serial killer's deadly game.

- Or you can grab the first three Jolvix Episodes in a box set.

A note from the author

If you got this far, I wanted to take a moment to thank you for reading and supporting my work. As an indie author, I put a ton of effort into each book—not just writing, but editing, marketing, and everything else it takes to guide a book through the whole process from a glimmer in the brain to a real, actual thing you can hold in your hands.

If you enjoyed it, please consider leaving a review. Reviews truly make an author's world go round. If you're interested in keeping up with book news, please join my newsletter or follow me on social media. And I love to hear from readers anytime at faith@faithgardner.com.

As always, I tried my damndest to fix every typo, but alas, I am only human. If you spot an error, please let me know! I appreciate every reader who makes me look smarter.

Acknowledgments

Mom, I can never thank you enough. You're my first beta reader, biggest cheerleader, and the reason I'm writing full-time. Then there's that whole giving-me-life thing you did. Seriously, you're the best.

My sister Micaela is not only a tireless beta reader, she also watches more true crime shows and cult documentaries than anyone I know. So grateful for your feedback and your recommendations.

Noelle Ihli and Steph Nelson, I have endless appreciation for your friendship and support. Your beta feedback and advice was so crucial to getting this book to where it is today. I owe you a hundred fancy seafood dinners and tarot readings. And Caleb Stephens, I'm so happy to have you in my corner! Our little writing cult helps keep me sane and I don't know how I'd do this without all of you.

I adore my enormous, hilarious, talented, brilliant family. Special shoutout to my husband Jamie: I'm so lucky to have you as a partner in this wild, precious life. Anything feels possible with you at my side.

My daughters are too young to read my dark books, but thank you, Roxie, for always giving me your opinions about my book covers. And Zora, thank you for naming the villain in this story. Simon wouldn't be Simon without you!

To every reviewer, supporter, Bookstagrammer, TikToker

who has helped boost my books: without you, none of this would be possible. So much appreciation and respect for all you do for writers.

And thank you, dear reader, for spending a little time with me and my book.

Also by Faith Gardner

Standalones

Like It Never Was

They Are the Hunters

The Second Life of Ava Rivers

The Jolvix Episodes

The Prediction

Violet Is Nowhere

What January Remembers

Pearl in Deep

Eve in Overdrive

The Slaying Game

Young Adult Novels

Perdita

If You Can Hear This

How We Ricochet

Girl on the Line

That One Time I Wrote A Rom-Com

Make Me a Double

About the Author

Faith Gardner writes suspense novels. When her head isn't stuck in a book, she might be playing music, cooking, or playing with tarot cards. She's also a fan of documentaries and scary movies. She lives in the Bay Area with her family. Find her at faithgardner.com.

www.ingramcontent.com/pod-product-compliance
Ingram Content Group UK Ltd.
Pitfield, Milton Keynes, MK11 3LW, UK
UKHW031320050225
4457UKWH00032B/373